T0031304

EDGE
of
STARS

EDGE

of

STARS

BLOOD OF ZEUS: BOOK SIX

ANGEL PAYNE

WATERHOUSE PRESS

This book is an original publication of Waterhouse Press.

This is a work of fiction. Names, characters, places, and incidents either are the product of the author's imagination or are used fictitiously, and any resemblance to actual persons, living or dead, business establishments, events, or locales is entirely coincidental. The publisher does not assume any responsibility for third-party websites or their content.

Copyright © 2023 Waterhouse Press, LLC
Cover Design & Images by Regina Wamba
Interior Cover Images: Shutterstock

All Rights Reserved.
No part of this book may be reproduced, scanned, or distributed in any printed or electronic format without permission. Please do not participate in or encourage piracy of copyrighted materials in violation of the author's rights. Purchase only authorized editions.

ISBN: 978-1-64263-368-9

For all the dreamers who dare to become doers.

Reach for your stars . . . always.

"When you can't look at the bright side,
I will sit with you in the dark."

— Lewis Carroll,
Alice's Adventures in Wonderland

CHAPTER 1

Kara

"YOU'RE A MISERABLE EXCUSE for a bride, Kara Valari."

My sister's tone, meant as playful, is threaded with enough of her real meaning to excuse my attempt at a laugh. A mostly failed one.

"I won't tell Madame Voracity if you don't."

"Won't tell me what?"

Kell joins me in whipping semipanicked sights to the doorway of the small dressing room where we're hiding— ermmm, *preparing*—ourselves for the upcoming festivities. Events that, according to our new guest, should coalesce into the happiest day of my life.

How I wish I could prove the woman right. But Madame Voracity, for all her glory and notoriety and longstanding relationship with our family, doesn't—and cannot—know what today is actually all about. Her image is larger than life, but she's not. She's a normal human being, just like the majority of the guests who swoon at the Pacific Ocean view while strolling toward the cliffside chapel across the patio.

They all have to keep believing they're bound for the biggest industry party this decade.

Though right now, that's far from Maximus's and my biggest stress.

That honor is in the hands of the *other* wedding guests. The demigods, gods, and goddesses who mix into the crowd undetected, save for the otherworldly beauty that's undoubtedly getting them some curious glances from LA's elite.

It's the largest gathering of Olympians this century— and probably the twenty-five or so before. And we're determined to turn it into the largest peace summit the pantheon has ever known.

"We were only saying that you've truly outdone yourself, madame."

Kell for the win on the potential sticky with the designer who's reminding me of a well-accessorized partridge. Madame probably meant well, dressing in something close to Mother's chosen color palette for everything, but her dress has decorative overlays shaped like wings, and her strappy heels are natural conspirators for the birdlike steps.

"I hope Maximus is steeled and ready," my sister adds with sugary diplomacy. "Because he'll be focusing on keeping his eyeballs in his head from the first sight of this girl."

"Creepy but oddly sweet," I mutter, though I'm distracted by my buzzing phone. As I expect—and hope—

it's from the man who turns my chest into a butterfly rave from the sight of his words alone.

My hotter-than-sin fiancé.

You ready to do this, little demon?

I tilt a goofy grin at his avatar on my screen, a photo I snapped when we were taking our golf cart ride to El Capitan Beach on the gorgeous evening in which he proposed. The sight of his windswept hair and brilliant blue gaze brings a perfect burst of bravery for my silly reply.

*Did you have to remind me of that last
part before we march to an altar while
every major player from Hollywood and
Olympus watches?*

His dancing dots last a mercifully short time.

*Heaven didn't kill us for it during
rehearsal.*

I tap an answer, wishing it could match my original cheek.

*But now heaven is the last of our concerns.
Why did everyone have to be here?*

Again, wonderfully short-lived dots.

*Would you feel better if we met to go over
the plan once more? There's time ...*

My smile spreads wider. Incredible man. If he were standing in front of me, I'd kiss him for all I was worth. Just the inner vision of it is enough to move my fingers again.

*Of course it would. But Kell and Madame
V are still in here.*

So we go to the backup plan.

*You have a backup plan for discussing the
big plan?*

His slight pause has me assuming his default to a wry chuckle. And then:

*Do you remember the storage closet? The
one we found during our tour?*

My lips barely hold in a giggle.

You really think I'd forget it?

I already know how he's answering that. With a small smirk of his own, coordinating with the sultry heat that rises in his cobalt gaze. The eyes that started so much for me. The intensity that torched my senses before his touch ever did. It's so easy to remember it all again now, since it was the same look on his face when he first pulled me into the closet during Mother's tiff with the wedding coordinator during our tour.

Luckily for us, the planner had a stubborn streak as long as Mother's. Their debate about the all-day rental fee might as well have been a NATO arms summit. In the way of all successful summits, the end came with compromises. Mother agreed to half a day plus set-up time for the camera crews, while Maximus conceded to giving me only three orgasms.

Only three.

The thought forms a much bigger chuckle in my throat, but I disguise it in the nick of time, going for a strangled choke. Kell doesn't believe the stressed vibe for a second, but Madame's all in with her concerned rush to my side.

"Oh, darling!" She runs a smoothing hand along the sparkling design of my fitted dress. Her hand presses at the area above my navel. "Are we feeling all right? Jitters are normal, you know. Just as long as they're only that."

This time, Kell's doing the choke-laugh thing, undoubtedly out of memories from the first fitting we had for the dresses. It wasn't a pleasant time for me, since I was stressed about my shapewear not doing its duty beneath my gown. Concealing a secret baby has to be an ordeal even under typical circumstances, but mine were—and still are— far from that. And every time Madame got me with an alteration pin, which seemed to be a lot that day…

"Yes," I murmur, forcing out a composed smile. "Only that, Madame. I promise."

Translation: *I promise the nerves won't eat up my gut until I almost empty my breakfast onto your creation.*

The designer lifts her bright-pink lips and pats my hand. "Good. So very good. You truly have nothing to be flummoxed about, dear one. You are *stunning*. The natural makeup, and the hair in this long pretty style... Why, the devil himself would agree with me, if he dared lurk nearby!"

The blood leaves my face like a thousand balls dumped from a pachinko machine.

"And everyone in that chapel is going to agree with me," she waxes on, oblivious. "Especially the one waiting at the end of the aisle for you!"

Yes, well... first he's got to meet me in the storage room.

I keep the thought carefully cloaked—or so I think. While Madame still primps my gown while humming along with whatever the harpist on the patio is playing, Kell eyes me with completely different intent. She's *not* laughing about the fitting day memories anymore.

But she'll have to deal with it.

Maximus and I don't have a second to waste.

"You know, Madame..." I push to my feet and feign a little wince. "Now that I think about it, I *am* a little woozy."

"Oh no," the designer gasps. "Ohhh no, oh no!"

"It's all right." I squeeze the woman's clammy hand. She clamps back hard enough to gouge the back of my hand with her talon-length acrylics. How the woman does the basics with those things, let alone the intricate work behind her wedding dresses, is a grand life mystery to me. "I think if I can just sneak outside for some fresh air..."

"I can help her."

My sister's overly bright line gets her my censoring glance. "I'm *fine*, okay? I can find—"

"Nonsense." The last time she drawled that word with such creepy intent, it was to a photographer who thought nothing of suggesting a three-way with the two of us and him. "What's your maid of honor for, anyway?"

The photographer didn't get that particular line—but as I remember the glass of old beer and cigarettes that Kell sniffed out on his window ledge and managed to *accidentally* spill onto his crotch and camera, I give in with a grudging sigh.

Madame Voracity sends a happy *tah-tah* while heading toward the patio to check on Mother's and Nancy's dresses. As soon as we head the other direction and emerge onto a private breezeway, Kell tugs my elbow and hits me with the determined slant of a brow.

"Time to spill, pretty one."

"You really think I'm pretty? Awww."

"Knock it off. You can't afford to be stalling." She pulls in a prominent sniff. "Your cover story to Madame Voracity was like holding my head under an In-n-Out broiler."

I roll my eyes. "Don't you ever just want to turn that thing off?"

"Don't *you* ever just want to trust me with the whole story?" She cocks her head. "Especially right now?"

I probably could have dealt with her first probe. But the second, offered on a plate of her concern and swimming in a puddle of her affection, is my undoing. In her nose,

I'm probably a cheeseburger, large fries, *and* a triple-thick shake by now. Which I sincerely wish we could take off and go grab for ourselves, this very second. My little sprout, seeming to plug into my yearning, gives it an encouraging wiggle. I answer the sweet thing by rubbing a hand across my stomach.

"It's okay, little one. It's going to be okay."

Kell walks a few steps, frowning down at the long skirt she holds away from her strappy heels. "You sounded the exact same way when you told Veronica you *like* this color combination."

"But I do."

"Kara, it's weird."

"It's *different*. Dusty rose and gold is kind of trendy … isn't it?"

Heavy air bursts from between her teeth. "I look like a slab of eighties bathroom granite."

"But a gorgeous one. The hairpiece gives your eyes a nifty Morticia vibe."

I'm not lying, but she narrows her smoky-make-upped look anyway.

"You were working on that one, weren't you? But do we even have time for it?"

I glance over, already conceding that part of the exchange to her. It's worth it if I succeed in gaining a little more of her trust. Maximus and I could use an extra ally at this point of the day.

No. Not just that.

At this point of the *game*.

The much larger picture to things.

The risky ruse that he and I are running, in the form of the most prestigious Hollywood wedding of the year.

"Okay. You're right," I go ahead and murmur. "Time isn't exactly an expendable commodity right now."

"So start talking, and fast," she counters. "Though for the complete record, I was so damn certain about this."

"Uhhh...this?" Because feigning confusion is suddenly the easiest buzzer to slam down. Because even if it's not a hundred percent confusion, my fallback of suspicion is just as effortless.

"*This*," she volleys, sticking harder to her conviction. "Whatever is up with the two of you. Don't bat those big browns either. I've known it all day. No, probably since last night. You barely touched your food during the rehearsal dinner."

I demure, rubbing at my stomach. "It's called having a demigod baby do the cha-cha on one's digestive tract."

"So what's Maximus's excuse? We were having the chef's special cut at *mar'sel*, and he only ate a couple of bites too. Everyone else thought you were tangling toes in each other's business under the table, but I wasn't having it. You two smelled like stress on matching skewers. I said as much to Jaden, but he didn't bel—"

"Zeus and Hades know I'm pregnant."

Her rambling stops, making way for her fully dropped jaw. "How?"

"They both think that Hecate might know too. Though if she does, she's pulled out a really good poker face."

"Wait. That's impossible. You and Maximus have been so careful. You even moved into that casita at the Terranea just in case the seedling decided to have a sudden growth spurt. Granted, if you're going to hole up anywhere, that's the place to pick..."

I shrug. "Maximus gets frustrated with the Wi-Fi. It's the sun bouncing off the ocean during the afternoon and how it hits the windows. Sometimes his video connection looks like a bad *Star Trek* episode."

"Oh, *no*." She drapes a melodramatic hand across her forehead. "Not Professor Hottie getting fantasy cast into Starfleet itself!" She side-eyes me with as much meaning. "Just not a red one, right?"

I roll my eyes. She's undeterred.

"But I'm still not getting it. Maximus is teaching classes virtually, and you've scaled back to remote shoots and interviews. And neither of you have been to a single industry event since the EmStar awards... Oh, *shit*." Her face loses color once her rant fades into realization. "The night of the awards...the billion-and-one photographers..."

"And the dramatic dip that Maximus insisted on in the middle of the entrance carpet," I supply.

"Oh, no." Rickety dread defines her repetition. "But still...how?"

"We're not entirely sure. But let's just say that Sprout had as much fun with the dip as Maximus and I did."

"And someone caught it in a picture."

"That was sold to a tabloid."

"Shit." Her head rears back. But not for long. "And *Mother* never said a word?"

"She probably gave it a fast glance and little else. At first look, it's just a trick of the stage lights."

She realigns her stance, looking ready to roll her eyes. Her fresh blurt is the stopgap for that. "So who found out first?" she charges. "Nosey All-father or Freaky Hell Man?"

"Not sure. They confronted us with it together."

"When?"

"The night Maximus proposed."

"Wait." Her forehead crunches as quickly as her other expressions. "When he whisked you off to El Capitan? After your first gown fitting?" She adds an incensed nostril flare. "Nearly *three weeks ago*?"

I step back and spread my hands on the air. "There's a good reason I didn't tell you."

"Out with it. You have sixty seconds."

I haul in a hurried but full breath. This wasn't the conversational path I expected to be skipping down with her, but here we are. No U-turns. Not with my sister looking like she'll yank either the whole story or my beating heart out of me.

"Zeus and Hades were certain that Hecate would soon spot the picture too. And once she did, she'd be coming for Sprout."

Even more color drains from her. "The only demigod-demon-human-witch hybrid in existence. Which she'd grow in one of her barn incubators if she had to, while the flies fed on your decimated body."

My grimace is instant. "Really gross but really right. And practically what Zeus said too."

Her shrug is equally fast. "Who said it's hard to rule a realm?" After I jump both brows, challenging if she really wants me to fill in that answer, she pushes on. "So tell me he also arrived with a solution for you? Or Hades did?"

"You think they'd have shown up otherwise?"

At that, I do supply her with Z's and Hades's certainty that Hecate's would soon put together our truth for herself. That once that happened, the goddess would see nothing but her end goal: overthrowing Olympus with all the forces she could rally, including harnessing my child's power. Whatever it cost her. Whatever it cost *me*.

That in order to prevent it, they were certain I had to be hidden. That it had to be in one of their two realms.

"So they ordered you to make a *choice*?" Kell inserts with a stunned gawk. "One or the other? Hell or Olympus?"

I try to let my face register most of my incredulous affirmation. This wedding gown, while one of the most beautiful garments I've ever worn, has too many beads to lose if I gesticulate an inch in the wrong direction.

"Like a rock and a hard place—if *rock* means ninth circle and *hard place* means a realm in which Hecate can access with any road she chooses."

Kell shakes her head. "So what happened? How'd you get out of it?" Her posture stiffens. "You got out of it, right? You two haven't been getting day passes for good behavior, right? I can't see Hades doing that. But if you went with Zeus and—"

"We didn't go with Z," I intervene. "Maximus told them *both* to go pound sand."

Her gaze flares. "And how far did the sparks fly?"

I'm ready with my own quick shrug. "Actually, they didn't. I think they were both certain we'd be back soon enough, banging on one or both their doors, and they'd be able to name more conducive conditions for hiding us."

Her nod is purposefully slow. A steady show of deep approval. "But you've been doing that for yourself, at Terranea."

I jog up my chin. "Effectively enough that even you're still convinced."

She rears back again. "Huh?"

I pull up my whole posture now. "Maximus and I haven't spent a single night at Terranea. Well, not yet. I really hope that can happen soon. I've stretched out enough on that casita bed to know I'd *really* love a whole night's sleep..."

Her huff breaks in on me. "Can you talk thread counts and mattress quality later? Because right now—" And then even cuts herself off, making room for another confused sound. "So where have you two been—"

"We've actually been staying at Rerek's."

"Excuse me?"

"Don't be mad."

"Mad?" she snaps. "Why would I be *mad*, darling? Ohhh, you mean why would I *stop* there, right? Why stay at *mad* when one can absorb the announcement that their sister has been voluntarily sleeping at the same place they were held hostage for a couple of days? You're right. Why would I settle for merely *mad* right now?"

She's winding up to fling more, but she's paused to see

if that's enough to knock me down a few pegs. She doesn't realize I'm not the same sister she knew even a couple of months ago. That her wry rants, even in the lowkey style that's nearly her trademark, won't hit bullseye on my guilt reflex anymore. I love her, still so much and still so intensely, but I can't keep showing it in the same ways. I can't keep taking care of her—or even Jaden—as I once did.

We've all grown up so much. Our worlds have gotten bigger. In a very short time, my own body will symbolize that. Now my heart and spirit have to, as well. I just have to find the right way to tell her that.

"Hey. You're not the only one who got screwed over by Rerek's wrong decisions." I'm justified about parking my hands on my hips to emphasize that, confirmed by my sister's sullen face. "That villa is where I got snatched away by Hades. Needless to say, I don't go anywhere near the formal living room."

"Oof. You're really right," she mutters before pushing out a breath.

"But you know what? Our ordeals combined would have been days at the playground compared to the captivity my child would endure under Hecate's thumb, meaning Maximus and I had to make some tough decisions. We remembered Rerek being so eager to help us all when he showed up at the EmStar Awards. We realized that since he had to maintain the hex across his villa for so long, the magic was probably still strong there. We were right. After I patched the hole that I created when breaking you and Jaden out, and then adding a spell of my own on top of it, the place turned into a fortress. Jaden's been a huge help in teleporting us back and forth from Terranea when we need it, but we only show up after the media's been alerted that we're going somewhere."

"And Hecate doesn't dare touch you while so much of the human realm is looking on," Kell supplies.

I'm nodding before she finishes. "If she *is* aware of the baby by now, she doesn't dare come right out and kill me to get what she wants."

After an extended pause, she sighs. "I wish I could tell you that no part of that makes sense. But it's solid thinking."

There's heartfelt stuff beneath her cynicism, compelling me to step over and pull her into a hug.

"I wanted to tell you," I admit. "So many times. But you and Jaden have already been through so much because of my journey with Maximus. And lately, there's been more for you to deal with. If Veronica had her way, we'd be planning this occasion into next year."

"Oh, far beyond that. You know she'd be wanting Sprout in the ceremony, so that would've meant waiting for the cute thing to become a toddler."

"And who's being disgustingly logical now?" I push away by half a step, letting her see the determination that's likely glommed on to my every blood cell by now. "But delaying this wasn't ever an option, for reasons far beyond the sapling's arrival date."

Kell cocks her head. "Why do I feel like there's a lot more to this story?"

Her query is all I need for approval on another lengthy

disclosure. This one contains the surprise meet-up that Maximus and I had with Persephone back at Oread, without missing a single word of what the goddess of fertility told us. I especially emphasize what Persephone exhorted—begged?—to us to do, in terms of today.

The task that feels more daunting than ever.

Which is why I'm ready to tear up before I even step foot down the aisle.

"Well, soonish Mrs. Kane, it sounds like you and your groom are going to need some significant help here. Like from a sister who's offering to do whatever it takes to pull this thing off?"

CHAPTER 2

MAXIMUS

I'VE ALWAYS PUSHED OFF superstitions as nonsense. Tools for the schoolkids who branded me a monster or crutches for uninspired horror writers.

Today, they're the bullshit I can push aside while stepping into the storage closet to wait for Kara. I even do it with a giant chunk of gratitude, glad for this chance to hold her before we're nothing but the main attraction for today's big event.

Bigger than I really want to be reminded of.

But forgetting isn't an option. Not the show that Veronica has staged, and certainly not the summit that Kara and I have coordinated on our secret burner phones. Flames that already feel too damn hot...

I react to the thought by sliding a nervous finger under my collar and tie. If I were only here for the chance to declare my love for my sweet little demon, my sweat count would be sliced in half. But that's not going to happen. Not when both of us know our wedding might be humanity's last chance for survival.

Thank *God* for this private moment we managed to grab...

Though once the door opens and she steps through, illuminated by the sun that's dipped low enough to limn her from behind, I instantly rethink my reticence about all the folklore.

It's got to be mocking heaven if one is marrying an angel.

That's it. That's the word for every dazzling inch of the female consuming my gaze now, in the gown that looks spun by spectral seamstresses just for her. From the sparkling accents that hug her neck to the bodice that tapers down her torso to the flounces of fabric swirling her hips and legs, she sucks the air from all my cells and the thoughts from all my synapses. Every conclusion except one.

Demons truly *are* the angels who got pushed out of paradise.

Maybe, I muse, it was because of jealousy. What seraph wouldn't want an eternity of standing next to this beauty? Her eyes, aglow like dew diamonds in the sun. Her skin, smooth as tawny clouds in that same light. Her hair, tumbling like ebony rivers around that idyll. But the best of all, her smile: a curve of open adoration and unending love that has me doubting my initial observation.

Maybe the demons were never forced out of heaven at all. Maybe they're just selective about who gets to see the whole kingdom. Best of all, with her as guide.

I'm ready for the full tour.

I show her so by taking the first step. At the same time, reaching out for her. My arms aimed nowhere else. My sights fixed on nothing else.

My heart bursting from no other sound than her voice, rich and silky.

"Good afternoon, Professor Maximus."

"And what a damn good one it is, Miss Valari." My own tone is thick as I cup hands to her waist and draw her closer. Then dip my head to capture her lightly glossed lips...

Until a light snicker tethers me back.

Not Kara's. Because at once she's biting out, "Seriously?"

"Sorry." Kell is recognizable even before I can fully see her. "I mean it. I was just thinking...that's probably the last time you'll hear it. *Miss Valari*. It's bittersweet. And if I don't laugh, I'll do that other emotional thing. Not cool after an hour getting all this done." She flows a hand, ta-da style, in front of her face. "Which I'll serve up as *your* cautionary tale, groom guy. Mess up your girl too much here, and people will know you've been laughing at fate."

I'm ready to snort something glib about desperate writers and fanciful children, but Kara lifts a more rueful smile my way. "She's probably right." Her fingertips follow the trajectory of her stare, trailing into both sides of my beard. "Especially because you look good enough to wreck right now..."

She gives way to a staccato sigh, communicating meanings that braid with my hoarse moan. But that's not the worst of the torment. Damn her, the woman adds a tiny lick along my bottom lip, striking flint to stone for a solid spark all the way to my groin.

I roll both hands down to her backside, uncaring if I knock every sparkle loose from her ass. I need to feel her form against mine. To revel in the shivers that are overtaking her too. The arousal that stutters into her every breath...

"Annnd that's it." Kell's declaration is a good friend and worst enemy at once. "Chain's being yanked, wrecking ball. Rubble isn't pretty."

Kara moves back with a low huff. "*Rrrrmph.* Speak for yourself, killjoy."

A similar sound vibrates from Kell. "What happened to the part where I'm right?"

"Where you're *what*, now?" Again, the interjection doesn't belong to Kara—nor to the sister practically tapping her foot in wait for an answer. The words are urbane, unruffled, and male. "Aren't stalactites supposed to just hang there and be pretty?"

Another growl from Kell, twice as irked as before. "I *told* you," she spits at Kara before her peeved pout toward the closet's newest arrival. "And fuck off."

"Well, I'd rather be fucking *on* something, darling Kell. Or some*one*...if you know any volunteers?"

I lean forward, making sure Prieto sees my clenched jaw. "If you're looking for ways to get your ring back on her finger, that's not it, man."

Prieto's smirk fades at the same rate that Kell's quirks up. "Nice work, brother," she croons my way. "And I was just going to say he's been dipping into the paint restoration resin again."

A long sniff expands her fiancé's aquiline nose. "Hmmm. But better the resin than sweet Clio's bedsheets, yes?"

Before Kara and I can muster stunned reactions, Kell handles the guy's assholery for herself. The crack of her palm across his jaw is muffled from outside by the towels and toilet paper stacked around us, though that doesn't stop a bang of insight in my brain.

"Wait. Clio?" I inject. "As in one of the *Musai*? She's the muse of history, right? The shy bookworm?"

"Define *shy*," Prieto drawls.

Kell's vicious sniff rips the air. She draws back as if readying a full punch for the guy but sags into a seethe when Kara hits her with a warning glance.

I join my censuring stare to Kara's when Prieto whips a new look at his betrothed, lips twisting with the sadistic cocktail *he's* prepared to mix for *her*.

"Okay." I straighten my shoulders and firm my jaw. "As much as I'd love to grab boxing gloves for you two and some popcorn for Kara and me, time isn't an expendable commodity at the moment." I pulse my hand around Kara's hard enough for them to witness. "You guys probably thought we were getting away for some fast face sucking. And also as fully as I wish that were the case—"

"You're planning something," Arden inserts as calmly as asking where we're going to honeymoon. "Aren't you? About all the whispers of the war?"

"*Potential* war," Kara cuts in, her form stiffening even more. I wish the change didn't triple her elegant, ethereal effect in that gown ... "Nothing has been that plainly stated."

"Not yet," Arden says.

"And not *ever*, if we can help it."

I peer harder at the incubus. "But you already knew that...didn't you? How? What *whispers* are you talking about? How loud are they?"

Arden sweeps out a reassuring hand. "Deep breaths, please. It's still well below the main gossip radar, at least in the underworld. A few of us are just trained better about the frequencies to listen in at."

"And they're chattering about it there?" Kara steps forward, a tremble across her delicate features. "How loud? How often?"

Arden arches his brows. A wave of something—simple reaction? Deeper emotion? Overt conflict?—is an odd flicker on his own face. It doesn't disappear either. "Not as often as the conjectures that your belly is cooking the world's most unique hybrid, my sister."

Kell sews her tension onto Kara's now. Neither of them is comfortable about the incubus's tendency toward the familial liberties, but it's not the most important point at the moment. Thankfully, Kara understands my gentle reminder in the form of my subtle weight shift.

"All right, let's just hope you're on a sharper edge than everyone else, Prieto," I state, "and we've still got the element of surprise on our hands here."

Kell's expression narrows. "Surprise? About what?"

Kara's the one to readjust her stance, giving me an entrancing view of her profile as she pulls a long breath in. "Right after we learned about the pregnancy, Persephone sought us out. She was as worried as us about Hecate's commitment to taking out Zeus and Hera."

While Kell's stare stiffens, Prieto cocks his head. "Fascinating."

"No," Kell says. "More like terrifying." She darts her focus between her sister and me. "How does she know? Hecate confided in her?"

"More than that," Kara divulges. "Hecate retrieved her from Olympus ten days early. Told her that she needed help and couldn't even entrust any of the Iremia *magistras* with it. The goddess needed help in 'keeping an eye' on us."

"*Very* fascinating."

Kell backhands Arden's shoulder. "Keeping an eye on you," she echoes. "I assume not in the *please watch my cat while I'm out of town* kind of way?"

Kara sputters an ironic laugh. "I'd let you scratch my chin if that were even half true."

During their exchange, Prieto's clearly processing the new input of information. "She came for Persephone ten days in advance. So she's been suspicious about *your* suspicions for a while now."

Kara nods. "Most likely the largest reason for Persephone's effort."

"Which came down to what?" Kell queries. "Don't tell me she was just rolling around to give you a friendly heads-up about stuff."

"No. There was more." Kara sobers by at least a dozen degrees. "She implored us to take action. To try to stop Hecate's crazy plans."

"Now that's past fascinating." Without altering his frown, Prieto prevents Kell's new bicep punch by snatching her wrist in midair. "Wouldn't Persephone stand to benefit in many ways from an upset of the realms?"

I hike up my jaw. "Not if it was going to take out the one she loves the most."

Kell's posture goes slack. "The humans?" Right before she tenses again, curling white fingertips around Arden's knuckles. "Is she positive about that?"

"*I* would be," the incubus inserts. "While this world has led the way in so many innovations and advances, they've done so at the price of their infrastructure. Not just the physical. For all of our disagreements in the underworld *and* higher firmaments, we have always found a way toward common ground and the steadiness of traditions. But the humans…they're tearing each other apart. Rendering their world down to the fiber of their souls." He sweeps a dark look around our little circle. "If any realm was already crumbling from the inside and ready to be quashed to dust, it's this one."

Kara drops my hand. I let her, already feeling the trembling fist she's forming. "Don't underestimate dust, *brother*," she grates. "It can form rocks. Cliffs. Galaxies."

"And peace?"

Prieto's challenge comes with a crane of his head in the other direction. My woman matches the position with a small but steady smile.

"Especially that," she finally declares. "And especially if every cell in my body has any say about it."

Her fade-off is filled with expectation—which Kell meets by stepping forward and yanking on her sister's hand. "And mine."

I press my grip atop their conjoined one. "And mine."

A few moments of silence, though they're actually good ones. During the pause, I watch as Prieto mirrors Kara's expression with a confident smirk of his own. When it reaches its height, he speaks.

"All right, then. What's the plan?"

CHAPTER 3

Kara

NOT LONG AFTER THOSE words leave Arden's mouth, I'm semi-sure he regrets them. But I've never been more thankful for his smug bravado and the question that transformed Kell and him into more than just the snarky representatives from our wedding party.

They're now our comrades. Co-conspirators for a plan that *has* to work.

Because despite the words I was tossing back at him, my stomach lurches at thinking of this world—my *home*—as dust.

This globe, even in its messed-up madness, is part of me. Threaded into all the parts of my being.

Nothing validates the surety more than the moment Kell and Arden exit the storage closet. As Arden pushes open the door and ensures they aren't being watched, an ocean-and-redwoods breeze steals past my nostrils and into my heart. My soul is next, reaching in response to the dark gold sunlight that surrounds Kell when she turns back to me with a quietly concerned glance.

"I wish I could say this plan is one syllable short of idiotic, but it already makes too much sense," she mutters, twisting her fingertips with mine. "But don't drag out this prologue too long, or I *will* lose my nerve."

"You won't be the only one." But I stop an inch short of putting action to my words, already taking note of Maximus's tug on my other hand. "I'll be right out," I tell her. "I promise."

She purses her lips as if already calling my bullshit. As soon as the door closes behind her and Maximus hauls me close, I admit that she's not wrong. And I'm not ashamed of it. Not by one iota of my incinerated senses.

All the cells that go up in flames as soon as he crushes his mouth over mine.

Then moans, using his mouth to open mine.

Then growls, plunging his tongue against mine.

It's the last thing we should be doing right now. But the most crucial thing we need. The steel rope to each other, like a tether in the storm we're about to face. A tempest that might be merciful—or terrible—to us. I yearn to believe in the former but know we must be fully prepared for the worst.

So here it is. Our version of training camp.

And I'm all in for the rigors.

We gasp against each other as if we've run ten miles. Laser our gazes as if our aims have to be sniper perfect. My heart throbs in my chest with that importance. It climbs into my throat, its thunder serious and scathing, as if this is the last time I'll drink in the glory of my amazing man.

My husband.

The words we have yet to say...though right now they're just a formality. The verbal versions of what already rings through me as perfect truth. Resounding reality.

So why am I waiting?

Why doesn't he deserve to hear it all this very second? The syllables already written in my heart and decreed in my spirit...

"Maximus." And now begging to be proclaimed by my lips. "My dearly beloved..."

But I'm silenced as soon as he kisses me again. Less deeper with his mouth but more intense with his pressure. Though it's not for long, the contact is enough to make my whole body vibrate. I shudder from the impact, wrapping myself closer to his tall tuxedoed form.

"I...I need to tell y—"

"Not yet," he commands beneath his breath. His lungs expand, causing my gown to shift against my breasts in wrenching ways.

Wonderful ways...

"Not yet," he repeats, demonstrating his direction by roaming his seeking grip along my spine. "Christ. How do I get into this thing?"

A laugh mingles with my new sigh, reacting to his greedy rasp. Just hearing what I do to him...and then feeling it, in every inch of the stiff flesh that's pushing from between his thighs...I'm joyous. Delirious. Rapidly ramping my desire to his level. Clutching at the ledge of his shoulder with one hand while destroying his pristine ponytail with the other.

"Zipper," I direct into his ear, resisting the urge to bite down on the flesh there. *Not yet.* His order is now my strength, an assurance of even better things to come if I'm ready to wait. "On your right. Along the side. Yesss."

I flow it along his neck, corresponding to how he scrapes the zipper along its metal teeth. As the nubs brush my flesh, I gasp and quake once more. Such fantastical flutterings. Phenomenal fires. Rush upon rush of the thermonuclear threads that solder us to each other, bound in gold and silver brilliance for all time.

My soul burns with the surety of it. Shines with its blissful severity.

But Maximus is brutally beautiful about needing to prove it.

I know that even before he feels his way beneath my underthings, aiming his knowing touch straight to the space between my buttocks. I'm even more sure when he keeps going, probing my trembling tissues from behind. And I'm past positive once he plumbs into me, sliding far and deep between my wet walls.

I mewl for him, trying to keep my volume beneath respectable decibels, but I'm fairly certain we've shredded *respectable* like every roll of paper towels on the shelf beside his head. Goodbye, mewls. Hello, needy hums. They're my litany into his ear as he sets up a merciless pace, pumping his digit into me over and over again.

The moment has come to indulge temptation, and I

give in by tugging at his earlobe with my teeth. But ohhh, the man is more than ready. He answers by doubling his pace—and his penetration. Another finger joins his first, stretching me in all the best ways.

"Maximus!" I can't help yelping. "Oh … *my* …"

The rest of it is taken by my stunned gasp, courtesy of his own nipping teeth. They're a harsh bite around the shell of my ear, and when I expect some soothing licks, there are more growled orders instead.

"Pretend it's me," he grates out. "Pretend it's my cock, taking your purity on our wedding night. Moan for me like it is, Kara."

I almost do. But I lean back instead, letting him see my rueful smile instead. "We both know that's not true."

"No?" Though his rhetoric is clear, he presses determined lips to my forehead. "Every time I'm inside you it's the first time, sweetheart. Because every time, I see … *you*. All of it. The honesty of your body. The clarity of your character. The fullness of your heart. It's all there …"

"And it's all … my purity?" I want to be rhetorical too. I want to be so right about this. About the conviction that's making *him* glow now too—even brighter than the light from my stomach, flowing out from the seam in my dress and illuminating the bottom edges of his face.

"It is," he affirms, lips barely moving as his gaze reflects the flames in mine. "And it's all mine. Now and forever."

My fires feed on his raw, rugged words like a hillside full of summer brush. Within seconds, I'm a high-hazard zone, and I don't care about anyone's defensible space. I want to burn. I need to incinerate.

"Yes," I rasp. "*Yours.*"

His gaze is hotter. Heavier. "Now and forever," he says from locked teeth. "Say it, Kara. All of it."

I stop to gulp as he increases his rhythm again. Driving my flames even higher....

"I'm...yours," I manage to choke. "Always...and forever."

"My bride," he growls back. "*Say it.*"

"Your bride."

"My love."

I nod at least eight times in succession, taking those cherished words in. Wanting to give him more than rote repetition now...but fighting to stay standing and sane as more of my body surrenders to his flamethrower fingers. The ferocity of their thrusts. The command of their caresses.

And then, before I can comprehend what he's doing, the reach of a third finger...across the ridge of flesh that craves his strokes the most.

I'm detonating.

Disintegrating.

Aflame in the starfire he's brought, a purity I can actually see now, white as heaven and golden as its gates.

A paradise only one man can fly me to.

The man I reach up to, cradling the edge of his face in my adoring grasp. The demigod I actually have words for now. Only three of them, yet so crucial. The most prized of my existence.

"Thank you...husband."

Maximus rewards me for that at once, his smile a

gorgeous outbreak in the middle of his beard. "I'd keep ordering you to say *that* again, but we might not ever make it out of here."

As he speaks, I soften my gaze into sultry suggestiveness. Slide a hand down, searching for the clasp of his slacks. The task isn't tough. I simply let my fingers follow his heat. "Well, we're not going anywhere until *you* get some heaven too."

A pout forms as soon as he sets me back by several inches. "I can't, beautiful. And we both know why." When I hit him with a flustered huff, he persists. "I can't lose control. Well, not yet." With his free hand, he squeezes my shoulder and then my elbow. "If that sunset light suddenly morphs into a David Fincher film, every god and demon in that sanctuary will start to wonder what you've gotten me up to—"

"Several mighty fine inches?" I jibe.

"—and then they'll get curious about things."

He pulls back a little more, letting that truth dig into my head as his perfect fingers slip out of my body. As he settles my dress back into position, I push out a grudging sigh.

"And with this crowd, *curious* leads to powers that can penetrate the walls."

Starting with Kell and Jaden themselves...

Damn it.

I'm not finished with the thought before Maximus reads it across my face, responding with a tender smile on his own.

"It's okay," he offers. "I'm serious. This just gives me a

better reason to get you alone again, after everything."

"Everything." I wish my echo were more than a tentative murmur. That I could render it to him with the same confidence he's projecting. That I could look into a magic ball and see the future as boldly as he seems to. I'd even settle for a gander at the next *hour*.

But even after the man kisses me goodbye with toe-curling skill, my divination game stays fuzzy. I have no idea what to expect from any of this—there's no user's manual for gathering the main players of every realm and forcing them to talk to each other!—which means I feel as steady as a newborn foal once I make it back to the bridal dressing room.

Kell's waiting inside but doesn't glance up from her phone as I shut the door. "Wow. You and Professor Hunk have really perfected the quickie. Jaden sneaked me a glass of pinot, and I'm not even done."

"Okay." I draw the word out, inflecting enough to imply my question. But I iterate it anyway. "Compliment or complaint?"

"Hmmm. Both. But you'll have to share the naughty deets later. Veronica's been getting testier with the texts. She's even citing some etiquette columns about proper delays on ceremony starts."

I tighten my eyes. "And that concerns *you* now too?"

"The etiquette police?" She rolls her eyes. "*Please*. But if any of our *elite* guests do ..."

"Good point." But while my assurance is steady, my senses aren't making the effort to back it up. My mind whirls twice as fast as before. I fight the temptation to feel so feeble about this. So unready…

"Hey. You okay?"

I push out a smile to answer her protective primp along one of my free-flowing curls. "Yeah. I—uh, I guess," I softly stammer. "Just wondering why I feel all of ten again, when we had to walk that first red carpet."

"I remember it too," she murmurs. "For the night the Film Institute honored Gramps."

"I had no idea what I was doing." I wrap my hand around her upheld fingertips. Get one gulp down to battle the emotional bulge in my throat. "Oh God, Kell. I still don't."

"And you're supposed to?" she rejoins. "Because everyone in the world decides to use one's wedding as an excuse to cast a spell they've never done before and hope it traps a bunch of Olympians long enough to talk out a peace plan?"

"Okay, okay," I concede, giving in to a chuckle. "Another awesome point courtesy of my amazing sister."

"Who's just here to support *your* amazingness."

While declaring it, she tilts back to retrieve my bridal bouquet. The luxurious dusky roses are bunched in a tight, perfect bundle, inserted with crimson diamonds that match the dark-red stones in my headband. I lift a hand to that piece now, tracing my fingers to the small hooks that have been customized into it. The holders for the most important piece of my trousseau.

"You remember how to hook the veil, right?" I murmur.

"Unless the process has changed from the first fifty times you showed me," Kell says, already securing the edge of the long silk tulle piece that I've been painstakingly working on with Madame. From the moment she asked me if I had any special ideas for customizing the veil, I knew exactly what had to be worked into the piece. The designer has outdone herself with my concept. I knew it before now, but it's breathtakingly clear as soon as Kell secures the final hook.

"Maximus is going to fry all his pasta when he sees this."

I spurt a small laugh, joining her to examine the star-shaped crystals cascading in the tulle down to my ankles. Their pattern isn't random. The carefully selected arrangement is a message from me to my husband, and I can't wait for him to see it.

"Should I assume that's a good thing?"

A blithe shrug from Kell. "Probably depends on who you ask."

I tug on one edge of the veil and spread it out, glad I took Madame's advice to sprinkle a few ruby-colored crystals in with the clear ones. At once, I see how the accents complement my headband—but most importantly, how they highlight the Valari crest earrings secured to my lobes.

My mind flashes to the day that I feared one of the heirlooms was gone forever. Its clip back had come loose in my hurried rush away from Maximus—from the attraction I'd stupidly thought to evade, as well—and I'd panicked, wondering how to best tell Mother that I'd lost half of the priceless family set. But I'd retraced my steps and remembered exactly where I'd last been aware of the jewelry. The process didn't just bring a rush of relief. It stabbed me with new awareness.

The realization that Maximus Kane wasn't just my flirting fancy.

That a much greater force was drawing me to him. A destiny that felt written in the stars.

Oh, God.

It truly was.

The surety clings to my mind as firmly as the stars in my veil, blown against my face as Kell and I cross the courtyard to the shallow stone steps that lead into the hilltop sanctuary.

Everyone is inside now, waiting.

There's a slow pop song of some sort, rendered by a harp and piano, swelling.

And now here's the throb of my pulse, racing.

It all gets faster and brighter and sharper as time ticks off a few more seconds. Clarity that I welcome because it brings the recall of a conversation from just three weeks ago, in which Persephone gave me a perfect collection of words. A pair of sentences that I knew I'd embrace in this exact moment…

Sometimes, one cannot hope for peace. But one can facilitate understanding.

I give in to a smile while strengthening my posture. Another long breath in and out, and I'm closing my eyes to again savor the crisp warmth on my face…

That, once I open my gaze, becomes blinding light.

But I see past it, as a figure steps forward. And I'm

36

rushing joyously for him.

"Gramps," I sob, trying not to snot out on his shoulder. He's so pressed and stately in his suit, which isn't quite a tux but measures a step above the austere underworld livery in which he last appeared. Back on that beach, at the side of his new master. On that day of such elation and then such confusion...

"Hey, ladybug," he murmurs into my hair, sounding unnervingly good. Strong. Better than he did when wasting away in the backyard casita of the Valari estate. "Just look at you. My sweet, sweet girl. The world's most gorgeous bride."

"Gorgeous?" I chuckle softly while stepping back. "Said the pot to the kettle?"

He looks ready to scoff but regards me with somber eyes instead. "We'd best get things started. Despite your mother's dogged intentions, some of your...guests...might be tempted to expand on the night's main attraction."

His purposeful pause already implies what he'd say as follow-up if he could. By *guests*, he's really only referring to one in particular.

Hades.

And by *Hades*, he means that the night might just be getting started.

But I can't reply with typical *I understand*s and *it's okay*s. Not without lying to my grandfather, which I've never done before. And do *not* plan on starting now.

"Maybe some *guests* will just have to change their minds." Hurray for Kell, who has no issue at all with lobbying to Gramps.

But does Gramps know something we don't? Something in

the works besides our carefully laid plan?

Even if that's not the case, does his hell guard job description now include an hourly report? And if so, to whom?

Are we all screwed before this mission even starts?

Try as I can for an inkling of that from Gramps's aura, there's nothing there for me to pull but the pride and love he's already declared aloud. That means his mild jitters are really just *grandfather of the bride* anticipation, or he'd learned how to sequester certain thoughts just for his master.

It also means a third thing.

That right now, there's nothing I can do to change any of it. There's only one road to take. One path to follow. One set of stairs to climb...

To a collection of moments I'll never forget.

For so many reasons than the obvious.

To have and to hold...

As I scoop my hand beneath Gramps's elbow and step forward, I look out across the waves bringing the tide along the rugged beach and cove below. No magic is necessary for the beauty of this twilight, with the magenta of the sky kissing the silver foam of the sea. For a moment, I remember the last time it all took my breath away like this. The night I flew over Rerek's villa, reaching deep inside for powers I had yet to claim or try.

Magical providence had been good to me then.

For better or for worse...

I only hope, as I ask it for a bigger bucket of help, that it's inclined to smile in once more...

So we can really make this day the start of the *better* part.

CHAPTER 4

MAXIMUS

"LITTLE PRO TIP, MY beautiful son? Today is supposed to be the *happiest* day of your life."

A chuff escapes me, helping with the small smile down into Mom's twinkling gaze. "I *am* happy." It's not a lie. It's just not the whole truth either. "Just nervous too."

And there's the massive understatement on top of it all. Which, *damn it*, she already seems to comprehend in full. I view it already across her face, with the wattage of her smile diving by double digits.

I brace myself for the witticism that'll double as her demand for information. Instead, she fluffs my boutonniere, tucks some stray hairs back from my face, and murmurs, "Well, nervous is normal..."

"But?" I say it as soon as her trail-off implies it.

A few more moments, in which she brushes nonexistent lint from my shoulders before shrugging one of her own. "I've seen you shake hands with *nervous* before. And *this* is something past that."

"Hey, if you're not ready to throw up, you're not doing it right."

She perks a brow. The expression just intensifies how pretty she looks, even in the simply cut dress that she purposely picked to not upstage Veronica. But the dress, in the merlot shade that the mothers agreed to wear, simply complements Mom's coloring better. The makeup adds depth to the blue specks in her eyes, and her blond curls pop against the dress's dramatic color.

"Clever," she remarks to my declaration. "Dredging up more Einstein for us today, Professor?"

I shake my head. "That's a Max Kane original."

She drops her hands. Straightens her regard. "All right. No more smoke screens. Are you having *actual* jitters, son of my soul? Because Kara has gone through too much for this, if you aren't completely stitched in for—"

"*Stop.*" I mellow the impact of my growl by repeating it with a tender wrap of my fingers around hers. "Of course I'm stitched in. Locked down. Charged up."

"Okay, okay," she laughs out. "You've even brushed up on the metaphors. Impressive."

A new shake of my head. But with this one, I give myself freedom to grin a little. To feel *a lot.* "I'm not the impressive one today."

I've rarely spoken truer words. Not just because of what Mom's just stated about Kara. Not because of everything she's been through already.

What the woman is about to attempt . . .

And accomplish . . .

She'll do it. She has to. I already believe, with the stuff in my soul that's real and true, that she will.

"Well, *both* of you are lucky," Mom returns to my assertion. "I always knew you would end up with someone extraordinary, but that's because you're so amazing. Luckily, I already know that *Kara* knows it." A thin sheen grows in her eyes. "She's going to cherish you, Max. I will always ask for—and expect—nothing less."

I rear back a little, unsure what to do about it.

What's going on?

Nancy Kane isn't a buttoned-up stiff. I've seen these parts of her before, through every phase of my upbringing. Bits and pieces of it even came out last month, when Kara and I showed up at the emergency response post after the earthquake. When Mom embraced me, I felt the edges of the sandpaper in the last few seconds of her hug.

But this, right now…

It's different.

In so many terrifying new ways.

All the ways in which I peer at the world as a father-to-be. And all the feelings that all those paths lead to.

All the ways I now comprehend Mom's tears.

And another truth.

That I owe her *my* truth.

"Mom…"

She rocks back by herself. I'm glad about it. The woman isn't a mindless dandelion. She already hears the meaning in my voice. My sober intent.

Tell her.

Tell. Her.

The time has come to let her in. To know you can count on her as an ally when the crucial time comes. It won't be much longer. When it does, and you're peering around for those who can be strong for you and with *you, you'll look to her be able to know—*

"Oh, my." She cuts into my thoughts with a concerned mutter. "I *knew* there was something." She balls up a hand but looks unsure about whether to writhe or pump the fist. "All right. Out with it, Max. What's going on?"

I reach for her clenched fingers. I look down, unnerved by the sight of her tension—but that's not the only reason for the spike of mine.

My mom is wearing new jewelry.

Expensive jewelry.

It's not a ring, thank fuck, but a piece that's just as revelatory. A bracelet. A really nice one. I've overheard enough chatter between students over the years to know what's considered trash and what's *ooo*'ed and *ahhh*ed at as treasure. The quality of the clasp. The care of the settings. And of course, the sparkle in the bling. Whether Z procured the bracelet in Olympus or Los Angeles, its stones are definitely the real deal.

As real as the duel to which my logic has now brazenly challenged my heart.

"I'm sorry. This is all ... a lot."

I know she sees the honesty of my remorse, though not for the apparent reasons. My regret stabs deeper, into the soul that sees the foolishness of trusting her right now. If *Operation White Lace and Peace Up* fails today, Kara and I will have a room full of fuming deities ready to play the blame game. Mom's day will be easier if she can look at the guy who put that bracelet on her arm and declare she knew nothing about the plan.

"—*imus?*"

My head jerks, the gray matter recognizing this likely isn't Mom's first summons.

"Sorry," I mutter again. "I mean it. It's just—"

"A lot." She chuckles it out while patting my arm. "Got it. And it's totally okay."

"I was actually just thinking…about you and Z." I run a thumb over her bracelet, knowing she'll figure out that I've snapped together a few facts. "You two have been spending a lot of time together."

A blush tiptoes onto her cheeks. I smile, relishing the sight. It's a rare one. When she replies, it's in a tender murmur. "We've had a lot of happy reasons to."

I form my hand atop hers. "Which is really cool…"

"But?" she fills in with my hesitation.

"I just want to make sure he's treating you right." I slide my free hand into her other one, thankful she's finally ditched the fist. "He can be persuasive. And persistent."

Her smile widens. "Yes to Box A. *And* B."

"Well, he knows you have a life, right? A happy one? He's not guilting you into dates or anything? Giving you the whole *let me sweep you away to our private villa* speech?"

"Yes to those boxes too," she supplies. "But *breathe*, baby. And give your mom a little credit. I'm not the starry-eyed missy he first seduced. Slowly but surely, he's learning that.

And getting used to it." When she glances up and notices my stubborn skepticism, she jogs her chin and adds, "He even went with me to weeding-and-wine at the neighborhood garden last week."

I'm ready to scoff, but it's impossible. "That's so random, I can't even call bullshit on it."

"He even flirted with Mrs. Worthington from your building. And he's likely out there doing it again now."

"Why don't we all go see for ourselves?"

The new contributor to our conversation isn't one I expected. Since we've passed the ten-minute mark on delaying the ceremony, I've been watching out for my best man to roll in at any second, deftly flinging his version of a fidget spinner.

But instead of Jesse in his wheelchair with the elastic hand snapper, we've got Rerek Horne in a shiny vintage suit, wielding a smirk on his lips and a sharp pique in his eyes.

"Horne." I walk over and shake his hand. "Good to see you. It's been a while." By *a while*, I mean a few hours ago at his place up in Malibu, but Mom still believes what the rest of the world does—that Kara and I have been bunking at Terranea for the last three weeks. "Let me introduce you to my mother, Nancy Kane. And Mom, this is—"

"Oh, I already know."

"You do?" Rerek and I spurt it with matching bewilderment. Not the fun and quixotic kind. We're a kinship of disquiet, wondering how far she's lifted the curtain of our ruse. More vitally, how much she's allowed Zeus to peek in.

"Wow. It's a real honor." She gushes through all five pumps of her handshake with the demon. "Your Paris Fashion Week looks were amazing. But not as awesome as your appearances on *Flounce*."

I dip a tight frown. "What the hell is *Flounce*?"

"It was my favorite part of the show, seeing what you'd wear for the elimination round," she goes on. "When you walked on set, it was like the chaos just got started!"

Though I'm still putting pieces together, at least Rerek regains his urbane composure. "Well then, I accomplished the mission." But all too fast, his smirk gives way to a new hit of his palpable tension. "Which regrettably, isn't *this* mission." He turns fully to me, cocking an eyebrow like the thing is tethered to his slicked-back hairline. "If I don't return to the sanctuary with our handsome groom in tow, Veronica Valari will be feeding valuable parts of my anatomy to a pod of orcas inside the hour."

"Relax," Mom exhorts, patting his burgundy satin lapel. "We'll make it happen. But FYI, the transient orcas are usually only around these waters in springtime."

"Not if they've arrived as part of Poseidon's envoy."

The demon is a complete gentleman about it, compassionate to the point of sweet, though it's not exactly something Mom hears every day. Not as a complete truth, anyway.

To her credit, it only puts a small dent in her composure. "All right, then," she murmurs, calming her bugged gaze with a long breath. "I can put this in the *weddings to remember* file for many reasons, then."

Outwardly, I'm able to indulge her quip with a smirk and a laugh. But Rerek's own reaction, a smile that doesn't stretch to his eyes, tells me a larger truth. That my facade isn't fooling anyone except the humans. He already sees—maybe even hears—what my head actually wants to say right now. What my gut twists in seven new ways about.

You have no idea, Mom. No idea at all.

CHAPTER 5

Kara

"**S**URPRISE."

As soon as Veronica whispers the word, my nerve endings turn to paranoid spikes. It's Pavlovian. That word, paired with her for-the-cameras smile, usually means they're about to weather some turbulence.

But every once in a while, the turbulence is joyous. Like in this second, as she approaches me at the back of the sanctuary just as the processional song begins. It's the song we agreed upon, *Someone Like You*, originally performed by Van Morrison.

Today it's being sung by another Irish star, one of my favorite pop singers from the last couple of years. I've been obsessed with her talent for two years now but have never crossed paths—or red carpet steps—with her to say so.

I won't get the chance today either.

Not if everything goes as Maximus and I have planned.

I push aside a fresh twinge of guilt, already anticipating the mental blank space the humans will experience after our vows. But if everything goes right, it will be nothing more than that: a blip that's nothing more than an odd brain fade, making them wonder how they could have forgotten the last few minutes of the year's biggest power wedding.

Okay, maybe more than a few minutes.

Probably more.

But the alternative isn't acceptable. Today *isn't* the right time to expose the human race to our huge truths. Not when a larger story is riding those plotting coattails. Not when they wouldn't just discover that the Olympian Pantheon is a real deal but that the gods are bickering and on the brink of dragging humanity into their crossfire.

I need a Maximus-sized chunk of self-control, and recreating the *Endgame* finale with the cast in *my* head instead... Not a smart play.

Not with the beautiful moments that *do* deserve my attention right now.

My mother's open, proud expression. Every note of the song, with its tender melody and words so ideal for Maximus and me. The redwoods that sway gently outside the chapel's glass walls and ceiling. The dark orange sunbeams that find their way through, twinkling on the jewels in my bouquet.

But even more beautiful than that...

That sunset flowing across the altar at the other end of the building. Those beams shining on the umber and gold head of the most beautiful male I've ever seen. Or ever *will* see, in the rest of my existence.

My husband.

I don't care about the formalities we've still got to go through. In all of my heart, he's already mine. Every regal, formidable inch of his towering, dazzling form...

All that considered, why does he still seem so far away? More immediately, why is it taking everyone so long to make it up the aisle in front of Gramps and me? Jesse and Regina are first, followed by Jaden and Sarah, then Arden and Kell. Mother and Nancy turn to hug Maximus and me before making their own side-by-side trip between the packed pews.

Finally, it's time for Gramps and me to go in.

For all my desire to sprint straight up to the altar, my legs have suddenly turned to applesauce. A nervous flush conquers my face, earning me tender stares from most in the crowd. Thankfully, my stress is coming off as a simple case of bridal excitement. Nobody, not even some of Hollywood's most elite actors and directors, suspects the bigger truth.

But the industry hotshots don't matter as much as the rest of the crowd. The guests who really have to buy off on my act.

The gods. And goddesses. And every member of their entourages.

I glance at them as much as I can, face-hopping fast in the guise of *thank you for being here* smiles.

There's a trio of muses I haven't met yet, notable by the musical thrum beneath their auras. A few rows on, I spot Persephone in her dutiful but miserable place by Hades's side. She pierces me with a fast but purposeful scrutiny, yet

I change nothing about my overall demeanor. The hell king doesn't miss much, and the poor goddess would pay dearly if he suspected we've met before.

I move on to where Poseidon is located, bracketed by his two guests, whom I assume to be Amphitrite and Triton. His wife embodies most of the classic historical portrayals, with her long, blue-streaked braids tamed by a wreath of sparkling seashells and ruby-encrusted crab claws. Triton is as stunning as his parents, with an NFL-star jawline and bold brow. He's nearly as tall as Maximus and seems to rock an equally impressive head of hair. His tight dark curls are tamed beneath a black knit cap.

Nearer to the front, I get to the row with all my Iremia sisters—Marie, Morgana, Aradia, Kiama, and Liseli—who beam and wave between dabbing their tearful eyes. My heart swells so much, I'm tempted to stop and race over to hug them all. It's easier to fight the allure when my sights pull toward the inside end of the row, where Circe and Hecate are already prepared for me. Their serene smiles and queenly nods are interrupted only by the dainty dabs at their own eyes.

Guess I'm not the only one floating a thick cover story here.

Except the two of them should receive extra performance points, everything considered. Well, one main thing.

The fact that they're only separated from Zeus by the sanctuary's center aisle.

As I approach that narrow breach, I resist the urge to

halt in place. To be the physical representation of everything I've been mentally fixated on. To shake them until whatever they call brain matter is knocked into place the *right* way, forced to see that there's more in this realm—in *all* these realms—than the threads that bind their egos.

But what good would my screaming really do?

Maybe this once, they'll open their eyes and see it for themselves. No screaming needed. Unity that can be found. Understanding that can exist. Love that can happen, no matter how many voices scream the opposite.

Maybe Maximus and I can *show* them…

With every step I take, it feels more possible. More like the man to whom I'm walking, surer by every second. He was once an unattainable dream. The teacher I couldn't crave, the fire I couldn't touch, the obsession who meant my ruin.

Instead, he was my redemption. Once I dared to believe it was possible, he took me to the edge of the stars…

And then beyond.

He reaches for me now, promising to do the same. I lift my fingers against his, sending him the same message from my soul, my psyche, my body, my heart. The sparks we've always shared, so unique and unmatched, zap into all those precious pockets of me. I hitch a tiny grin, watching Maximus jerk from the same impact.

And here we are…

Inside our own star.

The fires of our bond, rising and enclosing us. The colors of our love, twining with those flames. It's gold and red, silver and sapphire, amethyst and forest, and so much more. Galaxies on top of each other. A million points of light, each giving an endless flow of energy, until I'm sure my heart will burst from these incredible constellations ...

Until I realize that none of them are stars.

They're mirrors.

Handing back only what they see. Reflecting exactly what's in front of them.

We're those awesome asterisms.

The brilliance that grows from outside our orbit as well as in. Taking a little strength from the minister who stands between us, using the same surfer-Zen calm that earned him Maximus's trust to begin with, to guide us through our vows. Gathering more fortitude as we commit ourselves to those promises, grateful we chose to go for the traditional *to have and to hold* script instead of fumbling with memorized poems or crumpled-up scribbles. I already feel the truth beneath my man's rough tone. I hope, as I send my unblinking stare up into his mesmerizing cobalts, that he somehow knows mine too.

"For better or for worse ..."

My better *started from the moment I touched you. If the worst is yet to come, I'll stand by you to face it. All of it.*

"For richer or for poorer ..."

With you in my soul, I'm the wealthiest woman alive. You are my treasure, Maximus. My shining gold.

"In sickness and in health ..."

I'll be here for you. I'll be here through every moment. All the light and dark, the good and bad, the joyous and painful. You're mine, and I will never let go.

"To love and to cherish…"

And beyond.

No matter what that means. No matter where this all takes us.
I love you, Maximus Kane.

At the edges of my consciousness, I'm aware of those words slipping out on my tearful whisper. It's easier to hear what he says, equally soft but twice as gruff, in reply.

"As I love you, Kara Kane."

Thick emotion surges up in me, a flow of awe and exhilaration, mirroring what I capture from Maximus's mien. *Kara Kane.* My heart has dared to utter it a few times, but it's the first occasion I've actually heard it on the air.

It sounds…amazing.

Intoxicating.

But in many ways, perfectly normal. Like the sunset beams that outline his head, just…meant to be. Hecate might have interfered about how and when it happened, but the reality of this—the inevitability of *us*—it was as certain as our first breaths. We would have found each other if I were a shepherdess in Mongolia and he ruled a Fortune 500 empire in Manhattan. Somewhere, somehow, it would have happened.

The sun always finds a way to shine.

A soul always finds its way to its other half.

Mine stretches for his now, tying with its mighty fabric until we're tightly knotted. But I don't stop there. Out comes the steel thread from my spirit, stitching in frantic rows—especially as the minister murmurs something about kissing to seal the deal on our union.

A kiss I despaired of ever sharing with him.

But now, falter about even starting.

Because starting it means finishing it. And finishing means our gateway into the next part of this day.

We have to step free from the star. And into our well-prepared crucible.

Maximus doesn't want to do it either. It's evident in the persistence of his lips and then the rebellious vibration of his grunt. That's all before he drags up and away, though only by a few inches. He's still close enough that I can denote the darker blue rings in his irises, as intense as the brackets that appear at the corners of his mouth.

"You ready to do this?"

I answer his murmur with a small smile. The tension lines trace all the way up to his forehead, conveying his confusion, but there's not enough time to explain my whole reasoning to him. It's not *what* he's asked, but *how*. The gift of his concern, wrapped in the strength of his respect... He might not ever comprehend what a gift they both are.

But I have to shelve the explanation for now. Group it with all the other things we haven't found time for. So much we have to say to each other. So much we have to do.

So much we have to save for the moments when our life truly begins.

Moments, I pray, that aren't far off.

This has to work.

This has *to work.*

I panic, realizing I've rasped it aloud when Maximus

grabs my hands tighter.

"Hey." His murmur commands my head up. His face is firm with conviction. His nostrils flare, and his gaze is close to igniting just like mine. "It'll work. They're dealing with *us* now."

"The cuckoo Kanes?"

His soft snort is like a summer wind on the winter of my jitters. "If that's what it'll take to get through to this bunch, then color me eighty shades of cuckoo."

I pull in a steadying breath. "If I can't get this spell to work, my love, I might be sharpening your crayons."

"And doesn't *that* win the trophy for today's finest euphemism?"

The jibe, drawled so serenely that it's nearly obnoxious, has Maximus matching every inch of my startled pivot. But three seconds later, the description is no longer relevant. I pass up startlement for all-out alarm, once my logic rules out all the usual suspects as its source. Jaden, Jesse, Kell, *and* Arden are all as silent as watchful saints.

So ... *who* ...

Once I affirm the perpetrator, I struggle to hold in my stunned gasp—though am even questioning myself about that. Why am I this stunned? How is this hitting me as anything unusual?

Unusual.

In that one word, I recognize my mistake.

This isn't an unusual turn of things.

It's a *magical* one.

Orchestrated by the only person who's now rising from

the crowd.

The crowd.

Only now do I realize why everyone's as quiet as sleeping zombies.

Because they are.

How else can I describe what's happening? Or ... what's *happened*? I don't know how to qualify that, even as I struggle to measure the intention of the female who rises from her pew to greet me. The goddess who walks but seems to glide. Who curves a smile at me like Mother Theresa and Lucrezia Borgia in the same three seconds. Who folds her hands across her middle with the calling of a queen but the intention of a demon.

Hands that now feel like they're buried in my stomach.

I stop, almost doubling over from the first blow. The next. The one after that. The sensation is more than our strong little Sprout taking some jabs at my ribs. I'm as positive as I am discomfited about that.

But *comfort* isn't a word I have a right to in this moment.

Not with the complete stillness that's taken over the room. The nearly supernatural silence. A quiescence I long to be waking myself up from. A dream that looks too eerie and feels too real.

But I know better.

This isn't a convenient little vision.

I've known this reality before. I've *seen* it. Maximus too. We witnessed it a little over a month ago, in the main room of Rerek Horne's Malibu villa. The seconds before the chaos demon turned his zombied-out partygoers into fully frozen statues, clearing the way for Hades to sweep in and grab me. His simple pretext of an innocent dance was the jumping point of my abduction into the middle of hell…

"Well, shit."

Maximus's snarl brings a welcome shot of ferocity to the air—but only for the two seconds before I recognize the thick underlines of the sounds. His dread is a raw and awful reveal, not just because of the current I feel from every pore of his spirit. It's the stuff creeping into, and curling throughout, my own.

I let go of him to grab my chest, certain I'm about to endure the same fate as that hideous night at Rerek's. Positive I'm about to look up and see the demon himself, smirking through his trademark rock-star saunter, just like he did before delivering me to Hades…and straight down into hell…

But that's before my stare locks on to Rerek himself.

He's in the fifth-row pew on my side of the chapel, with huge eyes fixed and unblinking at the ceiling. His long neck is seized in a permanent moment of strain. I almost gasp again, assuming he's been killed, but the frantic pumps of his chest confirm a different truth. He's alive but locked down, paralyzed in one position…

Just like everyone else.

Po, Zeus, and all the attending demons included.

They're all immobile. Helplessly, petrifyingly so.

The description is more accurate than I want to admit but have to accept. Everyone in here, except for Maximus and me, is a frozen *victim* of the spell now…

"Even...Hades."

In my peripheral, I catch Maximus's confused startle to my stunned whisper. I look up, confronting the laser intensity of the rings in his dark cobalts, before blurting, "This time, she's even caught Hades."

My husband barely has a second to tighten his frown before Hecate smacks the air with a laugh that hits like a nun's etiquette ruler.

"Come now, sweet one. *Please.*" She strolls forward by a few more steps. "The cretin has gotten more wily over the years, I'll give you that, but there are still a few places his power can't crawl." Her grand gesture around the church only enhances the daunting effect of her strict black attire, despite the frothy layers of her long skirt and the shoulder cut-outs that bracket her high neckline. "It also means he doesn't get to take credit for *my* handiwork."

"Oh...no." I squeeze my fingers tighter around Maximus's long digits. Even tug him into a subtle step backward. Until now, I kept hoping I was wrong. Yearning for some other drastic explanation for this insane scene. Some logical kind of *human* science to verify the *why* for the freeze frame across the whole room...

But I'm wrong. My pounding senses tell me so. My pulse throbs harder, driving home the point. My own eyes stab me with the admission, forcing me to return the goddess's iridescent gaze.

The fact that it *is* a gaze, not a glare, should tell me even more. But I fight it, no matter how loud the thunder in my ears and the horror in my blood.

"How?" I finally stammer, though it's past a cacophony of mental chaos. I jog my head left and then right, trying to dim the assault of colors, shapes, and noises from the magic queen. But she's relentless. Merciless. Full speed. Nonstop. "Wait. *No.* It—it can't be the—"

I stop myself in the nick of time, though my effort is wasted.

"The grimoire." Hecate sashays forward as if preparing to simply offer us some tea. "*That* was your intent, my darling, yes? You're still wondering about the volume of spells—*my* spells—that *you* took from Hades's library?"

"With *your* blessing," Maximus bites out. "You already knew what happened to it. Hades all but accused you of guiding Kara to it in the first place so it would expose the magical elements in her blood, and you defended her actions. You were *proud* of her for getting it back."

He shifts forward, planting feet on the two lower steps of the altar, in order to loom closer over her. Hecate readjusts her proud stance. Or is that a smooth cover for a gut-deep flinch?

"You asked us about it again, when we were staying with you at Iremia. We told you the book was safely hidden. That we'd never let it fall into the wrong hands."

He's barely done before the goddess jolts again. This time, not because of him. *At* him.

"That was before you *became* the wrong hands!"

Her half-hissed attack has me flinging my bouquet toward Kell and forcing myself to ignore its loud *fwish* at her frozen feet. It takes another surge of self-control not to rub my stomach in reassurance during my frantic rush to my husband's side. Instead, I labor to send comfort to my middle in another way.

It's okay, Twiglet. Mommy's here. Please stop fussing, my love. I'll let you dance all you want . . . later. After we're done figuring out what the crazy witch lady is up to . . .

"What are you talking about?"

Hecate confronts my sharp demand with her severe glower. The depths of her eyes are like piles of diamonds, each poised to shatter a different window of this place.

"Oh, do not even attempt it, sweet one," she snarls. "Not with any of that nonsense. Not with me. Especially not now."

I force down a deep breath. Still, because I really am still dunked in confusion, I mutter, "Not with *what* nonsense? What are you even getting—"

"Stop. Just *stop.*"

Her violent enforcement of the command, with a hand flung up like she's about to unleash the gems in her eyes along my throat, has me backtracking so fast, I trip on my train and fall backward. The headpiece comes loose, bunching enough to cushion my gawky plunk—but not fast enough to assuage my spike of fear. With one hand, I brace against the rush of the floor against my ass. With the other, I'm spreading protective fingers across my navel.

Luckily, Maximus falls to my side with ideal timing. His form blocks Hecate's sightline in the barest nick of time. I use the advantageous moment to shake my head at him in a silent mandate.

We're fine. It's okay. Just help me up like I slipped a little, and nothing else.

Fortunately, the goddess seems to believe us—if she bothered to notice my fall at all. Once back on my feet, I'm able to see that her angry arm slash wasn't just for shutting me up. It was actually a summoning signal, ordering a figure forward from the shadows behind her.

The member of her team who struts forward, his arms outstretched, the glowing grimoire couched between them.

"Namazzi Wood."

More than anything, I yearn to sound more surprised by the man's arrival—assuming he's remained a man at all. Since Persephone told Maximus and me about the true identity of the Pendry Hotel's mild-mannered night manager, I expected him to show up again at some moment. Just not this one.

But there's no time for dissecting expectations and actuality. This juncture of real life and forced limbo ... Isn't it the perfect crossroads for something like this?

My mind's emphatic answer becomes my tongue's inflection of courage.

"Or perhaps you'd prefer *Hermes* from this point on," I challenge, despite knowing it won't alter his derisive smirk by one iota.

Sure enough, the shapeshifting snake seems to relax a little further, exposing fast glances of the actual creature beneath the physical shell that he used for our first meeting. Like "Namazzi Wood," his true self has dark-umber hair in nearly uniform ringlets that surround his face, and his sienna gaze is like a pair of dipping suns on a smog alert day. Pretty but filthy.

Indeed, even when he was fully disguised as Namazzi, the sneaky cretin didn't miss a thing. All his affected manners couldn't cover up that part. Though right now, I'm desperately wishing they would.

"Darling girl, I don't care *what* you call me at this point," he answers with cool but vicious ease. "As long as it's one of the key helpmates for our Queen Hecate." He turns a worshipful gaze toward the goddess. "The one who shall soon defeat Zeus and Hera and become ruler of Olympus's rebirth in *all* ways."

And here's my lesson about having classified the god so swiftly. Because here's the energy I never expected from him, even after the adoring look in which he swathed Hecate upon his initial approach. One peek inside his spirit, and I already know. The idol worship goes deeper. *Much* deeper. He's in such complete awe of her, it's ballooning into stark uncertainty. Like a cult member who's new to his movement, scared of what's about to happen but more fearful of missing out on the center of the glory.

In short, a disciple who hasn't been vetted all the way.

Though now, as I piece together several chunks of information, I have a damn good guess about when he was recruited. And how.

"Oh, my God," I blurt into the silence that chases his strange accusation. "*Hermes*…also known as *Namazzi*. It…was *you*…wasn't it? The one they were targeting last month, at the EmStar awards. The Pendry's catering team was responsible for the post-ceremony hospitality suites..."

"Ahhh." He presses a finger to his chin, nearly coquettish about it. "No mama-to-be brain for *this* one, Goddess. She *does* remember so well."

I move my head though am unsure about the weak wobble. I'm still not totally certain about my accusation, though his remark should be validation enough.

"Yes," I say, pressing harder on the point. "You *were* there, and hovering over every industry player that you could. Was that the goal? To literally be whispering in the media's ear? Setting them up to side with the best team once the assault on Olympus went live?" A new waver takes over my head, and I feel like a dashboard doll fighting off the fade from his smoggy sunset scrutiny. "Hermes, please tell me...that's not..."

But it is. I sense it from him before I see it push through his handsome intensity, so slick and easy, a declaration of belief that'd be breathtaking if it weren't so insidious.

"I am nobody's *target*, darling. But when the best opportunity of one's entire existence is dropped into his humble lap, it's best to pay close attention." But the statement, sounding so final, isn't his ultimate point. That belongs to the context of the next moment, as Hermes pointedly arches his brows in Maximus's direction. "Wouldn't you agree, Mr. Kane-*Valari*?"

CHAPTER 6

Maximus

I T'S NOT WHAT THE asshole's just implied. If it made anything easier for Kara, hyphenating my name would be the easiest decision since choosing my college major. Despite the circumstances of our first ten minutes together as wife and husband, they're still the best six hundred seconds of my life.

It's the totality of Hermes's implication. The allusion that I've used Kara, and her family, as some career stunt.

A lot like the one *he's* just pulled off.

Cockroach.

I'm sure the same slur spills out as I lunge for the smirking insect, taking hold of him by the lapel of his burgundy velvet suit. It's the only reason I don't repeat the word while hauling him up until he's grazing the floor with the toes of his matching spats.

"She's my *wife* now, you shit-dragging basement beetle. Call her an *opportunity* again, and I'll ruin that thing in your pants until you can't tell the difference between a boner and a piss."

For a long second, the bastard believes me enough to flinch. Not long enough. Once I loosen my grip, the cosmopolitan act is back.

"Ah, well. Suit oneself, I suppose. But don't come groveling when I'm nipping nectar and caviar in a suite in the heights of Olympus while you two puzzle how to raise your brat in a tenement off of 5th and San Juan."

"Is that what she's told you?" The interjection belongs to my scoffing—and never more beautiful—bride. "What she *promised* you?" She jogs her chin up. "A promise, I suppose, without filling you in on the potential risk. The very full cost."

The god scoffs. "Ohhh, little one, do you imagine me a green welp? Do you honestly believe this is the first flower attempted in this fine meadow?" And then he bristles while tapping at the curls that have escaped at his temples. "*Every* seed carries risks. *Every* new growth could be a bountiful tree or a rotten weed. There are no guarantees. *Every* commitment carries costs. But these odds…I am willing to accept. I am committed to nourishing. The harvest is too important, for *every* denizen of Olympus. I will water these seeds with my own blood if necessary. These grand victories will soon be ours."

"Yes, they *will*." Hecate straightens and lifts her head. She circles it around with dramatic pretension, posing as if she's not borrowing the stance from predecessors like Vlad the Impaler, Queen Bloody Mary, and Caligula. "In spite of what the disbelievers claim." She rolls an incriminating stare over Kara and me. "Dare I say *because* of them? Oh, yes. Perhaps I do."

Before she finishes, Kara's pulling up her own stance—but on her, the rigidity turns into a queen's stance that Hecate will never achieve. "All right," she states, scarily close to a taunt. "Go ahead and say it, goddess. As loudly as you want, as vociferously as possible. Because it will be your last chance to do so for any kind of an audience that's capable of listening."

"Nonsense."

"A profound truth from a perfect queen." Hermes bows so low, I wonder if he's intending on a curtsy as follow-up.

But Kara's already thinking faster, with three times the determination. She faces off with the god, her stare still set and her posture as high as Hecate's.

"Your loyalty is admirable, Hermes. And, given so many other circumstances, even justified."

The god looks ready to fling another indignant glare. Instead, he dials back to the disdain that probably feels safer. "I don't need justification. I have the truth."

"Right. *That*," Kara counters. "Because she's given you the full dossier of details about why her cause is worthy, right? Page after page about how she plans on confronting Zeus and changing the universe forever. She likely also said *you'd* be a vital part of that change and would have a unique place in the history of all the realms. How you'd be venerated once again by all the humans, restored to the initial glory that the entire pantheon enjoyed. Let me guess… Were there mentions of temples and feasts? Perhaps even orgies with virgins?"

Hermes flinches as if she's struck him. Then seethes from tight teeth, "Stop. *Stop it.*"

"So what if I said it?" Hecate declares, upping her own dramatic standoff game. "I still stand by all of it. Every last syllable!"

"Of course you do," I insert, barely tying back a vicious chuff. "Because that's the fun part of the adventure poster." That leads me to a hard stare back toward Hermes. "But there's fine print on the bottom of that thing, man. Did she let you see all that too? The parts about the lifetime rights to your soul and the permanent side effects?"

The god huffs. Shakes his head with threatening emphasis. "As I believe I've already stated, I am no untried welp. I do have a complete *mind*—"

"But a humble lap," I cut in.

"Which means a desperate soul," Kara adds. "The part of you that she's taken advantage of, Hermes. The part that wants to believe every colorful, pretty dream she's blown up for the poster, and *not* the part where you find out that *unique place* will be among a handful of surviving humans, at best. That the world she's going to change the most is *this* one."

The god stills his head. Drops his shoulders. "What are you talking about?"

Hecate grabs his shoulder so hard, the velvet looks permanently dented. "Darling, I told you they would try this. Do not listen—"

Somehow, one whoosh of Kara's hand is enough to clamp her silent. My wife doesn't pause to share my amazement. She remains brutally and beautifully on message.

"Planet Earth will be completely ravaged by this war," she declares. "If Hecate's told you otherwise, she's lying. Everything you've known about this realm, perhaps even grown to love about it, is that awestriking because of its intricacy. Its *fragility*. Vulnerable points that won't last when all the other realms decide to throw down against each other."

She pauses with weighted deliberation. This time, Hermes doesn't have half a syllable of retort. Shockingly, neither does Hecate—though the goddess looks as sure of her purpose as ever.

At last, Kara spreads out her arms. "All of this . . . will be a dystopia," she asserts. "And guess what human beings don't have time for, when they're worried about food in their bellies and a roof over their head?"

I stiffen my stance while supplying that obvious answer. "Temples." And the next one. "And feasts."

And I should have known Hermes wouldn't give up the head shaking for long. It's back, along with a contorted scowl, as he bites out, "Bullshit. Preposterous bullshit. Do either of you actually think me one of your simpering media sluts, to blindly believe every tale you weave like this?"

I cluck my tongue before he's done. "Do they really let you get away with all that language in the acropolis?"

"And *who* keeps allowing *you* these exemptions from fearmongering lies?"

Hecate flicks out the zinger with frightening grace, intensifying the effect by draping a protective hand around her protege's shoulders. She's just as intentionally feline as I step back, playing into her intention. But I'm past caring, or even explaining that the move is more disgust than fear, because I'm not done with my point. Not that it even matters anymore.

"Just like I said, my dearest," she croons past Hermes's curls. "Not worth a shred of attention. They only want to get into your head."

"For once, *darling*, you're not getting a word of argument," I volley. "Not when there's this much at stake."

"Oh, for the love of Apollo." Hermes earns back a few points of respect by stepping free from the goddess, though cancels the score by continuing his glower at Kara and me. "Do you think I am that vapid and selfish? That short-sighted?" He shoots out his arms, though keeps his tight grip on the grimoire with his left hand. "I am a fucking *deity* of Olympus. *Her* soul is *mine* too." As his arms descend, his lips part on a bleak smile. "Perhaps it might be the best thing for the realms, you know. If all the humans fell into their oceans. Good riddance, hmmm?"

I narrow my returning regard. "Is that also a line she fed you? And that you bought? Because that's what fucking deities do, right? Buy into every upsell on the truth from obsessive minor goddesses?"

Hecate's lips part. As her mouth seethes, her eyes flash. "*Minor* goddess?"

But though I still refuse to flinch, she settles into a new preen. Does she think I'm afraid of getting doused in her spectral carbonite? She's spared Kara and me for some reason, though that recognition is far from a reassuring one. Our friends and loved ones—hell, even President McCarthy and most of my department colleagues from the university— are being held as collateral against our help in her hideous scheme.

But why? And for what?

The goddess isn't exactly going to spill, which means I can't give up my drive at Hermes. No matter how infuriating the effort...

"All right, come on, man," I mutter. "I actually agree with you here. You're not a stupid pawn. So stop acting like one. *Think for yourself*, and then tell me this. What side suffers the most in a widespread war? Quick answer? *All of them*. Earth might end up as nothing but underwater islands, but the land of your soul won't get out unscathed. *Your* kingdom will feel this too, buddy."

"*Enough*." Hecate doesn't roar it, but I wish she would. Her feral hiss is enough to jerk at my posture, threatening a backlash I can't predict. But the blow for which I brace is nothing but a trembling silence. "Does *any* of this surprise you?" she grits at Hermes, who's now riding waves of clear confusion. "Snap *out* of it, dolt! I told you they'd try *all* of this, didn't I? Preying on your hesitations. Digging into your psyche. Hermes! Don't heed another—"

"What?" I cut in. "Don't heed exactly *what*, ma'am? A scenario that makes too much sense?" I swing my glare back to Hermes. "She probably took you to Iremia, didn't she? Gave you the grand VIP tour, along with the spiel about how you'd have your own luxury villa for little breaks away from Olympus when you needed them. You probably liked that back porch in the *sala*, perfect for enjoying your day's cappuccino before one of your private witch wenches delivers your custom-ordered breakfast."

Hermes rolls back on one foot, sliding into a skeptical scowl. "A little emotional baggage there, Professor Kane? I am more than happy to pass along my shrink's details."

"Not surprised you have it at the ready," I reply. "As long as we're all about transparency here, answer me honestly. You called for an appointment right after the tour, didn't you? Despite everything, you were still baffled about why you couldn't declare complete trust in the magical goddess with the diamond eyes. Because her goodwill came with a list of conditions. A *long* list. Stipulations that crept into strangeness. That hinted at the darker parts of her personality. I'll affirm to you right now, they're all true."

No more gloating from the goddess. But she's still tittering under her breath, adding an iridescent fingernail against her chin. "My truth or your predicament, Mr. Kane? Which is more believable right now?"

"She stands at the cosmic crossroads," I persist without hesitation. "You know that, man. She can easily pass between Olympus and Dis at will, with stops in Barrow, Boise, and Buena Park along the way. But those are just stops. She has no emotional tie to them, or you, or anything about the ground she's determined to burn on her way to Zeus's throne. You're merely an ego stroke for her, Hermes. That's it."

"Desperation," Hecate nearly sing-songs—though

there's a moment, fleeting but telling, in which a new crack appears in Hermes's cosmopolitan composure. For another second, he flickers his attention more on me than her. But the goddess takes notice just as fast and takes full advantage. "The human race has given up on *me*, not the other way around," she accuses. "Do you deny me *this* claim, demigod? That the precious art of magic has been turned into nothing but show business stunts? That the cycles of the moon are exploited on dating apps and social media reels? And what about you, Hermes? These days, your name is known more for handbags and perfume than the quest for metallurgic meaning and immortality!"

"But this isn't the way to get any of it back." I wrench at the tie that cuts off a lot of needed air. Right now, I need all the damn oxygen I can get. "It hasn't worked for your realm in the past, Hecate. And it won't work now."

Hermes's Botox-smooth forehead now looks like the trails after the Death Valley sailing stones had a good rager. "In...the *past*?" He jerks his gaze at his goddess. "You said we were making history. That nobody in Olympus had ever dared to dream so gloriously."

"Which was the truth!" Hecate injects.

"Technically," I bite out. "But let's define *glorious*." And then rush on before the goddess grabs another chance to intercede. "Over half of the world's notable disasters, from fire and floods to typhoons and cyclones, weren't *natural* tragedies." My air quotes are a fast embellishment. "They were the fallout from bickering Olympians."

Hermes rocks his posture back once more. This time,

especially with his fresh eye roll, it's so reassuring. "I *am* very aware of that, Professor."

"So you can jump to the part about imagining what will happen when Earth's burned up." It's an agonizing chore to keep my sights all the way on him, but I don't dare confront the look Kara must be attaching to her sharp gasp. *Trust me, little demon. Please.* "When you all have decimated this realm so much, you won't even have an Iremia porch for your fast vay-cays."

"*Untrue.*"

Hecate's nose pinches back in. She cups one hand into the other at her waist, exposing grinding knuckles. But from the neck up, she's returned to a former version of herself. The ashram earth mother, regarding my wife as if she still isn't keeping all of our friends and family in a spectral freezer.

"Kara," she chides, bright and bell-like. "This has all gotten so blown out of hand…"

My wife erupts with a bitter laugh. "You think?"

"*Sweet one.* Please. You know how highly I regard you." Almost like an afterthought, she glances at me. "*Both* of you. So you must know that my only intention here—"

"Oh, we're already clearly aware of it," my wife spits, throwing an agonized nod across the crowd.

"Necessary measures," Hecate defends, stiffening tighter. "For a divine purpose."

Kara laughs louder than before. Along with the volume, she draws out her icicles. "That's what you're going with? And you think it'll accomplish…*what*…exactly?"

"You would have barely glanced at me otherwise!" the

goddess erupts. "And all I want to do is talk—"

"Talk." No more laughter from my bride now, bitter or otherwise. Her voice is a sparse rasp. "Goddess, you have never just wanted to *talk* with me. Do you think I haven't suspected that from the start, when you insisted on isolating Maximus and me at the compound?" She slowly shakes her head. "But I didn't listen to any of those intuitions. Kept telling myself I had to be wrong. I was so relieved that you'd arrived to save me from Hades that night..."

"Hades?"

Hermes startles so hard, the grimoire nearly falls from his hold. As he bolts a new scrutiny to Hecate, he frantically massages the leather binding. While I don't want to take delight in his odd reaction, I do. It takes me a second to tamp my own relishing chuckle.

"Did your mistress leave that part out?" I prompt unnecessarily. The god's blatant astonishment already serves up the answer.

"You told me Hades *wasn't* a problem," he accuses the goddess. "You promised me, Hecate. You said you two were amicable and aligned for the cause. That as long as we had the Hollywood media locked up with the support of the Valaris—"

"Whoa." There goes any shred of temptation for any chuckle left in my body. Though I'm positive they've all fled for the red-tinted waves beyond the windows. And beyond.

"Excuse. Me?" But nothing about Kara's callout is an actual question. My woman is already at the level of command, hurtling it at Hecate as if about add weapons to the mix.

But in split seconds, she exposes her real firepower to us. The outrage so significant, it consumes every available part of her eyes—though not with the photorealistic blazes that I've witnessed before. This...is something new. Marauding but magnificent. Shocking but stunning. There's fire...but more.

At the edges of her optical flames, there are sparks. But not.

Because the sparks are actually stars.

Shimmering like tiny gold comets...until they track beyond the confines beneath her lashes and streak across her cheeks with blazing, searing force. The heat stops at last near her temples, leaving charred residue near her hairline.

"By the seal of Aegis," Hermes utters.

"Shit," I add beneath my breath, though barely. Raw terror consumes most of my volume. This can't be right for her or our Sprout. Healthy blooms don't happen in the middle of storms. "Kara. *Hey*. Breathe, sweetheart. You can't be—"

But she doesn't hear, let alone listen.

"I said *excuse me*," she growls again, angling her head forward like some kind of personal cannon.

Hecate, obviously unready to confess this part of her game, powerwalks back by several steps. During the trip, she struggles to resheath herself in a semblance of earth mother gentility.

"Now sweet one..." She trails off as Kara huffs with intention—and wisely keeps her silence while my wife looks across the whole crowd. Kara's hands are balled into near-white fists now, nearly matching the pale wash across her cheeks. This sight has to remind her of Dis's lifeless expanse, only worse. While our original plan included something similar, our goal was peace, not control.

The authority that Hermes seems to wrestle with again, concentrating on Kara in a new and intense way. For the first time, I feel like he's not just watching her but seeing her. And *feeling* her …

Along with fresh feelings of his own.

Perhaps some thoughts that are going to work in our favor now.

Please, I beg from within, sending the sole word to any multitude of powers, any force that might be willing to jump in with us right now …

"Please." Kara's reiteration is a world away. *Too* far. She wheels her gaze toward the goddess, all that magical star fire still pouring from her eyes, though the amber tracks across her cheeks are now streaked by anguished tears. "Don't call me that, Hecate. Ever again."

The witch queen borrows heavily from Vlad and Caligula again—but now she's tapping hard on the Mrs. Danvers vibes too. Only instead of reaching for a gothic candle, she wrenches the grimoire out of Hermes's hands.

The second she wraps her wraithlike grip against the edges, the tome starts to change. Too clearly and swiftly, it's starting to look different. The pages pulse with light. The lettering on the cover gains spikes of white-hot light. The whole thing is aglow with power. Forces I haven't seen since—

The times I'd rather forget.

The minutes that felt like hours, lying on the Dis castle stones, filled with the certainty I was going to die. Consumed by so much pain that I might have prayed for the extinction. Hanging on for one reason alone.

The woman who made it all worth it. Who was a living flame in that darkness, calling to me with the force of her life. A perfect vigor that pumps into me now, only twofold. The miracle of both heartbeats inside her beautiful body.

"And you would not have your precious grimoire without me. *Without us*."

Two words. Three syllables.

A complete change of the very air around us. At least long enough to shake Hecate off her game for a long minute. Another.

The same minute in which I struggle to rebuild my own stamina. Something that feels stronger than longing to roar out at my wife. Of all the bullets to give the witch queen right now, when her chamber is so ready and desperate …

But for all these seconds, the goddess is as affected as Hermes and me. Mesmerized by the proud silhouette before us. My wife, so diminutive but dominant. Swathed in beads and lace but emanating cave-girl power. A force that sucks the air from my lungs, the thoughts from my mind.

It's not just the protective spread of her hand along her stomach. It's the invocation of the sounds on her lips. A tone like sea wind in a siren's song. A cresting choir on an organ's swell. Ferocity buoyed by eternity. A power that doesn't emanate only from her larynx. It seems born from the very stars in her eyes. From the being who first made them. The life that existed before anything or anyone else.

Especially when her gaze flashes my way again.

Because now I'm not just witnessing those lights. I'm pulled up into them. Floating among them. A molecule and a universe in the same crazy moment. I don't even know if I'm still breathing, but I don't care. I don't need air anymore.

But I force myself to take it, as my woman crashes the air with a new spike of her rage.

"You used me, Hecate," she issues, low and lethally. "Just like Hades did, but worse." She drops one hand, using frantic fingers to scrape at the gown's beads. "Because you used all three of us."

While I despise the agitation she's come to, nothing can eclipse the joy from her words themselves. The soaring elation from hearing our greatest truth aloud.

All three of us.

"Yessss." I can't help but grit it out with victory, despite all the frustration that makes it out too. I fight to mentally catalogue the moment, planning to return for a more satisfying rewind as soon as possible. Relishing it now is out of the question. Not with Hecate already processing the revelation with visible machination, despite how her jaw works to get words but fails.

"Kara," she finally gasps. "Oh ... *my*. You ... you're ..."

"I-I don't understand," Hermes interjects, shifting his stance. "Goddess? Wh-What's happening? What are we doing now?"

Her minion's stammering is like a strange—and

alarming—switch for Hecate.

"Seize her," she dictates without another falter. "What the hell else do you *think* you should do?"

Weirdly, perhaps maniacally, I almost succumb to a laugh. By this point, Hermes's bafflement *is* bordering on comical.

"Ermmm...goddess? Are you cert—"

"Damn it, Hermes. Detain her, *now*. That chit's baby brat is the complete key to our victory!"

"What? *Baby?*" But the god is clearly still recovering from Kara's new power surge on its own, apart from the information bomb she dropped along with it. "I don't—"

"You're right. You *don't*." She swings the grimoire high and brings it down on the god's head. Hermes falls at once, buckled into a prostrate pose, but there's no escorting string of apologies—puzzling, until I realize she's turned him into a new statue for the room.

"Why do I have to do everything myself?" the goddess mutters, whirling back toward Kara and me. "Will I have to wage every battle of this war alone, as—*aggghhh!*"

I blink a couple of times. Double the count for shocked head shakes.

What the hell's going on now? How—why—has Hecate literally been pounded to her knees too? How has she been knocked there so hard that her precious cargo has popped several feet out of her grip?

Before I can start on postulations, mercy comes quickly. An answer. A damn fine one.

A distinct growl rolls across the air, shaking the sanctuary windows with its accompanying clap of otherworldly command.

"Leave them alone, Hecate."

The witch queen rolls to her side, indicating that the thunder's probably pummeling her brain worse than the walls. Not a shred of sympathy answers from my own head or heart. It feels too good to be acknowledging my flood of relief. But that doesn't stop me from drying out my next words to the point of gallows wryness.

"Hey, Pops. Took you long enough."

CHAPTER 7

Kara

CONFUSION THREATENS TO DERAIL my concentration—but most importantly, my fury. I don't give in, still pulling strength from the vital life I'm sharing this body with, knowing it's far too early to expose anything to Hecate but my rage.

Especially as the witch stumbles back to her feet.

She winces and pins me with tearful eyes, all but begging aloud for mercy. I grit my teeth, refusing to surrender a sliver. Zeus and Maximus lend me more conviction with their furious expressions, and I gratefully embrace the hotter fires of my own seethe.

But I'm not merely grateful.

I'm giddy.

Because I'm free. Cut loose from the disguise I've been torturously keeping up for the goddess. Pretending, to excruciating degrees, that I know nothing about her ultimate scheme—and her plan to use me as the ultimate instrument of her violence.

I can't take it anymore, nor do I have to. I'm so happy, it's impossible to be sorry for exposing the secret of our sprout. If I had to do it all over again, I'd even let *her* sing about it. There's no denying a minor twinge about the timing, which could've been hours or days or weeks better, but the aftermath still feels so right that I don't dwell. There are better things to think about now.

Starting with the glare I've already got ready for her.

I hold nothing back, no matter how flustered she is while clawing stray curls back from her face. All my denigration and disgust is here at full force, and it's amazing. Nothing's going to change that, not even the tiny wonderings about how and why Zeus is enjoying his own fresh taste of freedom.

Is it as simple as the obvious? Did the book that's now in *his* grip lend a cosmic life ring? Which came first: the goddess's golden egg, or his royal Olympian chicken? And if it's the former, what will happen if Hecate's able to summon the spell book back?

Oh, God.

What's going to happen if she claims even more power over the room—and her king?

What if this is just the beginning of it all for her?

Maximus and I planned so hard. Dreamed so high. We prayed we'd prevent a war but might have accelerated its arrival instead.

Oh, *God*.

I hate how sure that sounds in my mind and soul as I examine the goddess's stature. Fifteen minutes ago, Hecate swept up from her pew like a queen about to hold court. Now she's a monarch leaning toward madness, edging toward a fighting stance as Zeus approaches with a commanding stalk.

"Dial it down, my friend," he rumbles on the way. "*Way* down."

Hecate bares all her teeth. Watching her expression unfurl, I'm stunned by wonder. Less than a month ago, that grimace would've had me trembling in a weird mix of awe, fear, and admiration. Not anymore. Now that I know how she used those impressions to mold my thoughts and choices...to reshape my entire life...

The same thing she's trying now, shooting indicting glares my way. Reminding me of a traitor summoned to trial, still trembling with the belief that *she's* been wronged. Still clinging to her deranged cause.

But when she speaks up again, it's a direct spit at Zeus instead. "*Friend?* That's truly how you want to proceed here, *Majesty?* With *me?*"

She bursts into a high laugh, as if she's spouted the year's best joke. Oddly, the moment has me backtracking on some of my fury. Sprout has expanded more than my heart, strengthened more than my spirit. In this moment, I recognize my mind cracking open more too.

In those apertures, I'm able to acknowledge the method to the goddess's madness. So many centuries of service, believing in the Olympian ideals even when Z and Hera were shitting on them... I'm almost amazed she hasn't splintered sooner. In the saddest ways, her desperation is their fault. Her monarchs owe her a long, focused listen.

Thankfully, probably miraculously, Zeus actually looks to comprehend grasping that point, as well. At least for now. Which ultimately is what matters.

But he makes us wait for the payoff, disturbing the air with a long, reluctant growl. "Damn it, Hecate," he finally grits out. "You know it's exactly how I *do* want to go. You *are* still my friend. Don't you see it the same way?"

Hecate sniffs hard. Gulps with more determination. Her emotion is deep and disturbing—and still here at the edges of my psyche, trying to suck me back in.

I clutch a hand tighter to my middle and resist. *And resist.*

At last she rasps to Zeus, "You'd like me to answer that with a sweet nod and a serene smile, wouldn't you? That would make everything just so easy. Everyone put right back where you want us to be. Back into our nice little boxes."

As she pauses, her eyes glimmer brighter. A cold breeze comes from nowhere, lifting the edges of her damp curls. Such similarity to the night I first met her, but not at all the same—unless my soul-deep sadness counts.

"Oh, yes," she finally goes on, not-so-subtly goading. "That would please you, hmmm, All-father? Tucking us all neatly in, fitting under your thumb once more. Shoved into the whorls by all the pandering and the platitudes—"

"And the willingness to solve this without wiping out a whole realm?" I spew it because someone has to, and the witch will stop the hardest for me. But I make it clear that I'm not just ready to hit with words. I bunch my skirt higher, ready to throw myself physically into the effort.

Ready but *not* willing.

Don't make me do this anymore, goddess. Please don't make me hurt you.

I have no idea if she hears that. Sometimes, I'm positive she's making margin notes on every thought in my mind; other days she's a mask of mystery, giving nothing away. But this circumstance fits neither of those occasions. I can't figure her out because her emotions are like a storm front around her, blinding my senses with thunderheads of anger and electric flashes of stinging grief.

The deluge cuts into me. And at once, suddenly softens me.

"Goddess," I entreaty now, stopping before her with both arms spread. Despite my own internal squall, the moment's irony doesn't escape me. This is the pose *she* used, so open yet gentle, when first commanding my trust. The belief in her promise to guide me to my truth. Well, she accomplished the job—just not in the ways she expected. "Listen to Z. Please. He wants to work on this. Can't you hear that? Can't you *see*—"

"The same thing I've been hearing and seeing for centuries?" she retorts much too quickly. "Don't *you* see *that*, Kara? All of it? Do you see everything I was reassured about, even as my temples fell and my believers wandered off? Then as *his* did? Can you imagine the empty promises, one after the other, of revisions that would be explored when we turned into fiction and folktales? When nothing was done, even as our impact on the hearts of humankind was reduced to nothing but amusing adventures?"

I sag by several inches. "I won't pretend to know that I get it, okay? I really can't comprehend exactly what you felt...and are still feeling. But—"

"No." She counters by straightening with the same increment. "You *cannot* imagine. So don't try to tug on my tears, girl. Don't stand there and tell me that you have faith in the measure of my soul. *I* don't have faith in it anymore. It has been crushed—*shattered*—by this wretch and the shrew who sits beside him on the dais!"

As she slashes a trembling finger toward Zeus, I concentrate on calmly returning to my full height. Then, when I'm sure she's done: "I'm standing here because I must. You've given me no other choice, have you? Except the one I abhor having to make."

She lowers her hand—though this time, it's with balletic finesse. A repose that works the opposite effect on the fine hairs of my nape.

"Then allow me to choose for you."

For that very reason.

"Go ahead," I spit. "Make the move. You know I won't really try to stop you, given the situation." My nod toward my middle is terse. "But know this. I won't go as your eager little protege. Not anymore. You can put me on the game board, but I refuse to move around it at your bidding. And if you think my child will be any more malleable, especially if you eliminate me to get to her, then you've lost your war before it's begun."

"*Her?*"

Maximus's interjection is the beacon I need in this harsh, dark valley. I snap my sights over to meet his stare, only now realizing what I've blurted.

Her.

I nod his way, affirming it—because I know it. Somehow, in the middle of that new power that just suffused me for her—*from* her?—it became my truth. *Our* truth.

A certitude I need now more than any other moment of this day. Of this *year*.

It's a bolster all the way up my spine, spreading at the top into my whole mind and soul, as Hecate takes another step closer. Her posture is Mother Superior regality. Her stare is Gaia serenity. Her new smile is unflagging—and enraging.

"Oh, my dear girl," she murmurs. "You really believe all of that, don't you?"

I hitch my chin higher. "Oh, goddess. I *know* it."

But the flippant edge is more for me than her, and *she* doesn't hide her surety of it.

Damn it.

I'm used to dancing on the edge of Hollywood control games, not a tight wire between the mortal and magical worlds. The thread is higher than I expect. Scarier. Especially as she looks me over with new intent. Blindingly clear intention.

She's ready to walk on this wire along with me. And probably do a much better job of it.

"And *I* know that you'll agree to join me, sweet one. Or everybody in here will stay like this."

Because *there's* her hideous safety net.

I suck in air until it hurts. At the same time, before Maximus even knows I've sought his gaze for support, he looks across at his mom. An illegible profanity tumbles from beneath his breath.

I almost spit out the same words. But it's not a luxury I can allow. Not as I pin my stare again on Hecate, digging in for as much of her aura as I can. Desperately searching for a shred of bullshit to call her out for.

I come back with nothing but her cool certainty. And knowing arrogance.

"No." I thrash my head from side to side. "I still don't believe you."

"Neither do I," Zeus bites out. "Hecate. Come on. This isn't you, dear one. Granted, it's a good bluff, but—"

Hecate's hiss is a brutal interruption. It twists back on itself, becoming the thorny underline of her comeback. "You don't know me anymore, *Majesty*. But go on and believe what you will choose. After all, your judgment has been so good for guiding Olympus. Who needs grand shrines when people can *look* like you with a thirty-dollar costume and a nylon wig?"

"And *my* judgment?" I challenge. "I also call no joy. There are nearly two hundred people here. How long can you maintain—"

"As long as it takes," the goddess croons. "I mean, please, not *forever*. But if a human body isn't allowed to move or eat or hydrate…how long *does* that take? Add in a few more days for your family, who likely have stouter constitutions…"

"No!"

I pull in enough oxygen to shove volume into the protest, but it drains most of my strength. My knees buckle, and I double over, wrapping protective hands back across my stomach.

What do I do?

Surrender myself and this child to save my family and friends? And when that's done, hope and pray that Hecate will honor my oblation enough to let me live? To let me see and touch my daughter?

Not if she's determined about winning her war.

Which means I have to find a way out of here, no matter what the cost—including the sacrifice of everyone I hold dear.

Maybe even Maximus.

No, no, no!

But what other alternative is there?

There's new warmth pressing around me, and I look up far enough to recognize the refuge of my husband's embrace. But not the comfort. I feel him fighting for some to give, but the mighty thunderclap over our heads is proof of his fruitless search.

He's floundering as much as me. As clueless about an answer that'll save our wedding day from being the darkest one of our lives. But as rain starts to slash at the chapel's windows, glistening like liquid knives in the light of constant lightning blasts, we grip each other in the certainty of that impossibility. Holding tighter and tighter, as if this is our last embrace of all time.

Because it might very well be.

CHAPTER 8

MAXIMUS

"FUCK."

Normally, I'd write off the word on Z's lips as an egotistical ancillary to watching the room spin out of his control. But I wish his bruised pride was the only problem to worry about here.

That part is on me.

I'm the sudden storm guy. It's a solid fact these days, ever since I came to full terms with my true heritage. The squall I've summoned has actually been a strange comfort, expressing the deeper feelings that I can't put into words right now.

But there's a difference between a freak downpour and a full-on typhoon.

A tempest that's now brought the sunset's high tide right up to the edge of the church.

There's no mistaking what I turn and see. The ocean,

which was separated from us an hour ago by a high hill, a four-lane boulevard, and a sizable nature reserve, now splashes against the floor-to-ceiling window just beyond the front altar. Though the onflow succeeds in shorting out the sanctuary's electric lights, I have no trouble obtaining a visual on everything thanks to the lightning flashes that persist across the whitecaps.

The scene is apocalyptic.

I haven't even caused a typhoon. This is a *tsunami*—upon which the church seems ready to set sail any moment.

"Shit," I mutter.

"Fuck," Z repeats.

We're both muted by Hecate's stabbing shriek.

"*No.*"

She spins around, a dervish now dragging the soaked hem of her finery through the inch of water flowing across the sanctuary's floor. If this were any other time and place, I'd be gripping Kara's hand with an air of knowing humor, acknowledging how similar it looks to the wedding scene from her favorite rom-com film. But nothing about this is comedic. I hold my wife tighter, yearning that it doesn't swing completely the other way. Tragedies belong on muse masks and emo rock album covers, not in the aisle of our wedding chapel.

Not even in light of the terrible expression across the magic goddess's face.

"No!" She seethes it harder than before, her locked teeth showing like barbed wire past security fence tarps. "Turn it *off*," she drills at me. "All of it. Right now. Or your wife and child are mystical putty in my hands!"

"Stellae dicure aliud!"

I'm not wheeling a wide stare at my wife because I didn't expect her protest. It's because the last form I expected it to take was her rough snarl, as if she hauled the steel spikes straight from Hecate's mouth—

And wound them around *Latin*?

Oh, fuck yes. It *is* Latin, and it's never fit a moment of my life so succinctly. Beyond perfectly.

Stellae dicure aliud.

"The stars have something else to say."

She translates before I can, and I'm beyond giddy about it. On her lips, both versions are pure magic—perhaps literally. Either that, or it's an insane coincidence that as soon as Kara issues the challenge, she marks it with upflung arms and sparkling fingertips. At the same time, a new crackle of lightning stretches up and across the whole hill we're on. Its brilliance flares through the sanctuary windows, illuminating my woman like a silver supernova—with one blinding distinction.

She's far from nuclear-force death.

She's the spectral, astronomical opposite.

A newborn sun. A quasar in creation. A light so intense, it carries sound too. A sizzling vibration, as if a lightsaber is tangling with a Taser.

"Ag...gg...hhh!"

Hecate's moan is broken up as she stumbles back, tripping over the soaked layers of her gown. She flails and tumbles all the way into the puddle that used to be the church's center aisle, riding her own screaming flow of

Greek profanity.

I don't take the time to translate it this time because I don't care. Nothing dominates my attention more than my resplendent wife, who has me grinning and grimacing at once, one arm shielding my eyes while the other reaches for the back of a pew. I need the fast purchase, considering Kara starts exuding more than light. There's wind around her too, kicking up the water until her skirt is soaked and her hair is whipping. Within seconds her veil flies up too, and I'm captivated by the glow of the altar candles through the sheer fabric.

But then, so much more than captivated.

For the first time, I notice the embroidered design along the tulle.

It's *stars*. Yet not just that.

It's constellations. Specific ones.

The same formations that lit up the western sky over the Malibu shore at Rerek's place nearly two months ago. The stars that beamed their approval as Kara and I declared our love aloud for the first time. We'd already been wonderfully aware of it but hadn't actually spoken the words themselves. Not until those magical moments on the sand. The sea had swelled and churned as if rising in tandem with our passion...

With the same intensity that it fills my ears now.

Only without the enjoyable excuse.

I wheel around, hoping I'm the only one who notices it. Wondering—praying—that the waves bashing at the chapel's windows are concoctions of my imagination alone.

That I'm reaching and clutching the back of a pew bench from stupid apprehension, my exhausted mind making up the building's creaks and groans as it fights to keep the whitecaps outside.

For the first time in my life, I long to be the party idiot. A stressed-out lunatic, losing it more and more by the second.

I *really* wish my father's approach wasn't corroborating the opposite.

He's taking wide sloshing strides, tossing water at least six feet wide in his wake. His wildly bright glower gives me no choice but to fully look at him. It's what seizes my attention first, but not for long. Not when the more outrageous element is the load beneath his arm, fully explaining his dragging steps despite his sprinting stare.

He's carrying my mother.

Shit.

I have to force my eyes to stay open. She looks more like a mannequin, her eyes glossed over and her limbs still as stiff as support rods jutting from a concrete block. Though Z cradles her as gently as a pillow he's hauling to a sleepover, his expression tightens as if he's on the wrong side of a truth-or-dare round.

"Get her and grab her," he growls when my limbs join my mind, refusing to activate. "Your *woman*, damn it. Secure her, Maximus. Right *now!*"

As soon as he gets to my name, I'm lunging back through the wind and water. His voice—the urgency in it, so different than the imperial assholery that usually kicks in when he's ordering me around—is all I need to soak in now.

And there's my dropped vocabulary ball for the night. *Soak?* That would imply a relaxed dip, right? In these insane minutes, nothing's further from the truth. As in China-to-Argentina far.

So I'm not a delusional crackpot. But that's no therapeutic reassurance. The sanctuary's really shaking that hard. The waves are crashing that relentlessly. And the wind—

Shit, the sequel.

It's not emanating solely from Kara anymore. I know that because I've managed to lock an around her waist. The gusts that were just tearing at me from one direction have been violated by a raging crosswind, promising to tear my hair out of its double-strength tie like it's dragged my jacket halfway down my torso.

There's not a second to reseat the thing. I let it tumble off into the water, while the currents are still calm.

Because if my instincts are true, this tempest really *is* the *calm* part.

Sure enough, the fresh winds are emanating from the chapel's back doors, billowing back and forth on their hinges to the point that several inches are exposed between the portals when they reach the peak of their sways.

Sways that become pushes.

Pushes that become shoves.

Shoves that are too sharp to blame on the wind.

They're getting some significant help. Rousing shouts erupt beyond the thick wood, backing up my theory.

Still, I yank Kara closer. The hollers are too muffled to

identify as our security squad or more of Hecate's factions.

The doors bow in once more. Out. In. Unknowingly, my lungs start synching to their ominous breathing, down to every splintery rush. If, by some craziness, this *is* the goddess's auxiliary team, they're fumbling big-time on the back-up assault. Unless they still think that Hermes has the scene handled and nobody's bothered to give them the update. A depraved part of me actually wants to watch as the assholes barge in and behold their haughty lieutenant as his queen's iced-over afterthought.

But the fantasy is ripped from my mind as the doors finally give in, bursting open with a *whomp* of wild air and a charge of angry water.

I'm aware of it all, but not. Even the storm's raging ramp-up can't dissuade my grinning focus from the wide aperture at the back of the room—and the figure who's boldly paused there.

Regina Nikian has never let me down—and clearly didn't plan on starting now.

She takes half a second to nod my way before striding forward. Her leather-tied cornrows bang at her steel shoulder braces. Her elbows, positioned like forceful wings, support the hands she coils hard around her battle sword hilts. Though the weapons stay sheathed in the scabbards that hang from the thick leather belt between her molded breastplate and tasset-covered skirt, she's more than ready to draw them. I know it simply because I know *her*.

But while I wish, more than anything, for the chance to give the high sign for doing so, we have a bigger picture to worry about. With her entrance alongside the other three Olympian guards who've been maintaining a security perimeter on the hill throughout the day, a much bigger stress.

No.

We've got *stresses*. Multiple.

And terrifying.

The trees that formerly formed our welcome bower are now marauding invaders, sucked into the chapel with their branches stretching like talons. But after we all clear from their path by scrambling up the altar, there's no one left to target. Not even in a metaphysical sense.

"Oh my God." Kara's rasp is frightened and desperate.

I wish I could deny any responsibility for it, but it'd be a lie. Especially because I'm enduring the same stuff. More so as I join her to watch the surreal scene across the sanctuary.

The human and Olympians we love and respect the most, stiff as postmortem clay, are washed off their pew posts and into the torrent that's taken over most of the sanctuary. With the exception of the raised planters along the walls and the altar that's now our island, the chapel now looks like a storm channel alongside a graveyard.

"Bloody bollocks." Reg's double-decker idiom confirms that the scene's as bad as my gut tells me. "And this whole time I thought that if we were headed for a cock-up, it'd be out on the perimeter."

And her slang pile-up goes on—which means the big picture is worse than even my instinct understands.

And by now, it's scoping out a lot of the applicable

angles. Or so I think.

How much more of this nightmare is there? What are we *not* seeing here?

More crucially, how much more can I expect Kara to handle?

As soon as I think it, my mind ka-booms into its typical skirmish over it. How many times has Kara declared, and then proved, that she's tougher than I assume? That she can handle the hard stuff? That by thinking she's as frail as the fire pixie she resembles, I'm boxing her in just like Veronica always has?

But right now, Veronica's floating on her side in an eddy of drenched hymnals.

I swallow hard. It hurts like hell.

And am pretty certain *the hard stuff* never covered insanity like this.

A conviction solidified as soon as Kara shudders in my arms. And emits a sound of such loss, it's like a grieving animal. Low, lonely, agonized.

"They're dead. All of them. They're ... they're ..."

"No." Hecate says it as if we're back at Iremia and she's affirming the tea kettle is still warm. "Of course they're not dead, sweet one."

Kara goes stiff again. She shoves away, bracing on her own feet. Her arms drop, weighted by the taut coils of her fists.

"You mean not *yet*." Her seethe brings a violent blast of wind at the goddess. I still can't tell whether that ability is spontaneous or summoned, but neither does Hecate, and that's all that matters. "Because you can save them and you're not. You can return their autonomy, but you're—"

"No." Again with the galling tea-time serenity, except that the kettle's not the only thing with a fire up its bottom. The white embers in the goddess's scrutiny are kindled by the challenging flares at the edges of her mouth. "Not me. You know it, don't you?"

She spreads an arm out, flicking a finger high enough to make a passing floater jerk his knee up. It happens to be Arden. Nothing else changes about him, including his dark and somber expression.

"It's not me. *You're* the one who can save them, Kara. And you know exactly how." She flows her arm back in, extending toward my wife with graceful fingers. "Simply say the words. Tell me you're coming with me, and your loved ones live on. Or deny me and say your final words to them right now."

CHAPTER 9

Kara

I HATE HER.

And right now, I hate myself just as much.

Disbelief and disappointment join the self-loathing club as my VIP guests. They're perfect, here to keep making me wonder why and how I ever trusted that my destiny and happiness ever mattered to her. That her interest in my purpose ever counted beyond its fit into fulfilling *hers*.

Though even that investment is gone now.

If I was a cog in her machine before, I'm just a means to her end now. The courier for the prize she really seeks.

Over my dead body.

Fires flare in my gaze as soon as my mind rages with the quip, but Hecate only lifts an earth mother smirk in return. As inscrutable as the smile, I can still decipher the inner reply that's hooked to it.

Glad to grant that wish any way you like, sweet one.

I slide back fast. Hook my elbow under Maximus's with the same speed.

Nearly as swiftly as the tears that cloud my vision.

I can't surrender to her. I won't.

It's not a flight from wondering how she'd end me. It's the visions of what she'd do to my daughter afterward.

The *enlightening*.

The controlling.

The captivity.

More awful than anything I endured in Dis. Worse than what my family is going through now.

But what will they endure next? How merciful will their deaths be?

I have no theory to conjure for that. Nothing I have the courage to imagine.

Instead, I whisper the only words that *are* consuming my mind.

"I'm sorry."

The goodbye that this shrew demanded I give them.

"I don't have a choice," I whisper. "I'm sorry. I don't—"

Clink. Thwiiip.

"Wha…"

"You're right." Hermes's glacial growl turns my bloodstream into an equally Siberian river. I don't waste time wondering how he's broken free from his icebox. I'm only disgusted for not connecting the obvious dots as soon as Hecate started gesturing to the room like a triumphal princess. "You don't have a choice, darling."

I should know better than to believe his smooth

murmur. And I don't. Not that it helps a thing. Certainly not the pressure beneath the hold he's clamped on my free wrist—after transfiguring his hand into an iron cuff.

"No," I blurt. "*Please*—"

"The hell?" Maximus emits it on a low grate, but there's a full roar in his wide tiger's gaze. The burst never makes it to his lips. Instead, it shoots *up*, stirring directly into the clouds overhead. "Are you serious right now, asswipe?"

"Maximus." I can't believe I'm squeezing his arm as the calm one now. "The waves. We can't chance them getting any worse."

A low, hopefully reasonable, hum from Hermes. "Ah, how I appreciate a detainee who's smart about their situation."

And just like that, the shapeshifter has lived up to his power. Within seconds, his *reasonable* morphs into *sinister*, meaning Maximus's snarl turns into my revived strength. My silently rah-rah'ed home team. *Go, gorgeous demigod, go.*

"Little FYI, buddy," he bites out, homing in on Hermes. "I-Cuff-It-I-Keep-It Day hasn't been legal for three thousand years."

"Of which I am most aware." But the god's musical croon comes with a terrifyingly tighter dig around my wrist. He persists with the death-metal brutality, smirking like a lead singer toying with a screaming groupie. "And yet I am also most serious."

"That makes two of us."

Though another dangerous *thwing* of shifting metal accompanies the interjection, I welcome every beautiful British inflection of it.

Though just as quickly, reach for my right to walk the point back.

I've never seen Regina Nikian in full bad-ass soldier mode. The sight is more intimidating than I expected, with the numerous dents scattered over her armor and boots. This clearly isn't a kit she picked up at some Hollywood Boulevard costume emporium—not that any of us need the authenticity certificate, once she extends a sword that's likely capable of taking out all nine Westeros houses at once.

But she doesn't need the grandiose reference. After a nip of the blade's tip, in which she expertly nicked the buttons off Hermes's dress shirt sleeve, I realize our winter soldier is actually a precision surgeon.

"Rest assured, chum, I'd be chuffed to relieve you of your cuff, as well. Unless you've recently gained the gift of growing back appendages like a good little reptile?"

A surgeon *and* a comedian.

"Fuck the hell off, rank and file," the god spits at her. "Your king is no longer *my* ruler. And when my queen is running *all* of Olympus, she'll make you bow down before me and—"

A well-manicured hand descends on his shoulder, though it might as well be around his neck.

"There, there," Hecate croons past gritted teeth, filling in for his harsh chokes. "The little dear will learn soon enough. We don't want to spoil *all* the surprises, darling." She lifts her free hand into a new pose, as if she's turning a doorknob at forehead height. "Though previews can certainly be fun..."

Before her dulcet tone trails totally off, it sends a cowl of raised hairs across my nape. I'm no stranger to that stretched butterscotch voice—or the sticky circumstances it often brings once it descends.

And I've never hated myself more for being right.

Hecate's little wrist flick wasn't just for show—as I see with terrible certainty as soon as Reg is swathed in a shell of debilitation. Her mouth is fixed in its acerbic sneer. Her attentive stare doesn't blink. Her sword slips from her formless grip, clattering to the damp stones beneath our feet.

Maximus wheels around. "Reg?" And then grips her shoulders, shaking her with desperate jerks. "*Reg?* Come *on*. Damn it!"

I swallow hard, welcoming the punishing pain. Anything to detract from the sting at the edges of my eyes. And the same agony, squeezing around my lungs.

A torment that worsens when Hecate steps around, moving a hand along Hermes's shoulder in a strange, nearly sadistic massage.

"Retrieve the minion's sword," she instructs.

"Of course, my queen." The shapeshifter makes fire-under-his-ass haste. I clamp back a wince while he drags me along.

"Now grab Kara harder." Her voice still doesn't rise. "Because she's going to levitate you out of here."

And there goes that brief battle for self-control. "The *hell* I will!"

"Then hell is where *they'll* be going." She indicates toward the water, where the pew flowers and the chapel's potted plants now muddy the eddies between her floating victims. "Oh, and her too."

At the end of a blithe swipe, she topples Regina down

the altar steps—also toward the murky lagoon.

"Reg!"

But not before Maximus can help it.

Or not.

I scream *his* name as he rushes down the steps and catches his mentor by her hand. But he's left clutching only her gauntlet as the rising rapids seep under her armor, tripling her weight in seconds. I sob out, pleading for him to hold back as he lunges for her again, but the current whips her out of reach—in sad irony, right next to where Sarah is drifting along on her back.

"Maximus! No! Please! You'll—"

Words aren't possible past my audible gasp. Then my higher shriek. He probably doesn't hear either, since the violent waves have pulled him away and then down. I watch in horror, a matching torrent streaming down my face, as they swallow his head with their punishing force.

I whip a frantic stare across the waves, cursing the altar candles for throwing such schizophrenic shadows through the room. But I swear harder at my maddening, daring husband. Much harder.

If you die before we've left the church, I will break down every gate of heaven and kill you again myself.

That's the part I scream at him in my mind.

But the part I really want him to hear are the whispered words on my lips.

"Maximus. Don't this to me. To *her.*"

I swipe my free hand across my belly, blinking away furious tears—and helpless heartbreak.

"I need you, Maximus. *We* need you. Come back to us. *Please* come back to us."

CHAPTER 10

MAXIMUS

HOW HAS IT COME back to this?

Two months ago, I was tossed and turned through the muck of Styx, praying Kara would hear the call of my heart even from those disgusting depths. So determined to find her that I actually saw her in those waters, pulling me forward and willing me to survive.

But back then, I was almost drowning with desperation. Now, I'm just pissed.

Not only at the queen of the witches, though Hecate's antics have hopscotched her to the top of my Olympians-who-deserve-a-push cliff. Hermes is up there too, but in a different location. The ledge reserved for the kiss-ass snivelers.

But the summit of my rage is reserved for someone else.

The asshole glaring back at me from the reflections in the tumultuous waters.

He's absolutely there, all right. Ready and waiting, from

the second I find my way back to the tsunami's surface.

The flood that *I* caused.

The chaos I'm only stirring up worse, with every passing minute my rage goes unchecked. Like this one now, in which the storm clouds dance overhead in anticipation of more playtime.

Give it up, damn it.

Once I shoot the silent message upwards, I turn back to searching for Reg. The waves have calmed a little, but not enough. Not showing the mercy I need to spot my warrior friend between the swells, shadows, and light tricks across the raging lagoon.

Shit!

It's all your fault. Your *power that brought this tempest and its mire of visibility.* Your *rage and frustration that's keeping it here, ass bunch.*

It's the last message I want to hear but the first I have to honor. And heed. If I want the waters to recede, then I have to do it first. I *have* to get over myself and back down. Surrender. Ease back.

To the point that I let Hecate have her way? That I do nothing while the goddess bribes Kara into flying away with Hermes in tow, her jailor via one of the most disgusting abuses of a superpower that I've ever seen?

No. *No.*

But floating along in this lazy river on steroids... It's like doing the exact same thing.

Worse. It's literally *not* doing anything.

I've got to get out of this bowl of slop. And I've got to

do it *now*, before everything is too late.

Before I lose *my* everything.

"Reg," I mutter. "Regina…damn it. *Come on.* Where the hell are you?"

As if some higher power has heard the croak beneath my plea—I don't care which god, only that one was actually listening—a dread-locked head pops up over the water's surface, about forty feet away. It occurs to me that I've never seen Reg swim, but that steady fight against the current is also uniquely her.

"Reg!" I yell. "Hang on!"

Her strokes intensify, proving I've gotten through even over the water's relentless roar.

"Thank fuck," I mutter. Then again, just because I need it.

But too soon.

With the extra gallons pumping in here, the waters have picked up force. More than even the whitecaps at the surface are letting on.

Though Reg struggles to keep afloat with every effort she's got, the raging river doesn't care. It throttles her backward, weighs her down, and drags her away with horrifying force.

I block a spew of profanity by cutting loose with a primitive bellow. But I'm only half-done when the sound is sucked clear out of my lungs…by a new invasion of power in the air. In the whole room itself.

It trembles the walls. Shakes the chandeliers. Even threatens to shatter the huge plates of glass beyond the altar.

My mind compares it to a last-act alien appearance in a superhero movie, except I'm not on my ass in a theater recliner, enjoying the last of my chocolate raisins and popcorn. The sanctuary's actual stones are under me again, and my mouth is full of the saltwater that's been blasted at and over me with laser force.

But blasted to where?

Thirty seconds ago, this whole room was on its way to becoming one of the world's biggest aquariums. Now it's barely a tidepool, swirled with sludge that tangles around my ankles as I push to my feet—

Only to be knocked back down again—as the alien spaceship makes its full appearance.

No, not a craft from the stars. It's a floating *carpet*, made wholly out of *water*.

Instead of woven piles, the craft is formed of individual aqua spouts. Though every one of them is a miniature Cat Five rapid in its own right, they're crisscrossing to form the flowing platform that bursts in with the tumult of a world-class waterfall.

Suddenly, the form changes to match the noise. The carpet rears up and reshapes, looming closer now, like the approaching prow of an aircraft carrier. That's not even the craziest part. The conveyance moves with imposing precision and power but doesn't touch any of the figures that remain terrifyingly inert in the mud below. The array of humanity that can't really all still be alive ...

An uncertainty that can't get another speck of my stress. Not when there are living, moving people at the prow of the mechanized squall, which thunders closer every second. I cock my head back now, understanding what a sand crab must feel when a boat shoves onto its shore. I blink hard and fast, trying to comprehend the size, scope, and purpose of what I'm seeing.

Until none of that matters anymore.

"What…the…"

Bald bafflement makes me cut it short, once I confirm that one of the faces overhead is Regina's. And she looks three times more dumbstruck than me.

Four times, when the front of that aquatic—whatever—parts in the middle, wide enough to dump a torrent of water that re-molds into a set of liquid steps. Reg glowers, already communicating she'd prefer a lobotomy instead of a tumble down a staircase-shaped waterfall, though I refrain from a rebuke about the value of gratitude after being rescued from a king-sized toilet drain.

Not when I still don't have a clue about who'll get the thank-you note.

The *U.S.S. Tidal Wave* has to have some kind of a captain, right? Or did I hit the bottom of the pool when diving for Reg and am just having the craziest concussion hallucination in human history?

I'm spared a long wait for the answer. As soon as Poseidon strides into view, I appreciate the fact that we've met before—though I likely would've spotted him fine without the acquaintance. With water beneath him instead of land, the god comes fully into his own as a deity to be respected. His stature is taller, his exposed arms mightier, his hair more like an aquatic rock god's. Since he's kept the shell-enhanced beard but ditched the surfer togs for a barely there blue toga, the effect is enhanced by double digits.

But the most notable change comes from the way he moves. His steps, broad and bold, are no longer aided by his ornate cane. The staff has now become what it should be: the trident that rests casually in his right hand.

For now.

Casual is a fluid term under these circumstances, even for Po. There's nothing relaxed about the fire hose stare he aims at Hecate. He doesn't flinch even when Zeus sidles forward, a caustic greeting already twitching at his mouth.

"Took you long enough."

Po snorts. "I require a lot of lubricant."

My father shrugs. "Guess that's necessary, when one has to rely on gills for foreplay and a spiny dick for the finale."

Only the air's tension stops me from an audible groan. So that's where my crap humor timing comes from.

Reg endorses the point with an intentional smirk while finally sauntering down the stairs, not exactly how I thought the *aha* moment was going to happen. But nothing about this day is what I expected—especially as Hecate strides back over. On the way, she waves a hand of fresh command at Hermes. At once, the shape shifter clamps his cuff tighter around Kara.

My teeth grind. My nostrils flare.

If I leave this place without killing that shrew, that'll be the real magic.

"Took him *too* long," she amends to Z's quip. "As we can

all very well see. Though it's lovely you've prepared so well for the holiday boat parades, Majesty Poseidon. Shooting for the first-prize ribbon?"

A Mick Jagger smirk rolls out of my uncle. "Ahhh, Hecate. Always ready with the silky charm. But also as always, you're missing the point."

The goddess quirks a brow. "Which is?"

"That winning the game is about what you *don't* see."

As soon as he stresses the contraction, the sea king efficiently twirls his trident. Before his second spin is finished, a new figure emerges on the aquacraft's deck. The guy has a rugged but waggish face, reminding me so much of the morally gray bastard from *The Walking Dead* that I expect the barbed bat to emerge any second. But I don't think the character's tentacles, growing in place of Gentry's legs, possess pockets. I also don't think he'd want to be bothered, since his mere appearance has sent Hecate into borderline apoplexy.

"Awww, Hecate darlin'." He savors her anxiety with roguish delight. "You *did* miss me."

There's no filter on her vicious seethe. "As much as I'd miss a hemorrhoid, Proteus *darling*."

"*Ow.* And all this time, I thought *I* was your favorite shapeshifter."

"Careful, old man. Be *very* caref—"

"Enough!"

Z's demand rivals the new clap of thunder for which I'm undoubtedly responsible. Another unwanted apple-doesn't-fall-far moment, though I'm ready to own this one.

If Papa Bear's protective streak snaps everyone back into line, especially Hecate and her extortion threats, I'm all for it.

"This entire day has become a boil on everyone's ass." He swings around, impaling Hecate with a glare. "And it's going to cease. *Now*."

"Now there's a lockstep I can spark to."

Po's verbal thumbs-up comes with a close emulation of the motion, though it deserves respect in its own right. There's a new energy around the sea king, and I like it. *A lot*. The grizzled surfer has given way to a commanding god with phosphorescent power in his eyes—intensity that pushes across his protean's face too.

But the pulses don't stop there for Proteus. The light spreads, zapping down through the thick veins of the shifter's torso and arms. It's easy to know that because the shifter's bloodstream begins to glow with it—and then gains new texture as it goes.

But there's more.

Proteus's veins aren't just filled with iridescent power. Inside those fast-flowing streams, *shapes* begin to take form.

He's got miniature sharks in his blood.

Kara gasps. Hecate spits out something vicious in Greek. She lifts a hand, curling her fingers into a fresh claw. Between the digits, we can all view her intent now too. In those spaces, there are whole galaxies of orange, gold, silver, and purple.

But once more, she's too late.

And my gratitude hits an all-time high. Right along with my incredulity.

Make that pure shock.

As Proteus's new little pets chase each other down into his hand, engorging through his fingers.

Until his mini sharks give birth to an astoundingly big one.

This is no strange CG beast. It's a junior great white and throwing a toddler-grade fit to match. Its dripping teeth snap madly at the air—

Until Proteus shows it something better to nosh on.

Hermes's arm.

"*Yiii ayyyy!*" the minion screams.

"Oh *God*," Kara cries, though I'm stunned when there's no follow-up exclamation. But beyond that, proud. For a new bride covered in sea mud, kelp pods, and at least a gallon of Hermes's blood, she's astoundingly composed. Her gorgeous features, stamped with the relief of freedom, even give in to half a smile.

But only half of one.

Not far past her courage, I see everything she's longing to truly surrender to. Exhaustion. Uncertainty. Uneasiness. Sheer, unbridled fear.

All of it is there, and more, as she dashes her wide stare to me. I wish I could respond with something other than a reflection of her unexpressed anxiety.

What now?

Again, my sea king uncle doesn't let us down.

He's here as if he heard the question a minute ago. Flexed and ready, focusing down his water stairs but now extending more than his stare. He's offering to us—screw it, he's commanding us—with a huge, open-palmed hand.

"That's it. All aboard!"

A high, hysterical laugh erupts from behind me. Hecate's caving to full, desperation mode. "Oh, now *this* is the best part of the day. And here I thought you were getting too somber for your age, Po!"

"Fuck off, Hecate." He stresses his motion with a tough shake. Extends his fingers with tougher tension. "You kids want to be safe? You want your baby to be? Then get your asses in gear and let's amp this action. *Now.*"

CHAPTER 11

Kara

IF THIS WAS SIMPLY an awful dream, I'd wake up and be 9-1-1-ing for a trauma therapist. No. A priest. Because frying in holy water has to be my only available redemption for the catastrophe of this day. The hubris of this plan. The stupidity of thinking Maximus and I could pound even a tiny dent in the most stubborn skulls of the cosmos.

Instead, we're here, having to make this choice—our only choice—that should be easy in its necessity but is just the opposite. The most excruciating decision of my life.

I'm rushing toward Poseidon's vessel through a war zone. The broken, howling landscape that should be filled with the laughter, music, flowers, and joy of my wedding day.

Once Poseidon throttles us forward again, blasting out the church's huge windows on the way, that ice melts into my tears. It bursts from my heart as full and fast as the glass windows, now shooting like rockets into the redwoods. Unstoppable. Uncontrollable.

My husband pulls me closer to his side. Though his mud-caked form is solid, there are conspicuous tremors in his fingers. As soon as I turn fully against him, he pushes a shaky breath into my hair.

"I'm sorry."

We rasp it together but don't spare laughter for the great-minds-think-alike stuff. Nor do we waste the moments on depreciating the guilt. They'd be useless words. Pointless blame. We shared the dream of a beautiful peace; we're shouldering the weight of the ugly disillusionment.

Our systems use the time to combat the frustration in different ways. As his chest clenches on shallow breaths, mine expands and reaches for more room. As my shoulders shake, giving in and giving up, his are as formidable as cement blocks.

We grip each other tighter when our reactions sync again. Beneath my cheek, I feel Maximus's lungs suck back to his spine as mine do the same. We snap our gazes, forgetting all emotions to try to make sense of what's happening now. More accurately, where his uncle is speeding us. And how.

How?

It's worth giving myself the leave to repeat, even a few more times, as Maximus voices it in a better way.

"What the actual fuck?"

We're done riding Poseidon's jet-powered wave out of the church, off the hill, and across Palos Verdes Drive. We're now nearly past the nature reserve and heading straight into the moonlit waves of the world's largest ocean.

And now, suddenly . . . *under* them.

I'm ready to add my echo onto Maximus's words but am too afraid. Instinctively, my lungs clench tighter on their air. As soon as Maximus clutches me closer, I know we're on the same wavelength.

We're in survival mode, pure and simple, latched with a wild what-are-you-*thinking* glare at Poseidon. I don't foresee an overt reaction from the sea god, considering how calm he remained even when facing Hecate's temper. Exactly like then, his Bali-blue eyes are twinkling. His Oahu-worthy smirk is steady.

"Okay, the point is to get you both away from the actual fucks." He swoops in his hand, visually commanding us to breathe in. "Though it's probably okay to say *cluster* fucks by now." He continues, nodding toward Maximus. "Though, thankfully, you gave enough of all *your* fucks to flood me back into consciousness, so you have my thanks. That was impressive. Guess you've truly decided to go for the big waves with embracing the other half of the DNA."

"Wasn't exactly a decision." Maximus's retort is more a growl, though the whole line is clearly an afterthought beneath a more pressing subject for his uncle. "Though that's not what *this* all is. You going to lift the curtain, or the wave, or whatever the twisted Nemo is going on here? Should we be speed training to tread water over the Mariana Trench, hoping we make it to Guam by morning?"

Poseidon's tawny brows do mini dolphin leaps. "Well, there's an image. A wrong one, but still."

"So explain."

I swipe a hand over my stomach, relieved when the god

looks ready for just that, until his gaze darkens.

"And there's more of that Z-train DNA," he jibes, adding a smirk. "Though I suppose the boss bitch streak is a plus for your profession."

"Especially the part that suffers no dawdling," Maximus counters.

The smirk is abandoned. It comes as another unexpected relief. "Usually, I don't suffer mortals who forget that commanding the seas means commanding *water*, down to its basic molecular form. But we've all had a day like none other..."

The break he takes for an explanatory exhalation is perfect timing for my breath in, recognizing the snap of science logic in my mind. *Weird* science, to get eighties-style trite. I'm the girl who can quote Sophocles but usually has to ask if osmosis is a new eye shadow line.

"Basic molecules," I reiterate. "So you're breaking out the oxygen from the water to create a...what...breathing bubble for us?"

In the pause *I* now create, Poseidon drops a steady nod. "Your scientists have called it electrolysis since seventeen eighty-nine, but I've called it *necessity* for much longer."

Maximus jogs a brow. In the wavy liquid light, it changes his face in entirely new ways. I feel guilty for ogling his gorgeousness when so much of our fate—and everyone we've left behind—is still unknown. Thankfully, he's locked down better than me on the conversational focus.

"So you do this a lot? The mortal transpacific line?"

An interesting hitch of a shoulder from the sea god. "It's

better than a seat in coach between here and Tokyo."

"Well, I hope we clear customs too," Maximus returns. "Left my passport in the *other* ruined wedding tux."

My bone-deep fatigue moves in on the self-control, yanking out an inelegant snort. At this moment, though Maximus clearly doesn't want to hear it, his wry streak is my soul's savior.

His uncle also turns down a chance to bite at the sarcastic coax. If his plan is to ultimately drop us off in Japan, he doesn't confirm it.

Instead, with his features warming, he looks over our shoulder at a passing bull seal and says, "Ah, you made it back. Hello there, *filos mou.*"

The salutation is barely finished before the massive creature somehow passes through the odd bladder around us. No way will my science synapses jump in to help with an explanation for this part, so I'm captivated when the blanks are swiftly filled in for me.

The seal never makes it to the point of flopping on the floor. Its beefy tail section splits into a pair of hard-muscled legs while the fore fins follow suit, becoming brawny arms. All the human's middle parts start to fill in too.

And it—he—*is* definitely a man.

"Oh…my." I close my eyes and push my face back into Maximus's sternum.

"Damn it," he mutters, whipping off his soaked suit jacket. His frantic toss is fielded by an apology-muttering Proteus.

"Hey, sometimes the toga follows," the older man offers.

"But once I get into this lunatic contraption, all bets are off."

Poseidon bristles. "You don't have to take the ride. You know that—"

"Yeah, yeah. I *do* know." Proteus scowls. "As *you* remind me every trip."

"If fish were meant to travel at a bazillion miles a minute—"

"They would be stars and not fish." The sea king rolls out a weary nod. "As *I* do hear and acknowledge, my friend. But you know how to get out of here as well as in, so—"

"*Out?* And miss the main briefing?" Proteus moves his head to convey the opposite sentiment. Adamantly. "Not when this outcome is key."

"Briefing?"

"Outcome?"

Maximus blurts the first while I demand the second.

"What are you talking about?"

My charge is clipped and confident. This time, my instincts aren't off. They're the same spikes that poke me when someone's only being a friend for the social media clout or an endorsement contract has a clause with too many murky words.

"Don't you think we have a right to know?" I emphasize. "What are you two not telling us?"

Maximus tightens his hand around my waist while exerting the same scrutiny at Poseidon's lieutenant. "Come on, man," he wheedles from deep places in his chest. "Do you think we'll pretend you're just chatting about the latest kelp-patch gossip when you're the Nostradamus of Olympus?"

I wiggle far enough away to confront a corner of his stare. It's at its most intense now, a blue rivaling the ocean depths in which we're submerged and speeding through.

"And that means ... what?"

"That he sees the whole thing," Maximus explains. "Past, present—"

"And future?" I cut in, wishing there were more excitement than fear behind it. Also wishing my gut didn't clench in on itself along with Maximus's short nod.

"But not predictions," he says, lips terse. "It's *visions*, right?" he prompts Proteus. "Actually seeing. The sea speaks the world's secrets to you."

Proteus pulls in heavy air. "That isn't the subject of this conversation, young man."

Maximus copies the action. "So now it's a conversation, not a briefing? Or maybe your powers aren't all they're made out to be, since your bead on *the present* is damn sideways off the bubble. No way I'm a young man anymore, either. Not after the last two months of my life."

Oh, Maximus.

I send him the sadness and regret from all that's left of my soul. He's right, and I hate myself for it. If we'd resisted this—if I'd been thinking and realized what would happen if he didn't resist *me*—he'd be at his dining room table with Jesse right now, eating good pizza and grading bad term papers. Not standing here, subjected to the shifty approach of a harsh old man with harsher flares in his eyes, wondering if the god is planning to hug or shiv him.

Proteus chooses neither, and my mind jumps to both

sides of the gratitude spectrum. But not for long. The god still has words for my husband.

"Okay dokey, then. You're so sure about all that, Classical Literature Professor Extraordinaire? Then you know that *you* don't learn the secrets unless I'm captured and caged properly. So let the games begin, yes?"

"No."

The interjection hits such a perfect pitch between snarl and dictate, it's more than a moment before my mind discerns its source.

It's not Maximus, as I first assumed. It's his uncompromising uncle.

"Games are luxuries for those who have time," he states. "The sooner we clear the trench and get them completely under the veil, the sooner we *all* get to consider a little luxury again."

I swallow hard. "The...trench?" And battle to recall Poseidon's exact reaction to Maximus's mention of *the* trench a few minutes ago. Are we actually headed toward the Mariana—and what lies beyond it? Or *under* it?

I lean harder into my husband and close my eyes against a wave of dizziness but fail in fighting it off. It doesn't even help to remind myself that Poseidon provided the original lifeline when he and Nancy fled their persecution in Olympus or that nothing's changed about his intentions now. Regardless of his bold actions at the church, slaughtering his standing with Hecate and likely jeopardizing his relationship with his own brother, I can feel the god's overall mindset. He truly wants to help us. To hide us under some kind of veil.

But is that enough?

Miraculously, I'm still wearing my own veil—and I can see right through the thing.

Is *that* why he has to haul us nearly seven miles below sea level?

I try to suck down air. Halfway down, it tangles with a clog of nervous fear.

"*Errrnnnh*," I groan more than speak. "Sometimes the algae isn't always softer…"

"Mrs. Kane." Poseidon's interjection is firm but paternal, a gentle reprimand. "You're going to be fine. You *and* that special little one."

Proteus nods as if he's tapped into the same mind-reading app as his liege. With his brusque version of the Team Uncle vibes, he murmurs, "We're practically clear of the trench now."

"Wait. We…uh…are?" I choke out. With that communicative cat out of the bag, I turn around in a disbelieving three-sixty. "Wow. I didn't expect…"

"What?" Now there's a tease in Poseidon's tone, and I really do wonder what thoughts he's managed to pluck right out of me.

Though by the next second, my amazement has probably painted every last inch of my face.

And doesn't stop there.

This isn't the bottom of the deepest place on earth.

It's practically the opposite.

A long lagoon, sparkling like a billion Tiffany blue diamonds have been crushed into the water, is cradled by high canyon walls of contrasting texture. The rugged rock faces are almost like protective cowboy profiles, with their sepia crags forced to make way for lush vegetation. The flowering bushes and rustic trees push out from tall gashes between the rocks, breaking up the landscape in fascinating angles.

But in the biggest gap in the rocks, something much bigger is nestled. A multi-storied villa is breathtakingly tall and almost obnoxiously white, though the colored tile mosaics defining the edges of its numerous patios are the perfect antidote to the blinding whitewash.

As we drift closer, I notice other creative touches to the place. The outdoor furniture definitely didn't arrive after a few fast mouse clicks. The oceanic-themed craftsmanship in every piece is noticeable even from this distance. I'm able to take fast peeks at the interior too. The rooms are airy and open but elegant and stylish, with overstuffed sofas and chairs lit by wrought-iron sconces next to paintings from every major artistic era. If Arden were here, his shoes would already be soaked in drool. Kell would be giving him snide hell for it. Jaden would be tossing an eye roll at her for *that*. And Mother and Gramps—

Mother. Gramps.

Kell.

Jaden.

My stomach clenches again, but this time in anguish. And guilt. So much survivor's guilt, appalling and suffocating. My eyes behold the lush haven around us, all but ordering me to embrace gratitude for it, but inside, I'm back at the front of our wedding sanctuary, having to accept that Hecate might turn it into a sacrificial altar.

Or…already has.

I'm absolved from having to imagine that in full as Poseidon sweeps his hand wide, activating a new opening in the side of the bubble. A small flume of water stretches over the dock that looks perfect for a romantic music video shoot.

But I don't dare indulge a swoon about it. My sanity doesn't deserve that space. Why should *I* get it when my family is nowhere near similar freedom? When *they're* paying the price for *my* rainbow-crayoned dreams?

"Welcome to the island of *Kriti*. More specifically, to my velo," the sea king says, gesturing for Maximus and me to precede him up the dock.

My husband nods as gallantly as if his shirt doesn't have seventy mystery stains and his bow tie hasn't gone permanently MIA. As he retakes my hand and leads me toward the multi-storied villa, he states to his uncle, "So that's what you were referring to, about the veil. Your *velo*."

"Nicely deducted," Poseidon replies. "But the word also means cloak. Proteus and I have taken *that* part quite seriously."

Though we're nearly to the veranda, I tug on Maximus and stop.

"How seriously? Are you saying we're technically *cloaked*? Like stealth airplanes?"

"And the whole Iremia complex?"

I don't fault Maximus for adding that with such a

foreboding rumble. I held back from saying it because my own iteration would've had twice the seethe.

"Yes and yes," the sea king responds with swift ease. "But also no." His hand is already up, knowing neither of us will settle for the ambiguity. "Unlike this realm's militaries, or even Hecate and her magic machinations, the refuge you have here is as good as nonexistent."

"Do you mean it's a pocket dimension?" I ask.

"Yes...and no," Poseidon has the grace to add a self-deprecating chuckle. "But your theory is headed in the right direction. This gorge...it actually exists, in the here and now, on Crete. But to the senses of all visitors to it or spies *on* it, the lagoon and villa are nothing but cliffs full of sagebrush and a stream at which to enjoy a picnic. To them, we're nothing but vapor. Maybe vague spirits that they sense for a moment on the wind. We stay that way because every inch of Velo was constructed in harmony with the water. It's remained so through the vigor of the seven seas themselves."

I roll my head to the other side, hoping it might help for new perspective. The explanation is impressive and grand but thin on practicality, even to my science-compromised brain. Luckily, Maximus has used the time to come around and fully face his uncle with me. By now, his nod is as declarative as his stance.

"The commercial is impressive so far. So you're talking preternaturally powered hydroelectricity? Let me guess. *Yes* and *no*?"

The god offers a quick but appeasing bow. "It's not on purpose, I promise. I swear, I'm going to write *God Realms for Dummies* someday. Unfortunately, it's not today. Yet you've already been to Labyrinth and Oread, which means accepting that *walls* aren't always simple boundaries on a blueprint. But if you look deeper, *much* deeper, you'll know why the inclusion came so easily. *Maximus*...you'll know exactly why you endorsed all of it as fact."

My husband rocks back by half an inch, though his brows are still hunched. The ends of his fingers work nervously against the back of my hand. He's so baffled and frustrated, I can peer up at him and imagine I'm staring *down* instead. Feeling deeply for the little boy inside him, still struggling with his heritage. The boy who followed his mother out of the only home he'd ever known...to be brought to the shore to travel a huge sea. But not atop it. His uncle protected him, putting him in a strange shell to speed *through* it. Then that same boy, still so unsure when Uncle Po ensured it was okay to get out of the bubble and step out on the waiting pier. To keep going, toward the veranda at the end...

This veranda.

Oh my God.

There's no time to relish how right I am about it. Or even for Maximus to work out why his uncle is grimacing as if some pissed-off skunks have piled onto the lawn. But as suddenly as Poseidon has twisted out that new look, it changes again. The god jogs his head back with a new scrutiny at his lieutenant.

"Proteus?" he demands. "What is it?"

"We have to go," the aqua shifter barks, wheeling on one heel. "*Now*."

Poseidon doesn't move. Whether it's a good or bad sign, I'm clueless.

Maximus belies his own confusion with more rapid-fire squeezes around my hand.

"Where?" the god calls out. "And why are you clouting me with it only now?"

Proteus doesn't break an inch. "The future isn't finite, majesty. You of all beings should know that, especially after today."

"Shit." Maximus's hold turns into a tense clinch. "Does that mean—"

"You're going back to California." It's not a question for me. I fasten my attention on the lieutenant, already feeling his wave of terse confirmation about it. "You're headed back to the church itself."

CHAPTER 12

MAXIMUS

POSEIDON'S ANSWER DOESN'T LEND me a shred of comfort. Maybe it's because I already detect the sham, needing only my wife's strain for affirmation.

My wife.

A phrase I should be embracing with thorough—and carnal—joy by now. Instead, it's turning me into a protective ogre, charging my uncle like he's all three of the billy goats trip-trip-trapping across my bridge.

I don't care.

This Gruff owes me—Kara too—an explanation of why the grooves at the corners of his eyes are still deeper than this canyon. Why his posture is stiffer than a general strategizing a major battle.

Is that what he *is* right now?

What the hell has Hecate pulled in the fifteen minutes since we've been gone? Or has my mind completely lost its shit too, and has it been longer than that? I'm stunned that

Kara and I even know which way is *up* anymore ...

"No." I have to let go of her in order to clamp my uncle by the shoulder. We both skid along the pier from my contact, but we work together to stay passably upright. Still, I snarl, "You don't get to be Aqua-Lancelot here. Stow the sword, screw your noble ride into the sun, and *talk to me*."

My uncle rotates back as if the blade wasn't figurative. His ferocious expression imparts as much.

"You want conversation or *action*, nephew?" he grits, the volume modulated for my ears alone. "Why, of *course* Proteus and I can stay and make sure you two are feeling completely cozy and at home. Would you like a full tour of the villa while he recounts every detail of his new vision? Sound good? *Or*"—the top of his head is a sharp indication back toward the water bubble car—"maybe you're more interested in letting us get out of here to help your mother. Your friends. Kara's too."

If he thinks that's the key to relenting my grip, the poor guy is dreaming. But I can't pretend his words don't dent me. There's a dull burn behind the stressed scrutiny I slam back at his.

"Is that what's going on, then?" I dig in harder with my hold, barely suppressing the urge to fully shake him. "Is that bitch hurting them even more?"

Though he still doesn't give me quarter, there's a new element across his face—the silent acceptance and understanding of every part of my seethe—that makes it easier to get some air again. Some. But not enough.

Not a sufficient amount to call my breaths *easy* again.

Not nearly enough to let him go yet.

"I don't think it's clear yet," he finally discloses. "That caged bull look on Proteus's face? It's not a show. Something new has hit him. An unexpected alteration. Since Hecate's been the sneaky little mamba pulling so many of those lately, including the derailment of your wedding, then our jump to the blame is logically sound."

Here's the appropriate part to let my arm fall. I tack on a self-deprecating wince. "She wasn't the first one with the idea. About using the wedding for secondary purposes."

Poseidon rolls his shoulder. "Oh, I'm aware."

I bunch my brows. "You—"

"Were only paralyzed," he fills on. "Not unconscious."

I rock back my head. "So everything we were saying, after Hecate and the boy toys showed up ..."

"Was probably quite the enlightenment for *everyone* in the room," he clarifies, back to the James Bond-meets-Big Kahuna drollness, despite the circumstances. I'd ask him to lend a little of the martini-soaked surf wax if there was time.

"Enlightenment," I repeat, as if it's a new dirty word. In my personal dictionary, it is. But there's not a second to spare for explanations. I know that with piercing urgency now. The same tip of the knife that edges every syllable. "Damn it. So every ear in that room, god *and* mortal, knows about Hecate's plans."

And now a crack in the Bond veneer. "And that Hecate even *is* Hecate."

"And that she's from ... where she's from."

I go vague about it because I have to. If I'm more

specific about the queen of witches, I'll have to be more exact about my own heritage. Kara's too. The secrets of our blood, painstakingly hidden from the world. Not just the very-very VIPs from Hollywood and Alameda.

That crowd included a lot of everyday people as well. Our friends, who thought themselves trustworthy with us. Then there were the lesser gods and industry assistants, forced to be at the wedding because of duty or a paycheck. Measly compensation for nearly dying as supersized freezer pops.

Damn it, damn it, damn it.

"Yes. All of that," my uncle mutters. "Or worse."

"No. *Worse* is what we hope for," I growl. "But we *expect* chaos. Rapid and global."

"Unless Hecate's already dammed up the river."

I don't want to pivot completely toward the water, letting Kara interpret what she will from my hunched back, but I force my feet into motion anyway. She'll extract less from my posture than whatever feral forces are tromping across my face right now.

"So you mean sealed up the tomb?" I grit out, enduring my uncle's fast inhalation.

"Not the metaphor I wanted to slap you with, but now you know why Proteus and I are rushing things now. We'll make it," he vows. His grip on my deltoid is tight and damn near punishing, but I let him continue with the assurance I didn't even know I needed. "And when we do, if Hecate can't be…persuaded…to work with us on reversing the whole mess—"

"Jerry time?" I quip, imposing another deflection on my brain. Nothing in my imagination wants to start pondering what he means by *persuading* the goddess.

"Regrettably, Jerry's booked. Two bar mitzvahs and a fantasy cosplay convention. But we lucked out. Hypnos is free and says he'll do it for free pizza."

"I like Hypnos already." I almost send it out on a chuckle, but there's no time to waste. "And I'm grateful for you, Uncle. Honestly."

I break in on myself as if my cell's gone off on urgent reminder mode. It hasn't—no surprise, since I set it for seven days of honeymoon DND mode as of an hour ago—but I'm surprised it's still alive as I pull it from my front pocket. Guess the guy in the phone store meant it when he said *fully waterproof.*

"How do I keep in touch? Do you have phone digits? Or even an email?" I ask while opening my contacts list.

He narrows his gaze. "Living in the sea doesn't make me a rusty bucket, kiddo." After deftly thumbing numbers onto my screen, he hands back the device without breaking pace. "But you remember the part about velo being a literal cloak, right?"

My head rears back. "Okay." The word is slow on my lips, corresponding to the syntax I understand but the logistics I refuse to accept. "I did hear you. Every word. But how are we going to communicate? On *that* note, you remember that I've got a pregnant and nervous wife here?"

"Of course. But you know what works great for nerves after one's wedding was crashed by a delusional witch and a lackey who turned himself into a six-foot utility knife?"

Fresh comprehension hits me in a humbling wallop. "Okay. Maybe the hydro hideout *is* the best call for now."

Po hefts his jaw as if the whole plan has been my idea and not the other way around. "If that's the plan going forward, I suggest no pings in or out. Both Hecate and Z have likely guessed I brought you to familiar waters. They're probably ordering their stealth sirens to the Aegean as we speak."

"Damn it," I mutter.

"Hey." He looks ready to cuff my shoulder again, intense about pushing his support into me, but he's interrupted by a telling sound from the depths of Proteus's throat. It's past time that they get going. I know that now.

Before Poseidon turns, he murmurs to me, "I'm not your father, okay? It'll be *much* less than eighteen years before you see me again. And I'll arrive with news, good or bad. You'll get it all from me straight up, nephew. No fuckery on the board."

Choppy air makes its way up my chest and out my exhausted lips. I lift my view up and over the water, to where the crests of the gorge seem to come together in a deep V. Nested in that gap are whipped cream clouds, making it difficult to gauge any realistic distance out of here.

"No fuckery, eh? You're really going all-in for that one, with Hecate and her dice still on the board?"

As my uncle backs up, his confident steps offset by Proteus's impatient finger drums on a pier piling, one side of his mouth kicks up along with a lift from one of his fingers.

The speeder bubble starts bobbing on the turquoise water, salty foam billowing between it and the pier.

"Then it's a good thing I like to roll hard, yeah?"

As he leaps after Proteus into the conveyance, I watch for a few more seconds before they close the hatch and rev away. The pause is barely long enough for my soft but sardonic parting shot.

"Is it?"

CHAPTER 13

Kara

AS I WAIT FOR Maximus to walk back up the dock, I'm amazed I'm not swaying like the palms and oleanders that bend in Poseidon's newly summoned wind. My limbs are as flimsy as their stems; my will to remain upright is even more blown-out. Even the flagstones at my feet are looking like a great substitute for a mattress at this point.

I only stay on my feet by focusing on one thing.

Him.

My mighty demigod.

My incredible husband.

His wide steps are the timing for my breaths. His body, graceful and powerful, turns me into a grateful refugee watching a rescue plane on approach, only better. Faster. More beautiful. A new gust breaks a few more buttons of his shirt free, exposing the broad slabs of his bronzed chest. His hair, whisked sideways by the same breezes, is as virile and vibrant as his gaze. The rich blues that don't surrender their focus on me for a second.

The azure atmospheres that only haul me in deeper as he shrinks the universe between us.

Right now, that's exactly what this is for me. A world of our own. The inside of our own cosmic treasure chest, filled with flowers that have turned into gems and waters that are now mirrors, reflecting the energy of our love with twice the wattage. Soon even at triple power, as the gap between us is reduced to inches.

And he's *here* again. Lifting one hand to my cheek, the other to my waist.

During those perfect moments, a massive weight leaves my chest. The shed is a profound miracle, its abruptness hooking huge tears from the vulnerable spaces behind my eyes.

At once I fight the pull, frantically swiping at whatever's gotten loose down my cheeks. But Maximus is fast on the ball, tenderly drawing them away by folding fingers around my knuckles.

I'm less stupefied by his action than the expression with which he wields it. Both brackets at the corners of his mouth are lifted, conveying the secret he already sees. The fact that I'm bringing with all the weeping like an emo video girl out of sheer *bliss*.

"It's all right, sweetheart," he soothes. "All of it. Don't hide from me, Kara. None of it. You never have to again, okay?"

And *that* fast, the man has invited a hundred more emotion assassins into my tear ducts. I'm unable to fight them off, too obsessed with trying to justify my extended laugh. My man stares down with blatant perplexity, seeming unsure whether to join me or brace for a hysterical switch-up.

"Just be patient with me, husband," I console. "Hide mode has been a default since I was ten. Scraping it from the cerebral core is going to be like peeling off spirit gum after a ten-hour glitter shoot."

He slides his hands around my middle. Pulls me in tighter. "Say that again."

I chuckle softly but nod knowingly. "What part would that be exactly, *husband*?"

His approving growl accompanies his warm buss along my hairline. "Keep throwing in a bunch of those, and you can take all the time you need for the glitter."

A new laugh. "Don't let Kell hear you offering that. She loves the rhinestone sessions. One time, she even suggested filling a bathtub with them and—"

An agonized rasp cuts me off.

The sound that bursts from my own throat.

As my mind catches up to what my heart has blurted— and drives it through with a stake of reality.

Kell.

My biggest pain in the backside. Closest confidante. Clearest therapist. Constant wingwoman.

My *sister.* In every imaginable way there is.

I can't think of my life without her.

I refuse to.

She's not gone.

It's more than a protest of my spirit. It's a knowledge as deep as my bones, embedded into their marrow. The DNA that would surely be on fire if she breathed her last.

She'll make it through this. They *all* have to. Believing otherwise...isn't a choice.

"Kara."

Maximus almost ends it as a question, and I don't blame him. Not with a wife who's gone stiffer than the pier pilings. But his long sigh into my hair, coordinated with his fuller embrace, explains his choice of emphasis. No question needed because he already has his answer.

"She's going to be fine," he murmurs, dropping a kiss to my crown. "They all are. I know it."

"Me too." My hand finds its way to the center of his sternum. There's enough room to spread my fingers across the strong thrum of his heartbeat. "I do. I *have* to. But thank you for saying it anyway. I needed it...more than I thought I did."

My verbal pause isn't just for considering my full confession. It's tied to my physical shiver, which I can't even blame on the fresh rush of wind across the water. The air feels like summer and smells like rosemary, as textbook a Grecian island dream as it gets. And there's no one I'd rather be experiencing it with than the son of Olympus who rubs his big warm hands up and down my back.

"What you need most of all is some *rest*," he exhorts in a rough mutter, which has me reluctantly moving back from him.

"I hate to be so readily agreeing." The view beckons

my longing stare. So many places I've been across this world, from major city hubs to remote luxury resorts, but none of them have blown me away with such an ethereal aura before. Already, I conclude at least one major reason why. "My first time in a *long* time without a single appointment, meeting, or camera lens to worry about, and all I want to do is sleep through—*ahhh!*"

A chuckle rolls out of my husband as I repeat the startled cry, having forgotten that when a six-foot-seven male scoops a girl off her feet, the altitude is higher—even a little scarier—than usual.

"There, now. Dilemma solved," he wryly growls. "You're no longer on the *sleep optional* plan, Mrs. Kane. Though if you'd like, management is happy to provide some extra package perks for your slumbering pleasure."

"Ohhh. Please tell management I'm *very* intrigued," I tease back during his approach to the villa's main door, which seems to be located beyond a line of cypress trees and a stream that's fed by the lagoon.

Between the trees and the stream is a winding stone path. Maximus follows its quaint twists all the way up to a bridge, which crosses over onto the entry veranda of the villa itself. The whole floor of the platform is a sheet of transparent material—resin, glass, maybe some more of Poseidon's mysterious aqua manufacturing—that, whatever its mode of creation, is a perfect feature of the place. Beneath its surface, the little tributary expands until it reaches a landing that overlooks a broad sitting room and an expansive kitchen, becoming a waterfall that splashes into a scenic reflecting pool between the two areas.

At the far end of Lake Living Room, as I've already decided it should be called, are tall, clear cylinders with collection troughs at their bases. Once one of the drawers fills with water, it's sucked up into the tube and churned at dizzying speed. Despite the intense energy taking place in the big containers, there's no sound through this area except the steady shower of the waterfall and the meandering but mesmeric harmonies from windchimes that are hung from the high ceiling, accenting the lines of the curving stairs between the levels.

"Scratch *intrigued*," I say as we pause to take in the rest of the space. There's a peek of a dining patio for two, decorated in tropical fish colors. With that decorative tease in place, it comes as no surprise that one wall of the inside sitting area is dominated by a massive aquari—

And now the surprise party *is* official.

The massive fish bowl actually *isn't* an aquarium. It's another auxiliary finger to the lagoon that Poseidon brought us in through, and it functions as much more than a stunning interior design choice. It's a receptacle for another waterfall, narrower but taller than the one that feeds Lake Living Room. I look upward, seeking its source, but see only the balconies of the three floors that compose the rest of the villa.

"Wow and a half," I murmur, stretching out to see it all a little better.

"Po spoke his game true," Maximus says with similar reverence. "This whole place runs on hydro engineering. Beauty *and* functionality."

"Right? But *everything*?" I lean farther over, absorbed by curiosity. "There's a lot of space here. The upper levels—"

"Can be accessed in the *usual* ways." My husband's bark is just as obdurate as his arm around my middle, swooping from behind as my toes sneak out from the rail-free landing. "When actual wings spring from your back, or you're running on something more than three lattes and inhaled mud bits, you can try flying up yourself."

I nod, humbled by his vigilance for me even when this whole place is a tenable excuse for distraction.

"Thank you," I tell him. "Smart thinking. I don't want to be taking Sprout for an unwanted swim just by zigging instead of zagging."

"You're welcome." He leans around to softly buss my temple. "And you weren't *zigging*. Not yet, at least."

"But I was rushing. And all that speedway stuff is Jaden's department, not m—"

I cut in on myself yet again, enduring another skirmish between my heart and head. My practicality, calm and cold, orders me to remember the putrid plane that the church became before we left. The muck so dreary, I'd compared it to a battlefield. Decimated ground, strewn with the fallen.

But my heart knows what it believes. What hope it can still hang on to.

Jaden's not one of those muck crawlers. Nor worse.

Neither are Kell and Mother and Gramps.

I resolve it. I know it.

If Hecate did turn those swampy tides, sending them to eternity with grit in their nails and slime on their Verocity originals, I'd have heard it. No matter where I was or what I was doing, miles under the sea or even skirting the constellations in space, I'd have *heard* it. *Felt* it. They're my family. I only know one person's emotional frequency better than all of theirs. It's been that way since we were kids. Just as Jaden can hear me and Kell can smell me, I can *feel* them.

But what if things have changed?

I shake my head, already winding up thoughts for return fire—except that it'd be a mental civil war. My mind turning on *itself.* A shit storm of my own making.

What if nothing's the same now?

"Damn it," I utter. "That's not—"

What if you've *changed, Kara Valari? Only a Valari you're* not; *no more and never again.*

"No," I seethe beneath my breath, though pivot from Maximus as a precaution. "No! This is ridiculous. Self-sabotage because of your survivor's guilt. Which probably *isn't* that at all. You need to cut it loose, Kara. Cut it loose right n—"

Cut what *loose? The ring you accepted until death do you part? The child that's a part of your being for much longer than that? The elements that have transformed you into an entirely new creature? A* woman *now. A magical new being, different than the girl you were two months ago.*

"But they're still my family." I drop it to even lower decibels than before—though every syllable vibrates with my ticked-off ferocity. "I still know them. They still know me!"

They'd never shut me off.

Not even after what I did back at the sanctuary.

What I *had* to do.

Surely they know that. *They have to know it.*

"Kara?"

Only when Maximus's prompt comes, startling me with his proximity, do I realize that I've rasped the protest out loud.

"Who are you talking about?" he asks, sounding sincere but frowning with concern. "They have to know what?"

I circle around, fully pressing to him again. It's a sly move, banking on the effect it'll probably have on his bloodstream, but I'm not immune from the effects either. His bulk, so formidable and sheltering, is a well-timed soothe for my hammering pulse. The embrace he returns to mine, like bands of steel in a storm, are my new lifeline back to sanity. I wrap my own arms up and around his neck, tucking my head against his shoulder with a heavy but happy sigh.

Happy—but not relaxed.

"Ermmm...nothing," I blurt as quickly as I can, with as much surety as I can fake. It's dirty pool, and I know it, but it's cleaner than what this day has become for him. The last thing he needs, after everything that's happened, is a bride who's drenching him in tears because of weird communication issues with his in-laws. "And...nobody," I say just as fast. "I'm babbling. It's silly. Honestly. I'm burning off the last of the adrenaline."

His brow furrows. His head tilts over. Damn it; he's not buying it.

Time for more nefarious moves—easy to come by, as

soon as I reach up and comb my fingers through the long strands that bunch between his ear and shoulder.

If I needed any support for my decision about the ruse, Maximus's blissful groan gives that right up. Though his rough baritone evokes other times when I make him feel good, there's discernible exhaustion at its edges now too. The man is as worn as me, if not more. Just as afraid about the fates of his loved ones, back at the church. Just as uneasy about where *we* go from here, on the bigger scale of things. Living at Rerek's place was never going to be permanent, but perusing the available real estate listings in the suburbs won't be our nighttime popcorn activity anymore.

I know it—and one look at my husband's terse, tired profile is sign enough that he does too.

And that really settles it.

I'm not going to be one more weight on his psyche. I'm his *wife* now, the one who should be helping and supporting him. His ally and partner, not the weeping albatross around his neck. We're facing entirely too much right now. He needs the woman he first fell in love with. The fire we sparked in each other. The words we gave to each other. The courage in which we stood together.

The hope we found in everything.

The bright horizon we can still find now.

"Hey. What are the chances this place has an actual bedroom?"

The finishing dance of my eyebrows earns a roguish grin from my gorgeous husband. And then, after a sweep of his fingertips across my forehead, "We won't know if we don't look."

"Ohhh, excellent pro tip, Professor." It gets my coquettish inflection, encouraged even more by his brief but bold laugh.

This is what I want to be here for. To ease his loads and lighten his heart, no matter what kind of darkness threatens to overrun it—or us. To let him know that he's not alone. He's no longer the *odd one*, in either his humanity or his divinity. By showing him all that, I'm walking for the light, as well.

But I keep the poetic symbolism to myself, especially as we ascend some stairs and start opening doors on the next level. Being the practical protector is also another favorite headspace for my husband, and I'm happy to let him indulge it as we discover a painting studio, a well-stocked workout room, and an expansive library.

"Well, hurray for happy surprises," Maximus murmurs, earning my fervent nod of commiseration. "This is definitely going to be helpful."

I pause and nail him with a new stare. "For … what?"

"For the times when we're stabbing our own palms to keep off our phones."

I nod again, bizarrely mellow—and unsurprised—about the revelation. At least I now know what was so engrossing between him and Poseidon out on the dock. The moratorium makes sense. If we're here because the sea king can effectively hide us, why thwart the cause—or in clearer terms, why help Hecate, Hades, Zeus, or any of their recon teams find us—by dropping a geo-pin on ourselves?

It's not going to be easy—I concede that much right

now, knowing that we'll be rattling at our cage for answers long before Poseidon and Proteus make it back—but just for right now, just for this little moment, it actually feels like a breath of freedom. A respite we've been given to focus on the most important element of this day. Well ... what *should* have been.

Each other.

"Hey. Come on." I slip my hand into his. "Let's save the literary therapy for later. What's on the third floor?"

CHAPTER 14

MAXIMUS

IT'S WHAT WE'RE LOOKING for—only better.

The third floor, being the last level with a hard roof overhead, is the home of the villa's master bedroom.

As in, the whole third floor.

"Okay, *now* the surprise party can start," Kara quips, taking in the cream and gold theme that's elegantly appointed to everything. I do mean *everything*, including the spacious vanity and bathroom area with its jet-equipped tub, to the sunken seating areas with floor-inset views of the lagoon's glimmering surface, to the gigantic wave-shaped bed that's quickly defying every description in my flabbergasted mind.

Finally, I have it.

Bacchanalian.

No, damn it. That's not it either. It's one of my notorious favorites, meaning I don't toss it around lightly, but this time it's not enough.

I dig deeper, though all that comes to me are echoes of

smug chortles. Po and Proteus laughing at me from across the miles.

And there goes my imagination, chugging through the exhaustion to get to the melodrama. The stuff that *has* to be pretend. If those two are actually taking time away from Hecate's situation right now, simply to check in on Kara, me, and the sex party playpen...

Thoughts I stow for later. Thankfully, gloriously, they don't really matter right now.

In this exact moment, I have all the only components that really matter to my existence. What I readily wrap in my arms, following Kara's lead in not even bothering to strip fully. After I shed my shirt, I'm a goner. Falling to the heavenly mattress next to her and focusing fully on everything I could possibly want or need.

My wife, my child, a pillow that smells like ocean mist, and a dream that beckons better than the lagoon's hypnotizing waves.

In my dream, there's an ocean. I can see again, this time across miles of the vast waters, topped by foam that might even be softer than the orgy-ready castle bed. I ride the rollers without effort, skimming right then left like a boardless surfer, and conclude that subconsciousness actually *is* my friend from time to time.

The sky gets lighter, a peachy dawn blending into a sun-drenched day, before dark corners appear again at the corners of my vision. But the foam takes me farther, carrying me into a lavender and gray twilight, until I'm drifting next to dolphins and whales that sing to the stars for me.

Until their songs become screams.

And they're breaching high, whirling through panicked breaches, leaving me alone with the quivering stars—

And I realize it's not their terror at all.

Though the cries are far away, they're familiar now. Too damn familiar.

The stars shake once more. Then tremble on their invisible axes, before their gasses churn, their filaments flare, and their glow is worse than the first goop that threatened my vision. I throw both arms across my face, fighting their painful pulses, until realizing that those thrums are an attempt at communication. At *words*.

It's not Morse. But not basic English either.

Xypnísei.

I hold out a hand, silencing the lapping water around me. But not the distant shrieks. The screams I *have* to find now …

Xypnísei.

At last, my mangled mind connects the translation—from its original Greek.

Xypnísei, Maximus.

Wake. Up.

In the same moment, I know why the shrieks are resonating so deep. And now, shattering every inch of my heart.

I can't jolt into consciousness fast enough.

Before I'm fully there, I'm already back at her side. Folding myself around her. I don't care about the beading that scratches the inside of my arms. Part of me is stunned that so much of Madame Voracity's handiwork has hung on this far. But most of me is grateful for the realization of how lucky I am to be doing this. If fate, or its master, hadn't interfered on our behalf in Palos Verdes, my wife wouldn't be here.

As for where she might be . . .

I stab my mind into compliance before it can spin off into that horror.

"Kara." More constructive tasks demand my attention anyway, like the fervent croon I issue into her ear. "*Kara*. It's okay, sweetheart. It's me. It's only me."

Still, she flails. And whimpers. And sobs. "I'm sorry. I'm sorry! Didn't . . . have . . . a choice . . ."

"A choice? About what?" I'm as gentle as possible about it, hoping to ease her out of the dark dream that's got her. My poor girl. No soft seafoam rides with the whales for her.

"No choice," she repeats, then again. "I had to go. I had to . . . understand . . . please?"

"Of course," I soothe. "They understand, okay? Kara?"

"*No*. They don't! Maximus? Help me. Make them—"

"I will. I'll make them."

If I could leap into her nightmare this second, making good on my promise with whoever *they* are . . . But I can only demonstrate the point by holding her tighter, wrestling her closer as I move onto my haunches then dipping my lips close to her ear.

"I'm right here, sweet wife. I'll help you. I promise."

"Mmm, *ohhhh*. Maximus?"

Reluctantly, I shift up again. Only by the few inches

that I need to see her face—and confirm the new awareness in her eyes. Still, there's enough groggy drag in her blinks to make me try for the details ...

"Hey."

"Hey yourself," she murmurs, still adorably croaky. "What's ... going on? What's the—where the freak are we?"

"Magic hydro hideaway?" I prompt, though she's already straightening with more cognizance.

"Right, right. With the orgasm-worthy library and lakeside living room."

My chuff is instant and uncontrollable. "And *there's* why your test essays always got moved to the top of the grading queue."

She swings back around with sultry new angles across her face. "No *other* reasons?"

Five syllables. And *that* look.

They're all she needs as friendly reminders of my body's interesting ... condition ... before we fell asleep.

In *this* room. On *this* bed.

Details I'm pushing under the figurative rug—because of *this* bigger issue. "I had to wake you up. You were in a pretty unhappy place."

The sultry flair goes dark and moody. But not after she goes for the flirty hair toss. "But in a dream. Nothing real. Not worth rehashing. A simple dr—"

"You mean a nightmare, in which you were arguing like somebody was about to burn you at the stake."

"Maybe." She's dropped her stare to my lips, but not fast enough for me to miss the troubled tightness in her deep irises. "All the more reason not to revisit it."

"Unless the people with the torches were friends," I persist. "Or ... family."

It's her final straw. I anticipate as much, already steeling for the mighty huff she expels. I *don't* expect her to shove all the way clear from my lap, winding herself and the dingy tatters of her dress in one of the bed sheets on the way. The tangle results in an audible rip from somewhere south of her waist, likely more of her gown giving in to its own stress, but she doesn't bother to check. She's set on hitting me with as much of her ire as possible.

"Are you seriously still going there, when your near-naked wife is making eyes at you in the best sex bed ever created?"

And we're officially clear of everything I *was* prepared for.

At least she's able to preen, if only a little, with the line drive she's nailed to my throat. I'm unsure where that places the actual balls she's talking about here, but there's one fact I *am* damn certain of.

They're as ready as she is.

Really. Fucking. Ready.

She lifts one side of her mouth then the other, slowly savoring my fascination with her luscious mouth. I make a note to ask about the lip stain she used for the wedding, since its dark-cherry hue still clings to the fullest parts of her pretty moue. Tempting forth some ideas for my own mouth ...

The best of which I finally endorse ...

By pushing forward and lunging over.

By covering all those cherry-tinged curves with my greedy mouth.

By absorbing her startled moan with my primal growl.

She's already extending her sexy little sound into a mewling-sighing combination that triggers several Richter magnitudes between my legs, but I refuse to let them climb to impossible levels. Not yet. Only to the point that I know, without a doubt, how pliant and ready she'll be once I raise back up by a few inches.

Sure enough, as I pull back, her gaze is hooded and her limbs are limp. But confusion and indignation creep back across her expression. She pulls in a huge breath, clearly readying a demand to go with the mood, but I've got the upper hand of preparedness—and use it.

"So. You ready to tell me about the torch bearers *now*?"

The breath leaves her on a half-snarled sigh. "Why does it matter?"

I sober up every inch of my own face—including the scrutiny I refuse to relent. "Because I love you. And, as I said not too long ago, will continue to do so for the rest of my days. Everything about you is my concern, especially the stuff that scares you to the point of screaming in your sleep."

She rolls her eyes. "I wasn't screa—"

"I heard you, Kara," I break in. "I could hear you in the middle of *my* dream."

"Ah." She folds her arms, dipping a droll nod. "*Your* dream. I see. But we don't get to hear about the torch carriers in *that* one?"

"They skipped right by me." I spread my hands with a shrug. "They must've heard you and Twiglet were the best party to hang with."

"Well, they can forget *that* hot tip." Though her words are agitated spews, the fingertips she reaches to wrap around mine are quiet coils. Grips that get stronger as soon as she sucks in more air. "Exactly how *I* want to."

She doesn't relent there. Her beseeching touch stretches out again until her nails dig into the flesh at the base of my fingers. They're the only parts of her hand that aren't trembling.

"Please, Maximus," she whispers as our stares lock again. "I need to forget." Then, as she flattens her other hand to my chest and starts gliding it slowly downward, "Will you help me?"

CHAPTER 15

Kara

I DON'T GET VERY far. My hand halts as soon as his muscles tense beneath it, and I swear I can feel his heart beating in every one of those hard, hypnotizing moguls.

I want to explore further, wondering if the same pressure is punching him everywhere, but we're not just here because we asked to borrow his uncle's place for a little island getaway.

Velo.

The veil.

I sigh, wishing the definition was all-inclusive. That I could hide away in full from the fear and agony that are invading every spare molecule of my psyche. And now, even my dreams. Intruding on them so much that I'm yanking Maximus out of his own slumber. The REM stages he doesn't get enough of, thanks to the demigod DNA that often rouses him at ungodly hours.

I should be pleading for his forgiveness right now.

Instead, I'm roaming my hands all over the ridges of his lower abdomen, slinky and slow and merciless, until he's hissing as my fingers graze the area just above the wiry curls that peek over the unhooked waistline of his tuxedo pants.

His...pants.

Oh, God. How have I been ignoring that this fine male is in *this* bed with me, naked to his waist and staring at me with those heavily hooded cobalts? Have I been that absorbed in my stress to miss all these amazing details?

The tidbits I'm *not* skipping now.

Except for the fact that I dared to call them *tidbits*.

Nothing is a *tidbit* when it comes to my beautiful mountain of a husband.

Like the parts of him that I explore with careful, naughty caresses. That I savor with slow sultriness, moving my touch outward. Skating away from the moguls of his abs, to the places where his muscles are long, sleek ski runs. It's triple-diamond representation, leading back down to the triangle that points straight to—

Here.

A bulge that turns his crotch into hills of perfect, erotic heat. And fascinating hardness...

His hiss is twice as fierce. I layer it with my appreciative moan while dipping my hand in and around the soft cotton of his black briefs. My sound is born from frustration as much as appreciation. How I crave to simply tear everything off him, though I still acknowledge the wisdom of the coverage—most importantly because he still doesn't look wholly in for this plan.

"Hey." Though my voice is an interrupting prod, I keep my hand where it is. I may be stressed to my limits, but I still know a good decision when I feel it up. "What is it? Still debating choices for my punishment on the shrieking-dream thing? Because I think I can help..."

"No," he all but pants out. "Of course not. But—"

"What? You *like* looking like a grumpy toad now?"

At least I get him to a half-grinning chuff. "So that's the way of it, Mrs. Kane? Got the ring on my finger, and now I'm a testy toad?"

"*Grumpy* toad," I correct. "And I'd much prefer something like *hungry lion*. Or *rough and ready stallion*." After absorbing the jerk of his cock through the center of my palm, I squeeze his length with saucy emphasis. "Though at this point, maybe both apply."

He's ready to lean into the point as much as I am—every throb of his body and rush of his breath tells me so—but he chooses to shift his bottom half back while everything north of his waist is a new ball of tension. The most prominent part is his face, which welds me in with a look of dark contrition. He's not certain about it, but my searching stare isn't enough to unseat his quiet regret.

"Woman...we have to *talk*."

I take almost too long to answer. Extending past a comfortable couple of seconds but shorter than a full ten-count.

"Okay," I say, as if agreeing we can order in a pizza with anchovies. "I agree."

But agreeing to the toppings doesn't mean a full plan to *eat* them.

"Thank you." He pushes it out with full sincerity, despite the telling drop of his shoulders. "I just think it's important tha—*fuck*."

Never have I witnessed him sucking air back *in* with such a stunned rush. But if I'd given him the tiniest hint about my own pizza order, I'm sure he would've decided we go for frozen pot pies instead. Well, whatever the newlyweds version is.

Newlyweds.

There's exactly the word I need in my head right now. The confirmation that steels every inch of my daring move.

Chicken pot pie isn't for someone's wedding night.

"Kara. What—"

My small laugh shuts him off. I can't help myself after noticing how straight his shoulders have gotten again.

And how wonderful his erect flesh feels once I'm making direct contact with it.

"You have your way of talking and I have mine, Professor."

At once, there are more changes in him. His stomach goes taut. His arms shoot out with the same conflicted apprehension, as if to physically set me away. I raise my head fully so he knows that I won't resist if he does. I'm determined he knows what I desire here, but not to the point of going creepy cock stalker on him.

But he's swelling against my hand now.

Hardening.

And seeping.

Once I use those heavy drops to slicken my strokes

along his shaft, there's a strangled sound from the middle of his throat. It's sexy as hell. I tell him so with my own mewl before urging him back so I can pull his boxers all the way free.

More lusty sounds ramble out of him. This time it seems like words, maybe even in another language, but they're broken up by harsh sighs and deeper grunts. But despite my confusion, I'm massively turned on. Tingling. Needing. Getting more erect in all *my* right places...

Until I'm quivering from it.

The vibrations are so violent, I'm shocked I can slide back over his body with something resembling coordination. Or so I go and prematurely assume—before my knee catches inside my gown and tears away half the skirt from my bodice.

Maximus smirks up at me. "Now *there's* a new communication style. What are we calling it?"

While I struggle to readjust, more of the dress submits to the torque. Enough of it gives way to expose part of my waist and upper thigh.

"Maybe you have some ideas, Professor? Since you *are* the one trying to make up a new language and all."

His lips curl a little higher, with that mix of sultry and masculine only he seems capable of. At least to the point of all the places it awakens inside me. Damn it, I'm aroused even in the pits of my elbows and the valleys between my toes.

"Anything to keep the lectures interesting for my favorite students."

"Ohhh, I see." And nod as if we're simply discussing classroom seating changes. "Any particular pupils in mind?"

I'm ready to extend my own attempt at purposeful and sultry, but my sudden yelp breaks into the quest. It gets a repeat as I'm lifted up then flipped back, landing prone in the midst of more dress rips. Or maybe that's the sheets I can't seem to escape. I can't tell the difference anymore, and I'm not sure if I want to.

By the time I'm reoriented enough to look back up at Maximus, he's got a whole new outlook of his own. No more babbling languages. No more sultry smirks. And definitely no more pot pies or pizzas to order.

Though he's definitely ready to close his teeth in on *something*.

"Particular pupils, hmmm?" His gaze roams my face, starting with where he brushes fingers at my hairline down to the curve of my chin. During his journey, he tunnels that touch deeper into my hair. Tugs at my roots with rougher determination. Defined possession. Brutal domination.

My breaths come faster. *Oh, God.* The pain…it feels so good.

"You know, it takes special effort to be my favorite."

My air snags again. "I'm willing to put in the effort."

He pulls a little harder. When I let my head rock back from the force, a hiss escapes my lips. His eyes tighten at the corners. His irises darken, a combination of twilight and midnight in their fixated depths.

"To do whatever it takes?"

I'm ready to nod as fast as I can in spite of my ongoing

perplexity. How is *he* the one not wearing a stitch but controlling me like *I'm* the one kneeling naked at his feet?

He's not ready to stop either.

"Kara?" he growls, outlining it with more impatience.

"I heard you."

Master. It's on the tip of my tongue, ready to be slipped in with all the snark I can roll up, but he's not the only one with fun mind games at the ready. "And I'm ready to answer too. Just depends on what *lengths* you're asking for."

Once I demonstrate the reason for my emphasis, sliding a hand down and around his erection once more, he's forced back into reaction mode. When the low chuckle in my ear coincides with the jumping flesh in my grip, a special thrill zaps my veins. An even better version hits with the next flurry of my heartbeat. This adventurous, ferocious man is now my husband. If fate wills it, we're going to have a lifetime of trying to outwit and out-sex each other.

But even that won't be enough.

For now, I revel in the glory of the gorgeous smile he beams down at me while maneuvering the middle of his body to notch to the center of mine. But it's not as simple as usual, with the layers of different fabric still between us. The sheets are easy enough to yank away, but my dress is still intact in all the not-so-advantageous places. It'd be a funny coincidence if we both weren't so ready to get conjugal.

I don't give the man any doubts about my standpoint on the subject. As quickly as physically possible, I grab at the zipper along my side—the one that's *not* torn open yet—and help out with a vehement tug.

"Here," I tell Maximus. "For leverage."

He frowns. "For *what*?"

"Do it," I counter, even attempting to start the new rip for myself. "Whatever you have to."

Just as fast, he gives in to waggling brows. "To your Madame Voracity original?" Yet doesn't waste a second to widen the gap, rending the sparkling fabric until there's enough room to push it up and out of his way. "Well, you *are* serious about that extra effort."

I take my time about picking out a comeback line for that, but they drop off my consciousness like pebbles off a cliff once the sensual notes beneath his words dig into my psyche. And my pussy …

"As long as you're serious about naming your *lengths*, Professor."

Luckily, that's the one that decides to stick around. I must know it's going to earn me a new flash of his devastating grin, though the expression only lasts until he lifts the last layer away from the part of me that's trembling the hardest. Soaked for him the most. Ready for everything he wants to demand.

He keeps me wondering about that, shivering and anticipating, as he hitches back after his hard-won victory. I even get a little impatient—he fought to get me like this, only to nothing?—except my whole answer is already written on his face.

The way he's looking at me.

At *that part* of me.

Gazing as if I'm a work of art. A rare gemstone unearthed.

The woman he worships.

Every one of the comparisons is another light in my own fire. The inner heat that melts my walls for him. Makes me liquid for him.

He sees it all. And starts preparing himself in return.

Letting me watch as he strokes himself. Takes his own liquid and rubs it up and down, hypnotic and heavy...

"Lengths like this one, beautiful?"

I breathe in deep, savoring the essence of him on the air. His vanilla mixed with my cinnamon. The musk of his arousal twined with the honey of mine. When I finally release my breath, it comes with one syllable of lust-infused sound.

"Yes."

Maximus pushes back in. Makes room for himself between my thighs. Still, he growls, "Wider. All the way, sweetheart."

"Yes," I gasp out again.

"Now spread your arms out. Surrender to me, wife."

"Yes. *Yes.*" I'm sprawled for him and loving it. Open wide and loving *him.* "Take me away, Maximus. Please. From all of it. Take me far, far away..."

CHAPTER 16

MAXIMUS

BEAUTY AND THE BEAST.

The thought isn't a welcome one. But once it's lodged in my head, it's like werewolf's tracks in cement. Ingrained. Irremovable.

Like my memories of this illicit moment will be.

Even now, I'm unsure if I'm proud of that fact. But it *is* a fact, as unignorable as the need in my cock. The lust in my veins. The animal cravings that position me now, taking advantage of my beauty in the clothes I've torn off her body. In the powerless position I've ordered her to take. Spread for my invasion. Ready for me to maul.

To fuck her so hard she forgets everything we've gone through to get here.

Not completely. Not forever. But for now ... I can.

And I do.

In the space of one savage stab.

In the space of her hurting, joyous scream.

In the primitive force that takes over, rolling my hips tighter inside hers. Giving her exactly what she wants as I take exactly what I need. Her heat. Her hold. Her surrender.

Her sanctuary.

The oblivion I need as much as she does.

I plunge into it the same way I thrust into her: with as much force as I can. As I fill her with my sex, I stretch out to lock her wrists beneath my grip. Crucifying us both, in a desperate attempt to wash away today. It's only temporary, I know that already, but it's a salvation we both need. The right we'd envisioned for today, before Hecate infected it with so many wrongs.

But this...is right. So damn right.

And so good.

So. Fucking. Good.

My brain resounds with the refrain as my blood unites with its light. As it explodes up my cock, flowing from me in a billion points of liquid luster. As Kara returns the explosion with the same brilliance, bursting but squeezing around me. Coaxing out my life but giving it back too. With her cries of perfect climax. With her sweat-slicked fingers, bunching around mine.

And ultimately, with her kisses. Open-mouthed, passion-filled...and tear-stung.

Even after we pull back, the sobs continue to come. I don't try to stop them or even soothe her. She needs this part as much as everything else: the emotional release to pour out along with her physical burst. On both accounts, I battle to stay inside her. To be here for her aching soul and hurting heart as much as I was for her climax and kisses.

In a way—well, more than one—I need her tears too. They're as much my expression as hers. The rage and confusion and frustration that are as tangled as her dress and these sheets. A morass that, maybe now, we can work together to *untangle*—and then cope with.

There's no time to waste about it either.

As soon as her sobs abate, I pull out with slow gentleness. But I don't go far. There must be sixty sheets across this gigantic bed, so I use one to clean us up instead of stepping away to find towels. That task is far down on the priorities for this respite. Though I wish the top of the queue could be something like *want to do that again*, I'm bumping even that priority down by several notches.

We have other things to get to first. Subjects we can't treat like basic surface wounds.

"Maximus?"

In the simple three seconds of her murmur, I'm even more certain of the fact. There's so much of her in the word—her exhaustion, confusion, uncertainty—but a lot is missing too. The fear and trauma that are still only a few hours old. She exposed some of it in her outburst after her climax, but I can see it all getting packed away yet again. Carefully put aside, making room for the front she thinks I want to see.

No. For the facade *she* needs.

The Kara who's an expert at doing exactly this. Stowing away the ugly days, the monster people, and the clawing fears for the sake of being perfection incarnate. Faking it until she makes it for the sake of prying cameras, see-all reporters, and rabid fans.

Except that now, she's them. And *making* it has turned into *becoming* it.

This is her survival mode.

Which leaves me with the stickiest conundrum of my life.

How do I pull her out of it but keep her breathing? How do I emotionally kill her so she can truly live?

A tender tug on my beard snaps my attention fully back to the moment. "*Maximus*." Though my eyes haven't shifted, her smile coerces me to actually focus in on the moment. And I'm troubled about *her* spacing out? "Hey. Where'd you go?"

She gets my fast but soft chuff. "I'm right here. Promise. Everything okay with you and—" I cut in on myself with a contemplative look. "Hmmm. Guess we can officially move on from Twiglet now, right?"

For reasons I can't fully dissect, her answering smile helps me breathe easier. "I know it sounds weird, but I can feel her now. And even, sometimes..."

"What?" I prompt, trying to ignore her pure sexiness with her teeth against her bottom lip.

"Sometimes, I even hear her," she confesses. "Not in any kind of creepy way. It's more like...whispers from my soul, you know? Places that are so new inside." There's an attempt of a smile at the edges of her lips. "So it's not like the two of us are having quirky conversations and tea parties."

"Good." I'm compelled to kiss her nose. "Because for

the record, I like tea parties. But only if they have that sweet cream stuff and not just butt—"

As soon as she whips her head to the side, I chop myself short. She fills the suppression with a huff so harsh, I take a quick look for injuries.

"You know what? I'm starving," she suddenly says. She pushes to her knees while gathering up the edges of her skirt. "You think your uncle stocks the kitchen with anything for normal folk?"

"Normal." The reiteration inspires me to one last chance at witty banter. "You sure we can actually claim that one?"

Probably should've labeled it as the *desperate* chance— which ends as most of the ilk usually do.

"Maybe it's damn time that we do."

I'm eating the bitter air molecules in the wake of my woman's adamant exit, at the end of seven words that she's bitten out in place of so many more.

The sentences that, even if I followed her step for step downstairs, she'd still refuse to speak to me.

For right now, she needs that pride in her posture. The steadiness in her steps. And the walls in her psyche.

For right now.

It's not a phrase sitting well on the isthmus of my patience, though persistence helps me ground it a little better. The words say it all. This is temporary. No bride, in any realm, wouldn't be bruised to the middle of their spirit from a wedding day like this. In the future—the *far* future— maybe she and I will be able to watch *Worst Wedding Day* compilations and laugh together. *Hard* and *long*.

For now, only the balance of this night is the applicable subject for those adjectives. I'm going to give her that, as much for my sanity as hers. We'll both be more rested in the morning, which isn't that far off. It already looks and feels like late afternoon, which makes sense given the handful of hours that separate us from LA's time zone, so the concession isn't gigantic.

But my love for this woman...

Absolutely is.

The admission itself becomes my mental mooring, already telling me this is the right call. Agonizing but right. Kara and I have had to put on masks for everyone else in the world, but not each other. We've never waited to face our truths together, no matter how horrendous or painful. That we're doing even this minor duck-and-hide now, on our wedding night... I grit my teeth, trying not to compare it to stepping on a schoolyard crack or vertically planting our chopsticks in the rice.

This won't be forever.

I'm willing to take the gamble for our love—which is better than forever.

This is for eternity.

*✳

"Triple chocolate ganache cake with one layer cherry liqueur and one mango mousse, frosted with Swiss meringue buttercream and chocolate-dipped strawberries."

And if there's any additional reason to seal why I want to be married to this female even when I'm ninety, here's the moment I get it. I tell her so by leaning across the narrow kitchen counter that separates us and pushing an empathic kiss to her giggling lips.

This is absolutely the last scenario I imagined for us on our wedding night—perched on a couple of padded bar stools on opposing sides of a blue-and-gold damasco marble slab in a spacious but utilitarian kitchen, with at least twenty dishes of half-eaten food between us and the sink—but I also can't think of any elaborate restaurant that would be more ideal. No candlelit setting that would have us laughing so freely. Grinning so fully.

And kissing…like this.

With the chance to lean in and urge her mouth open with mine. Taking advantage of the freedom to linger like this, with my own lips still wide, swiping in at her tongue with the flat of mine. Waiting until she pants at me in return, grabbing at the collar of my open dress shirt, until we're making out more like the giddy teenagers we're acting like. With rolling lips and clashing teeth. With wet, suckling sounds and wanton, lusty moans.

Until a punishing *ding* breaks us apart.

Kara falls back onto her chair, pressing cute fingers to her madly flushed cheeks. "*Why* does that sound so much like the timer on our porte cochere light? Which always seemed to be set to an *earlier* time when Kell was out on date nights?"

I crunch in my brows. "Never for yours?"

Her expression sobers by a small fraction. "Never met anyone I wanted to stay out like that with."

"But now that *this* dude has, apparently, beamed you up to the Starship Enterprise?"

Her smirk returns, twice as adorable as before. "But the transporter clang is much more fun."

"So far, so good." I wave to our shameless sea of dishes, upon which there's everything from strip steaks and seasoned fries to escargot and an outrageous cheese assortment. "I still can't believe this place has a working replicator."

"No. It's a *kouzilina*," she corrects with a wagging finger and impressive inflection. "Or so your uncle has dubbed it. Says so on the instructions there on the wall. And as long as you don't go for any seafood..."

I chuckle, though toss a grimace over to the gray blobs that were produced in place of the shrimp scampi I first ordered. "Talk about a lesson learned the interesting way."

A fresh laugh, light and brief, from her. "Guess I won't be worried about having to hail you on the Federation-friendly frequency anytime soon."

"And *there's* the well-done geek gotcha for the night. You've been holding out on me, wife," I accuse while she opens the replicat—kouzilina's door and pulls out a huge slice of what looks like the intense dessert she just detailed. "Isn't there a clause in the California marriage license laws about having to disclose Trekkie status before the rings go on?"

Kara leans forward as if her dessert fork is about to be a gavel. "*Not* guilty as charged. I hardly know the difference between a Vulcan and a tin can. Jaden was always the guy to boldly go and find the new creatures in the final frontier."

I don't correct her butcher job on the famous prologue. There's a much more important subject to address.

"You mean Jaden *is* always the guy?"

She lowers the fork—though I no longer expect a cute *order in the court* to follow. Dejection defines her again to the point that the elaborate cake is forgotten.

"We don't know if that's still true."

I reach for her hand. "But we don't know the opposite."

"But we *do* know the extent of what Hecate's capable of," she snaps. "What she'll do, and who she'll do it to, in the name of her cause." A tremor claims her whole form, which looks more fragile than ever in the tattered remains of her wedding gown, the bottom shreds now enhanced by a sarong skirt she's created from a throw blanket out of the library. "You know I'm right. Maximus, she's driven to the point of blindness. All her means are justifying her righteous ends."

"Not arguing," I return. "But she's also *smart*."

"Which means what?"

"That she knows better than to follow the stunt at the wedding by sending anyone out of that room in a body bag."

Her frown is tight. "Why?"

"Because it cuts off the chances of ever winning you over."

She ditches the frown for a full flare of shock. "Does she think she stands a chance *now*?"

"I really think she does." Though she still gawks like my statement is an order to the kouzilina for fried ox tongues on Pop-Tarts, I keep going with the defense. "If I've learned anything from forced proximity with the pantheon over the last month, it's that they hate rejection, defeat, and all versions of the word *no*. Many times, they'll just pretend that none of them exist."

She's not done with the sharp stare. But I take hope, sensing she's starting to move toward the same. "So she may be more merciful...for strategy's sake."

I pull a hand free long enough to tap the tip of my nose, indicating she's hit the theoretical bull's-eye. But I quickly drop the gesture, owing her all the honesty of my answer— even its shitty second half.

"At least until she figures out how she can get her hands on Sprout."

I expect the sudden leech of color from her face. I *don't* expect the contrasting flames that consume her eyes at the same rate.

"Does she also figure I'll levitate her to the top of the Burj Khalifa and then throw her off before that happens?"

A grin splits my face apart. Damn it, the timing is crap— but the moment is also ridiculously right. I can't recall the last time she was this outrageously bold except for the first time we ever kissed. The school year wasn't even a week old, and she confronted me about feelings I didn't want to admit, let alone act on. Heated yearnings. Forbidden fires.

Lusting longings that assault me all over again.

Only this time, I'm the one having to do the confronting.

A face-off that begs me to be forgotten.

It is *your wedding night, asshole.*

Granted, commemorating the world's worst wedding on record...

Which means maybe thinking about how the rest of the day can count?

Which might mean not *discussing whether her siblings are alive or dead?*

"What?" Again, my wife swings me back to the moment with her queenly edict. "You don't think I'd do it? Or *can?*"

I haul her hand up to my lips and press her knuckles with a reverent kiss. "My love, if you want to drag that shrew to the top of Mount Everest, I'll be the one at base camp cheering you on."

Her tension eases. But not nearly enough. Still, she hitches up one side of her mouth before murmuring, "So is that where your mind's already gone off to? If I'd known earlier that roasted yak and *thukpa* would make your smile that big—"

This time I cut her off by going for a full lip-lock. Damn good decision. She welcomes me with open warmth and floors me with her sweet, generous passion. But that's just the beginning. As if she's seen the inside of my mind, and the little mental trip I just took to that night in my apartment, she moves to maneuver us closer together. Except *unlike* that night, there's a marble countertop between our bodies. Inwardly, I'm already cursing the thing, since even standing isn't going to help us at this point.

And here I go again, thinking like a mortal guy.

A mortal who married a flying witch.

Well…a *levitating* one.

Who's now filling my mouth with her husky laugh and my equilibrium with her stupefying conjuring, lifting me up off the floor as she executes a beguiling mid-air twirl.

"Holy…shit," I chuff out in uncanny time to the pair of circular swirls she directs at me with her hands. Now *I'm* turned in the same horizontal way she's gone, only I'm facedown and headed for her shapely uplifted arms.

She lowers us at the same time, and I already vow this'll be a main feature of my life's highlight reel in my last hours in this realm. But—thank *God*—that time is *not* now.

Now is solely for being here, present and aware of every second of this moment, as I lift my hands to smooth the hair from her eyes and my lips to adore her with all the awestruck adoration in my soul.

"True confession time," she says once we pull a few inches apart. "That's the first time I've ever tried the Cirque twisty."

"Worthy of a standing ovation." I quickly kiss her again to stress my sincerity. "But as long as we're turning this into tell-the-truth hour…"

"What?" She widens her eyes. "Oh no. Did I hurt you?" Her hands frisk as much of me as they can reach— which I wouldn't be so hasty to negate once there's only my briefs between my ass and her frantic touches. But she's too genuinely upset to be taken advantage of.

"Not a scratch. Honestly." I stress it as soon as she punches up a skeptical scowl. "But also honestly? Roasted yak isn't my thing."

No more narrowed eyes my way. Her gorgeous browns are as wide as the *O* of her mouth, slamming me with her mock distress. "Whaaat? Oh, that's it. We can't be married anymore."

I tilt my head, adding a little sarcasm of my own. "Maybe we can try putting it on pizza."

Her frown halts in its same place too. Her hands stop atop my shoulders. She nods toward the magical food maker. "Let's try it. Ask our fun friend here."

"Ehhh…" I shake my head. "Don't think it'll be the same."

"Ohhh, yeah." She lifts one hand long enough to snap her fingers. "Can't believe I forgot about your connoisseur standards."

"Which, to be honest, are more Jesse's thing than mine."

Her head tilts to one side, emphasizing the splay of her long wedding curls against the marble. "So you're being a pizza snob in his honor?"

"If it was only that simple." My reply is quieter than I originally planned. And more melancholy.

Of course, Kara doesn't miss a single nuance of it. *Damn it.*

"If everything was still just that," she rasps.

"Not even asking for everything," I return. The low utterance takes me to the edge of pathetic brooding, but I don't care. Maybe getting her to open up means *I* have to do it first. "Just the day Jesse and I were plowing through a pie while grading papers—and something more delicious happened to my day."

The focus on her features gains a new kind of intensity. Deeper degrees of understanding.

"So *that's* where you really went." There's a smile in her voice even if it still doesn't breach her expression. But she

178

gives me a better gift in the caress of her fingertips along my jaw. "I remember that pizza."

"You do?" Here go my brows again, crashing back toward each other. "Wait. Did I offer you some? No. I would've remembered that part. Well, goddamn. Guess who's not getting a host of the year nomination?"

Upside of my mortification: her emerging giggle. "I wasn't there for food, Professor."

"Ah. Right."

It hardly has any volume, and I like it that way. Mashed this close to her. Remembering our origin story together. Acknowledging how every sexually charged minute of them is directly feeding these. Liking that feeling too. Liking it a hell of a lot.

"You were there…for the earring."

As I gently tap on the jewelry, which has stayed on both her earlobes since this morning through some insane cosmic benevolence, she counters, "Or so I told you."

I dote on her with a soft kiss to her left lobe. Then the right.

"I'm grateful for these earrings way more than the pizza." And then seal my candor about that one with a meaningfully long kiss. "Though I might've gotten well acquainted with the cold knob in my shower that night, battling thoughts of how you'd look in them and nothing else."

A shiver claims her whole form, and I've barely begun with trailing my index fingers down the sides of her neck.

"You know, you probably could've convinced me to do something about that."

"No." I'm strict about it for a reason. "You're the most magnificently sexy female I've ever known, but you're also a perfect and rare gift. I wanted to wait for you. And I probably should've—"

Her own fingers are suddenly smashed against my lips. She pushes hard enough to make me wonder if she's morphed them into steel chopsticks.

"Probably should've what? Invited me over for afternoon tea, instead? Scones and sweet cream and all?"

I huff. "Your scones shouldn't have even been on my mind, Kara."

She ropes her hands around my nape, using the purchase to readjust herself beneath me.

"Well, yours were on *mine*."

Until her legs are spread and her sarong is bunched around her waist.

"All right, fine." I groan it out because her intimate heat already permeates the crotch of my briefs. And her wetness. *Shit*, and even her little tremors. "I wanted your scones too. And your...sweet cream. Badly."

Not until I cross that final word does she ratchet her hold harder, clearly not negotiating the equally brutal kiss on her mind. And it *is*...merciless. The polar opposite of teatime manners. A primal, dish-breaking mating call. Her dark animal roaring out to mine.

And mine...slashing back.

Rough. Relentless. Lunging into her with all the untamed need I felt that fateful day. The urges, wild and terrible and beautiful, that made me push her into my apartment wall and screamed at me to do so much more.

I'd growled them all away, taking pride in my nobly drowned urges. Justifying myself as a higher species, able to kill the selfish beast within. Professor Higgins on a self-righteous repeat loop.

Idiot.

I see the ugly truth of it now. Knowing exactly how I'd tried to run from providence. To duck from my destiny. To deny *our* inevitability.

"Fuck." I can't fight the searing blade of it any longer. The slice it makes all the way to the middle of my marrow. "Kara…"

"What?" Her whisper is benevolent but strident. Her hands, spreading under my shirt and along my shoulders, are strong but giving. "Maximus? What is it?"

I drop my forehead to hers. It's agony to keep the contact—not because of what's here between us but what's not. The sparks we first combusted. That shocking but earth-changing heat, so intimidating but irreplaceable … Where is it now? Has Hecate taken that away from us too?

I refuse to accept that.

More than anything else, I refuse to let her take away *us*.

Maybe the fight does have to start with me. With how much I'm willing to give up, and give in, to get the prize back.

How much I'm willing to expose.

It starts right now.

"That day," I grate, stroking the sweet space between the base of her neck and the beginning of her collarbone.

"Damn it, Kara. I was really stupid. Denying this. *Us*."

She flows her hands back in, not stopping until they press together over the hammering din of my heart. "*Hey*. It was scary. I remember. And I was stupid too."

I don't say a word. Right now, I have to believe that my silence speaks better. That she's using the long, uncomfortable pause to assess the pounding pulse beneath her fingers and the yearning emotion that locks once more into her gaze.

At last, one of us screws up the courage to speak once more.

"Maximus?"

I bore deeper in my spirit, summoning the strength to do the same. "Yeah?"

"Let's not be stupid anymore."

I slide one hand up to her cheek. Stretch my fingers out toward her hairline for the sole purpose of keeping her head in place—and her huge, breathtaking eyes right where they should be. Commanding my fortitude—and calling to my cock—in every way that I need. Every degree that I crave. Every inch that matters.

"That, Mrs. Kane, is the most exceptional idea you've ever had."

CHAPTER 17

Kara

THE ORGASM S ON the kitchen counter were amazing—but half the intensity of what Maximus gave me on the stairs. And then on the couch, in front of the wall-sized aquarium-that-isn't.

He's passed out cold to sleep now, his head against a pile of decorative pillows with his dark-gold hair spread against the couch's bigger cushions. I've long forgotten where he ditched his dress shirt and underwear, and I'm far beyond caring. With one leg splayed straight and the other bent to keep his foot secure on the floor, he's almost like a model posing for a Renaissance *artiste*: a glorious proxy for Adam in a garden or David asleep with his lions, characters used as excuses for some kinky guy with a paintbrush.

The things I'd like to do to him with my own paintbrush...

I hug my knees to my chest in order to stifle a small laugh. *Who needs a paintbrush?*

I only wish it was so easy to giggle about my new nightmares.

But they haunt me even when I'm awake. To the point that even now, in the throes of exhaustion, I don't dare go to sleep.

Like that's helping.

I can still envision the storm. I remember how cold and afraid it made me. How I couldn't stop shivering despite my gown being completely dry. In my dream, it was restored to all its original and gorgeous detail, and I walked so regally down the aisle in it.

But around me, there wasn't soaring music and smiling faces. The air was consumed slanting rain and flying debris. I felt like a doll, able to watch the chaos, but only from a detached glass shelf.

Until they appeared.

Like they do right now, occupying every shadow of my imagination.

Mother, Kell, Jaden, and a huge crowd behind them.

But it's not really them now, either. They're only forms, identifiable solely from the characteristics of their wide, accusing eyes. The black oil that covers the rest of their forms...it wipes out everything else, including their limbs and their mouths. They can't push their way free or even scream for help.

And yet they do.

They take over my head. Invade my heart. Torment my soul. The misery in their moans. The desperation in their shouts. The terror in their throats.

Why did you leave us here, Kara?

Where did you go, Kara?

What have you done, Kara?

I curl up tighter. Smash my hands over my ears, silently begging the air itself for any help. But the chaos in my psyche rages on as if the villa's been scooped up by the Wicked Witch's hurricane and plunked on an airport runway.

Stop. Stop. Stop.

But it all keeps blaring. Their screams gain more layers.

Where are you, Kara?

Why have you abandoned us, Kara?

*What-what-*what *have you done, Kara?*

"My best!"

I sob-sough it into the night from the second my escape onto the patio is final. The double glass doors nick shut behind me, bringing a second's worth of comfort.

I look back to check that the sound hasn't roused Maximus. Once that's confirmed, I sprint across the flagstones and then down the dock. I can't ignore the feverish scratches at my sanity any longer. I can't keep running from it or battling to pretend about it.

I can't keep the brave walls up for another minute.

In this case, not another second.

A tiny speck on the clock that feels like eternity, before I reach the end of the long quay and finally sink to my knees.

And let the heartsick tears pour out.

And every racking, roiling emotion along with them.

"I did my *best*, okay?" I cry at the wide waters. Part of me hates them for keeping such deep azure repose and glass-smooth calm, but the other part is giddily grateful for the exact same things.

Even more so as I swipe my face with both hands,

fighting to clear the grieving salty tracks much sooner than I expected. Though Maximus and I have likely been here for close to twelve hours now, this is the first moment I've had to simply sit with these feelings. But also the confusion around them.

What do *I even feel? What's even real?*

I wish I had half a laugh to give back to that. In any other place or time, it'd be a pathetically sappy song lyric. For all I know, it might already be. I sincerely *wish* it was. In a song, it'd be two to four fleeting minutes of metaphorical meandering and symbolic pining. But this... it's the unfiltered honesty of my heart. The pure pondering of my soul. And they're both fissured like every sidewalk in downtown LA right now. Chunks of feeling and longing and responsibility and ruin, pulled apart by forces far under the surface of what everyone thinks or assumes.

Even me.

The girl already raised with several levels of *sur*reality, having to perform that mental separation every day—often several times a day if Veronica was in fine form—now wondering which side of my brain is up and craving my mother in more ways than I thought possible.

"Mother."

I rasp it as strongly as I can, knowing that's how she'd demand the iteration regardless of the desolation that drove it. The surety makes me smile—only a little at first, but it grows outwardly as I look inwardly. If she's here so strongly in my head, maybe she isn't dead. So was she truly spared? But for what? Hecate wouldn't be dense enough to just let everyone go. Not without milking whatever advantage she could from the situation.

The deliberation takes me back to square one. Stark fear. Impotent despair. They rush on tracks that collide and fume in my new, clenched words.

"Mother. Talk to me. *Tell me.* Please...*please.*" Splinters dig into my palms as I press harder and harder to the deck, hands stiff against my sides. "What do I do? How do I know if it's the *right* thing to do? How do I pick? I...can't... I... don't know what..."

But the tiny wood pricks aren't why my cheeks are soaked in tears again. I'm as adrift as if my shoulder blades turned into sails and followed the wind out to the ocean itself. But even with a sextant, a compass, and nautical GPS, I'd be lost. In the middle of the nowhere called my mind.

What am I doing?

And why am I trying to figure that out *here*, when I should have ordered Poseidon and Proteus to take me back with them?

I shouldn't have jumped so fast at the sea king's ultimatum. Didn't all my experiences with Hecate teach me anything about trusting deities of *any* kind?

But isn't Maximus a deity?

I plop back onto my butt, blinking at the water for a long second before an addled giggle invades. "All right, all right," I mutter, hoping to assuage whatever higher wisdom that threaded the thought into my synapses. No way did it happen organically. Not every battery in my body drained to these critical levels. "But he's the exception."

To save more face—not that my existential counselor cares—I weave a weary finger into the air. The motion tracks my sights back across the lagoon. Its moonlit swells, aided by the strengthening breeze, are more than welcome in the frenetic flurries of my senses.

I pull in a huge inhalation. Though I'm significantly calmer now, lungs suffused with night wind and nostrils taking in myrtle and eucalyptus, I'm already thinking about getting up and returning to the villa. As much as this scene should be in a *Kriti* tourism reel, there's one important factor missing for this island visitor.

But maybe the land's famous fairies have been flitting into my thoughts—and, in the quixotic way of fairies, conspired in my favor. I stick with the theory, thinking *somebody* will need to be thanked for the heady pleasure of watching my birthday-naked husband on approach down the narrow dock.

"Do you little imps take Venmo, or is this going to take gold pieces and a full-on shrine?" Though right now, I'll gladly agree to either. Or both. Maximus Kane's form, in full pagan warrior mode, is worth any finder's fee on the planet.

I'm not done with the conclusion before he approaches so close, I've got to arch my head back to meet his gaze. Not a rough chore; perhaps one I'd also pay for. The tips of his hair are getting mildly lifted right and left, and the riot of stars in the sky behind him start to reflect in his intense blues.

I sigh. I think. Because I'm pretty sure I've forgotten how to breathe.

It's as if he already belongs up in those cosmos.

Is he *sure* he's only *half* a god?

Or is there something Nancy Kane isn't telling us?

There's no way I'll find out now, so I pivot to a subject that *does* have an answer.

"Hey," I say, reaching out for one of his hands. His fingers are chillier than mine, so I pinch a curious frown nearly at once. "Did I wake you when I left?"

"Well, if delayed reactions count," he replies tighter than I expect. "When you weren't there, I searched the house like a madman. Thankfully, the master has the lagoon-view windows."

"Doesn't *every* room in this place have a lagoon look-over?" My crack doesn't gouge the smallest dent in his tension—seriously, he's practically growing fuming tumors now—I wrap my other hand around the five demigod fingers still in my clutched possession. "I'm sorry I made you worry. *Hey*, I really am."

The huge hills of his shoulders rise and fall. His nose pulls in one more time, air moving into him with focused intensity, before he responds.

"I know that. And I accept the apology."

"But…" I prompt, chasing his lead.

"You could have woken me up, Kara." He's subdued with the volume, not having to talk over anything but the lapping water and a few cicadas that survived past summer. "I know you probably wanted to let me rest, and I even appreciate all the concern that went into that call. I also respect that your brain has been messing around with you since before we got here, for all the really understandable reasons, and that you likely wanted to escape somewhere to properly sort out the bedlam."

I sniff hard. Gulp even harder. How he sees this clearly

into me ... it's incredible but unsettling at the same time. A part of me is astounded and grateful, feeling this thoroughly aligned and acknowledged. But does that mean to thank the man by giving him a bath of my scared, silly tears? He's been through as much as me, if not more.

"Thank you," I manage to blurt, keeping my shit mostly together. "For saying all that. For ... getting it."

"Yeah," he murmurs. "I really do."

"But..." I stretch it out longer this time, also adding a knowing smirk.

Nevertheless, Maximus makes me wait out a lengthy pause before his growly undertone gets to work again.

"But this, here ..." He lifts his free hand and flicks a finger back and forth between our chests. "It's not just you and me anymore. I know that *you* know it too, but coming out here to sort your head, when there were a lot of other places to get the job done..." He curls his hand back in until his white knuckles glow in the moonlight. "What if you'd fallen in? And what if I was still asleep and never heard it? What if there was the slightest possibility that you and Sprout—"

"Maximus."

As soon as it blurts from me, full of aching emotion, I lunge to embrace him. Though I'm speaking everything more overtly, I already feel the matching severity of his feelings. Like the nightmares he had in hell, I can't see everything from his mind in vivid color, but the reactions are enough. His worry. His terror. His conflict. And yes, despite his staunchest efforts to control it, a stab of frustrated anger. At me.

"I'm sorry," I whisper into his neck, where his stress has caused a damp sheen under his hair. I burrow closer, feeling guiltier. Searching for something to say to make it better. "You need to know how much I mean it. But you also need to look out here. Hardly a ripple, right? And I do know how to swim. If something *had* happened, I could've—"

"Just glided back to shore?" He jerks back far enough so I'm nailed by his strained glare. "All right. *What* shore?"

A fast sweep of an assessing look, and I'm grimacing. He's right. This gorge isn't like miles of the Malibu shore. The framework for the water is solid rock all around, most of it high and steep and unclimbable. Even the land side of the pier is wedged as if a drill were taken to rocks older than dinosaurs.

So he's really right.

But he also really knows it.

In the minute it's taken me to confirm that with my own eyes, he's gone from being a little terse with a wide layer of clemency to totally flipping the mix—minus the gentle part.

His demeanor takes me back to the first day of the semester, when everyone in that Alameda lecture hall forgot to breathe as he strode to the podium. Many of us just gave up on air for an hour, especially me. Notably from the moment that his look got close to black before he kicked my harassers out of the room.

In this moment, I wonder if *I'd* be next on the list if not for the water below us. The shimmering depths that he's treating more like lava.

Overreaction? And even if I really think it, do I express

it? The man *has* pointed out a pertinent landscape hazard and calls the university science guru his best friend.

But maybe there are things *he* doesn't understand either.

"Well, I'm sure the lagoon has some shallows—"

"Which probably have craggy rocks or gossamer sand and slope toward the underwater trench that got us here."

I stiffen my shoulders, avoiding a show of my reacting shiver. Once again, his point is valid—but it's starting to feel like he's lording with it instead of talking about it. Overly punishing me for the point, which happens to be a damn good one.

So it's official. I *am* the new stand-in for the classroom bullies.

I take a second to pull in a breath, hoping the air will also bring a politic way of offering that to him. But the man beats me to the follow-up.

"But maybe that's a *good* fact for you now, eh? Another trench to hide in is probably an excellent discovery for the woman who refuses to talk to her husband."

And maybe oxygen is overrated.

Not when there's two tons of blindsiding fury to take its place. And consuming confusion. And piercing hurt.

Pain that pushes me hard enough to shove away from him. To scramble back up to my knees. To use the vantage point, if only a few inches, to punch down at him with a look that shakes me with its vehemence.

"What the hell are *you* talking about?"

CHAPTER 18

MAXIMUS

IN A CRAZY WAY—MAYBE two or three of them—this is the most exhilarating moment since we got here.

No. Not so crazy at all.

To the degree that I know my wife doesn't agree, I'm as certain of it as before. And more positive as every second ticks by, thick with all the stuff that's rushing out of her. Every awful conflict. Every turbulent agony. All the *feelings*, grabbing and piling on each other so fast that I can't identify a few. Several?

But it's okay.

Better than okay.

Beyond better.

I admit it in full as I cop to the initial shitshow of an excuse I used for my pique. The woman grew up ten miles from me and was probably doing mermaid-like laps with a private coach while I was still dogpaddling with Jesse in the Central Public Pool. Does that mean I'd stand back and wave from the veranda if she really slipped and took a splash into the lagoon? Of course not. But I'd probably be joining her with a laugh instead of a glower. If the water was nice enough, perhaps we'd do some casual exploring together...

Not a confession she needs to hear yet.

Definitely not now.

Not when she's finally coming out of her caves for me.

Not when I'm ready to move in and seal those escape routes forever.

The resolve pumps through me at full force, especially as I push all the way back to my feet. But even with my superhero stance and unwavering stare, I have trouble accepting the right method for the message.

Unbelievably, it's a taste of her own medicine.

The right pressure to trigger the full avalanche in her tunnel.

But since she's chosen words for this particular moment, as belligerent and insolent as they are, I'll give them the same effort. Just this once. Just because she's looking so delectable, with that brilliant bronze rebellion in her eyes and the Greek keys of the sarong halfway down one hip, that a bit of munificence taps at me.

"I think you already know, pretty wifey," I drawl. "But you also probably already know that I'm not *supposing* any *meanings* here."

As she falls back onto her heels, her head tips to one side. "*Wifey?*"

"You get the better meaning when I do."

And there's the line I should have stretched for a few

hours ago. The dip into hard love that I've never used with *any* lover before—but never even been inspired to. No other woman has ever impelled me to such a strong reason. Such forceful fathoms of anger.

Born from such depths of persistent love.

Once that recognition is full, so is a new kind of calm in my mind—counterbalanced by the thick, hot need in my body.

Inescapable now. Inevitable.

"You want to be my *wife*, Kara?" I ask with that same steady flow. "Then you'll think about opening yourself to me like one."

As I expect, she huffs. And seethes. Her arms twist across her chest, pillowing her pretty breasts against the meager remains of her wedding gown's bodice. The poor cups weren't built for a thunderstorm, a muck wade, and a trip across half the globe in a bizarre water bubble.

The whole ensemble will be done with its ordeal soon. I'm positive about it.

"You know what? That's enough," she finally spits out. Her head starts to weave like the best Act One Kate, preparing to read her riot act to Petruchio. But unlike the asshat in Shakespeare's story, I'm not going to deny my woman a thing. She's getting the exact opposite. As much as she can take. Everything she'll say yes to. "I've been completely honest with you, Maximus. *Always*. Even after everything we both went through—"

She stops as soon as I raise a hand. "I didn't say *honest*. I said *open*."

"There's a difference now?"

"There's a difference always." I'm unfazed by her garrulous eye roll only because I've logged a lot of self-control practice. And, to a small fraction, because she makes the look maddeningly cute. But it doesn't steer me from the ultimate point. Not by one letter. "Are you being honest with me right now?"

Another eye roll—and a little toss of her shiny mane. *Goddammit.* "I already told you—"

"Answer me."

"Yes," she spits. "I'm being honest. Just like—"

"Then tell me why you woke up screaming in my arms this afternoon. And why you've barely slept since then."

Her expression constricts. Her head is agonizingly still. I find myself longing for the eye roll again in place of what I know is back. Her resistance. Her staunch, stubborn gates, keeping me locked out of her innermost spirit. Her darkness ...

"It's just bad dreams, okay?"

I take a firm step. Dip my head toward hers, hating but thanking myself for making hers tilt back.

"Fine. If that's all it is, then tell me. *Open* to me! *Talk* to me. Let me hold you and help you—"

Her arms flail out. "There's nothing to help with, okay? I can deal with this, Maximus! I'm not a five-year-old who thinks there's a possessed doll under the bed who's going to feed on my soul. I don't need—"

I wave her into silence by raising my hands as livid flags. "You know what?" I seethe into the thick pause. "Fuck this."

And then hit her with an equally fierce glower.

She stumbles back by a couple of shaky steps. "Ermmm…Maximus?"

"Take off your clothes."

And here, at last, is where the demeanor gets tough. Her eye roll *and* head toss, even together, don't win against one moment of her stunned blink-blink.

"Wh-What?"

The stuttering sough is enchanting too. Luckily, I half-expected this part—and everything she unfurls at me afterward. More fast blinks, confirming my command was the last thing she expected. But during it all, the rapid rising and falling of her chest—telling me something else.

That she likes it.

"You heard me, Kara."

I yearn to demonstrate the point by tugging at the loose knot of her sarong, but I breathe deep and resist—showing her my own version of *open*. It's all here, on full view for her. The strain in my stance. The rise of my cock. The hunger in my eyes. That especially. I'm yearning for her…in so many damn ways.

"Get as naked as me," I emphasize in a guttural growl. "*Now.*"

Profound pleasure—nope, I'll go straight for delight— suffuses my veins as soon as she moves, silently obliging me. It's a little surprising when she curls an arm high, starting by getting free from her gown's bodice instead of stripping free from the looser, easier sarong. But I lift one side of my mouth, wordlessly approving the choice once she bares the erect buds at the centers of her breasts. They're already so taut and red, the areolas puckered and pinched.

She likes this.

I don't care what her pinched lips and narrowed eyes are saying. Her body is already learning the lesson. Revealing itself to me.

Opening...

"Turn around while you take off the rest," I instruct. "You came out here to look at the water, so you will."

As soon as the sarong drops, I'm behind her, molding my bare skin against every inch of her that I can. I press my hands to her belly, savoring the small bump there now, before bending and fitting my lips against her ear.

"I understand why you were drawn," I say in a sparse whisper. "It's nearly as spectacular as you, sweet woman. See all the colors that the moon makes on the water? They're like the different shades of your fire...your passion. All the ways you surprise and amaze me, each and every day. And look there, on the horizon. There's no telling where the starlight ends on the water and begins in the sky. That's us, sweetheart. The same light, in different forms. The whirling particles that were destined to meet and come together."

"Maximus." She utters it like worship, small soul-felt rasps that mesh together nearly as one. "Oh *yes*."

But then she's quivering against me, rocking and writhing, and I already know what she's asking for. Pleading me, with flesh against flesh, for. How I tease her, sliding one hand until my fingertips play with the edges of the curls at her core, though nothing more.

"Please," she chokes out. "*Please.*"

"Soon," I soothe back. "But not until you listen to me. Not until you understand."

I steel myself for an aggravated comeback, maybe at a full shout. But I've underestimated the fortitude of my girl. The way she nods to me instead, jerking her head like a possessed but lusty doll, does things to my shaft that I hadn't expected. Her obedience is my downfall. Her willingness translates to my wetness, already soaking my cockhead with astounding fullness.

I don't let it go to waste.

With a terse groan, I roll the drops around my crown. With a darker sound, I bend in to find her entrance...to ease the tension for us both...

I'm there. Except...not.

My cock notches into a tunnel. Except, as soon as Kara bursts with a sharp hiss, I already know it's not the one I was aiming for.

But holy *fuck*...it feels so good.

My balls swell. They're not the only body part heeding that memo. I grunt hard as my mind reels, a tangle of need and lust and carnality—

That, remarkably, weave themselves into a new blanket of coherency. Spreading themselves before me with vivid, even electric, colors. Eagerly and swiftly, my bloodstream plugs in.

I dictate to her with unalterable authority, "Get on your hands and knees, wife. Use your clothes for cushions."

Holy shit. Even with the extra charge in my favor, it's

going to kill me to watch her move.

And oh God, how it does.

In all the best ways.

A kinky man I am not, but this has to be one of the best sights of my life. This addictingly headstrong woman, tenderly trusting me enough to fulfill my direction, even as her rosette still grips me so tight that my tip stays rooted inside her.

Now go deeper. Stretch her farther…

I shake my head to free it from the taunting devil on my shoulder. Damn it, there's no angel on the other one, figurative or otherwise. I'm not in need of either. This decision isn't based on the temptation towards wrong or the inclination towards right. This isn't a simple multiple-choice exam.

But it's not a pop essay either.

It's more.

It's an illustration of a vital point between us. A lesson that isn't just essential for Kara to see. I've got to figure this out too. How to see when she's masking the real things of her heart, especially her fears and ragings, when she thinks something or someone's more important. Someone like me.

But I have to learn how to see it better. How I *haven't*, before now, is a testament to the challenges of our journey so far. So many corkscrew turnpikes and high-speed switchbacks. *Too* many blind intersections.

In order to ensure it could go any further, maybe our engine needed exactly this. Fried spark plugs. Bald brake pads. A complete strand on the shores of a Crete lagoon.

We can't keep ignoring the dashboard warning lights. And Kara can't keep stowing her truths in the trunk for the sake of irrelevant optics.

I can't keep letting her.

I have to learn to push—even if it makes us both hurt.

I hesitate, unsure about how to fully embrace the resolve. Whips, chains, and floggers really aren't my way, but I *am* a university professor. Tough love is an unspoken career requirement.

Her instant and incessant moan provides that easy answer.

Hell. Fucking. Yes.

"Oh, sweetheart." I utter it with syllables that tremble in time with the shivers through her body. "You're so wet." And the pulses in her pussy. "So soaked for me."

"Yes," she readily pants. "*Yes*, Maximus. Please. More. Stroke me…right…*th*…"

She breaks away, the words swallowed by a new moan, when I pull my touch totally free. For the moment, I have what I want. The lubricant, dripping sweet as honey, for where we're going next.

I use the nectar around the aperture that's gradually getting used to my girth. She tenses, but I soothe her with calm hums before scooping fingers into her body for more.

"Oh!" she cries out, head falling back. "Oh, no. *Yes*. Maximus, I'm so…so…"

I bend over, swiping my other hand into the lagoon just to make sure everything's sliding around well—and perhaps as a symbol too. A sign of reverence to the waters that are lending us their azure alchemy, flowing the wavy light across our bodies in ways that are almost angelic.

As I prepare to take her in the most demonic way.

A thought that has me forcing words up my dry throat. "You want this, sweetheart? Like this?" Because even devils would agree that doublechecking is singularly smart— especially when one's woman takes the better part of a minute to reply.

"I'm...not sure," Kara whispers. "But if it's what *you* want, then—"

"No." My parched larynx is now a ripping thunderhead. As I watch the lagoon waters vibrate from it, I drop my body low. Lower still. I don't stop until my chest kisses her shoulder blades and my lips slam her nape. "Not what *I* want. Not what you *think* I want. Only what *you're* craving right now, beautiful. Only what *your* body desires."

It might be a little unfair, joining my mini lecture with matching circles against the button at her center, but the woman's barrage of intense frissons is worth the guilt hit.

"I want..."

"Yeah?"

"*Maximus*. I want you...to take me to the stars."

And now she's accommodated for a full year of guilt. Well, at least enough to cover the extra flex I allow in my hips, flying my own concentration of nerves toward the heavens for which she's so sweetly begging.

"Stars are made from pressure, sweetheart." I work the words against the sensitive parts of her neck while working more of her arousal along the place where I'm slowly fucking her. "From atmospheric fusion. Atomic pain." I scrape her jaw with my teeth. Push my cock in a little more. "But... where they're done, it's the most astounding light in the heavens."

Beneath me, she shakes harder. Her moans emanate from places deep within. Her body squeezes and tucks around me, and I'm already seeing the light. The sparks that absolutely must be shooting from my erection already. But no. There's no letting go yet. There can't be. *Not...yet...*

"Do it," she grits out. "Take me there. Just like this, Maximus."

CHAPTER 19

Kara

AM I GOING TO regret this?

Parts of my body already say yes. I'm full and resistant. The stretching is unreal. His invasion is agony.

But along the underside of those sensations, there's discovery.

Knowing I'm giving him profound pleasure. The strokes of his fingers, promising the same to me. Sensations I've never known, heightened by the obscene strain on those illicit parts of me.

The pressure.

More. More.

The pressure.

Harder. Deeper.

"Push out, Kara. Open for me, sweetheart."

The pressure . . .

Before the light. And the sparks. The fire of Maximus and me, returning with an intensity I never thought possible.

The bright, bold flames we've been missing…for how long? I can't bear to think about it. How have I not even realized they were gone? How did I not feel the impinging cold?

Never again.

Not after this.

Not after this exquisite explosion.

The release, wild and wicked, cruel and carnal, detonating me to cinders. Pulling me apart until there's nothing left to protect. Nothing left in my comprehension but my screams, my truth, and my tears.

The sobs that take over before my shivers are through. The pain that takes over, invading deeper than Maximus's body can penetrate, until it's deluging out of me. Spilling from me, salty and bitter and embarrassing, but *real*.

The reality I wasn't *questioning* when I first came out here.

The reality I was *seeking*.

It's so clear. So catastrophic. And, as Maximus joins me with his bestial bellow into my ear, so consummate. A completion I never fathomed. Not in *that* method, at least.

I don't take a lot of seconds to keep processing that. Not when there's the fullness of this moment to savor, in ways obvious *and* obscure, bringing new understandings that are darting through my head brighter than the fireflies flitting in the tall grasses atop the cliffs.

The brilliance of it all is incredible, bringing me to a small laugh that pushes Maximus out a little. He doesn't help my composure with his small grunt, which says nothing but everything at once. I already feel how thoroughly I rocked his world as well as the other way around, but beyond that mental connection, I don't see what his revelation specifically was or what I gave him besides a climax that shook him like a skyscraper with a pulled cornerstone.

"Guess a penny for your thoughts wouldn't help right now," he mumbles, nuzzling along my neck.

I hold my reaction to a smirk. "You have pockets in places you're not disclosing, Professor?"

His grumbly hum sends more delicious tingles along my skin before he kisses my earlobe again. "All right. How about some H2O for your ... ehhh ... notions?"

Once more it's a struggle to hold off on the giggles, but I sigh so thoroughly that his cock slides a little more. He pulls out decisively but pauses to pivot for a few fast splashes to his groin with the water around us. It takes him no time to face me again, stretching out on the blue-and-white throw. He beckons with one arm, and I lay down in a mirror pose of his. Except we're not quite matching figures—a fact for which I've never been more grateful.

I snuggle into him, taking refuge in his brawny size and calming strokes along my back. No. Right now, it's not just post-coital shelter. It's emotional necessity. A craving I thought I comprehended after our very first touch, now seeming almost like immature fancies compared to this.

The ways I see into him now ...

But not with my abilities as witch or my powers as mage.

With my love as his woman.

And the ways *he* sees *me* ...

No.

The ways I need him to see me. The openness I still have to give him in full. *Starting right now.*

"So … you're not wrong," I softly offer. "I do have … notions."

The hand along my spine comes to a stop. But only for a second. "About?"

"Your point. The one you began earlier, when you were comparing us to the water."

He scoots a little closer. Though I adore him for the added warmth, I'm sad about surrendering the view. His nudity really is better than any naughty gallery art.

"Once you got poetic, you referenced the reflections on the surface. But before that, you talked about all the things that could exist below the ripples on top. Even beyond the shallows. Hidden caverns. Crevices nobody can see when they're taking the pretty view at face value."

I'm not sure if his chest appreciates the speech, but that's the audience my new nervousness picks for it—until there's a commanding finger under my chin. When it's joined by its pal at the indent beneath my bottom lip, I have no choice about lifting my gaze to fully meet his.

"Face value," he echoes, the roughness solely for my ears to absorb. "Like the way the whole world looks at you."

I swallow hard. "Until you called me to your podium after class that day."

He smiles, but it's fleeting. More prominent is how his eyes darken to troubled indigo and his jaw develops a subtle tick. "The most incredible thing that ever happened to me. You changed my life."

I brush fingers across his furrowed brow. "For…the better?"

He relaxes his scowl, though not all the way. "In every miraculous way I can think of, my beautiful bride."

"But?"

We've both flung the prompt too many times today, but I can't think of anything more eloquent. Not when I sense its necessity from his spirit as well as his voice. Still, the relief that comes with the second half of his intention, a flow of nothing but determined devotion, is enough to swell my heart and race my pulse. It's the kind of Professor Kane fantasy that would soak panties across half of Alameda University. But I'm not secretly gloating. I'm outwardly grateful. How this man is all mine is a mystery I might not ever fully solve—nor want to.

"We fell so hard and so fast," he offers then, quiet and contemplative. "Which, to be clear, I wouldn't have stopped or slowed if I could…"

"I know." I trail my touch along the rugged edge of his face, treasuring the combination of his hair and beard beneath my fingertips. "Me neither."

"Then there was a trip to buy fruit and some damn good sushi at Yamashiro, I think—"

"Before hell broke loose," I finish for him. "Literally. And several other ways too."

He accepts that the way I hope. With a heavy sigh but a quirking chuckle. "It's been a nonstop parkour run. If stuff like boulders in the Styx and cliffs in hidden witch haunts also count. And they really damn well should."

A smile tempts my own lips. "You forgot the daily disguises during the drive between Rerek's place and Terranea."

"Still can't decide whether I like you better as hungover rave girl or fussy old lady with the fake poodle in your purse."

"You mean Pookie?"

"Oh shit." But the grumble doesn't stop his heartier laugh. "I can't believe you named that mangy thing."

I respond, mockingly serious, "If Pookie were here, I'd order her to bite your nose."

"Well, that settles it." He nods. "We're burning the old lady outfit when we get home."

"Hmmm. Yes, sir." My tone is milder as I add the flat of my hand in my caress along his jaw. His gaze intensifies. I push in even more, enforcing how this isn't some humor-as-barrier move. That I haven't forgotten a single piece of his point. That I want to stay open now, not just honest.

I tell him so too. "Costumes and concealment and the constant defense plays…" It deserves an emphasizing sigh. "We've been so busy fighting *for* us that we haven't had time to simply *be* us."

A new breath leaves him, as well. It's heftier than before, spilling over my senses with focused ferocity, casting a strange but welcome kind of spell. I didn't think I could feel closer to him, but the truth of it is clear. A hundred new doors have opened between us, each leading to a new level of our love The intimacy goes beyond the rings and the vows; it transcends even the woozy wonder of our tender first dates. It's exactly what Maximus claimed: a bond like the stars themselves, pulled to each other like light and space and gravity. Destiny that was sealed in the cosmos, no matter how Hecate messed with the timing.

Magical thoughts. And star-bright surety. But between it all, we're now learning what every couple, Olympian or demon or human, has to. The intimacy, not just the sexy sleepovers.

It's a big mental glob to take in, but the process brings me to a wider grin than before. When my husband emulates the look with his own tender stare and reverent smile, I tug into his beard, urging him closer. And then more. *More...*

Until we're sharing desperate breaths. And heavy husks. And throbbing heartbeats.

And passion.

All of it...and more.

The long, wet mash of our mouths. The longer, savoring lolls of our tongues. Vibrations and connections. Wantings and hungerings. For this once, for this now, seizing the chance to forget what we've been through and just celebrate what we are.

A little closer. A little wiser. Stronger together.

The beginning of a family.

As soon as the thought fills my mind, there's a flurry of sweet flutters through my belly. I startle so suddenly, Maximus yanks back as if I've accidentally kneed his groin.

"What?" he charges. "What is it? Are you—is Twiglet—"

I cut him short with a laugh that's probably too sharp. But I can think of no better restitution than taking him by the wrist and guiding his hand across the tiny thumps against the inside my abdomen. "I'm fine. She is too. Except—" I stop before he can even react with more terrified eyes.

"Holy—" But I'm not quick enough. His pupils are blown, taking up space in his irises like a pair of rogue black holes in twin nebulas. "Is that...my God, *Kara*..."

I laugh, trying to infuse it with enough warmth to quell the heart attack my husband's surely about to have, but it looks like I'm again too slow on the proverbial ball. Maybe a quip will help instead.

"Hey. Tell it to the little linebacker here, mister. Though maybe we should go for *Bigfoot* instead of *Twiglet*? Or...start talking about that actual name again?"

For a long second, Maximus doesn't answer. I don't mind. The look on his face, adoration mixed with wonderment, is the best configuration of his features since the moment he first declared his love. But this...moves me even more. Clutches every chamber of my heart and ounce of my soul. Two minutes ago, I was certain I'd never discover more depths of love for the man. But here I am, as astounded as if we've jumped back into Po's bubble and dived to the bottom of the Aegean to uncover a precious treasure.

Maximus sits up straighter and leans in, practically confirming he shares the conclusion. His action pulls at what's left of my gown, wrapping it around his lower waist and groin. It covers a little more than Proteus's provocative getup, but not much. I have to command my sights north of his sternum, or the subject will again get shoved away like the eucalyptus stamens blowing off the pier. As pretty as the sight is, I refuse to adapt *Stamen* as our daughter's next nickname.

"Okay, then." Maximus aids the cause with an easy pragmatism beneath his tone. "Let's do it. Do you have anything special in mind?"

Besides giving myself permission to ogle your loincloth for a few seconds?

I beat off the thought with a roller-coasterish giggle. At once, it's layered with a push of unexpected tears. It's only a sheen, not even blurring my vision, but a strong enough sting to explain itself. Or maybe that's all this man's doing. This incredible, formidable man, so readily signing up for a role he never expected. So clearly and completely loving me...and everything about our child.

Okay, now the real tears set in. While I readily write them off to hormones, *overwhelmed* isn't understating things when it comes to my heart.

My husband waits in patient silence, letting me collect pertinent thoughts before speaking up again. I yearn to kiss him—and everything else—even more now, but again, I have to focus on something better than *Stamen*.

Something *much* better.

Something that's going to be worthy of the realms' most magnificent child...

"Well, I like the general theme of trees, but this baby *is* royalty..."

Maximus nods. "So, fancier than *Loblolly Pine*."

I don't hold back on the laughter this time. "How do you even know that?"

He barely skips a beat. "Fancier than that, though?"

I bop fingertips against his shoulder. "Yes, Professor."

"Gwynedd? Fruella? Hapshetshut? Edithinia?"

"How do you know *those*? And no, no, no, *no*."

He takes the wise route, dipping into a moment of contemplation. Since he's giving me the opening, I go ahead and soak up the sight. This time, all of it. Nobody in their right mind would blame me. My husband is the epitome of masculinity even with a lap full of sparkly Italian fabric and a mane full of bright-pink eucalyptus stamens.

That's it. Name decision or not, I'm nearly ready to lunge.

But, thank all the gods, Maximus Kane knows, *without* knowing, that I need a rescue.

His grin broadens with gorgeous confidence. His eyes brim with a special kind of joy.

"What about . . . *Nikoleta*?"

My heart skips. My lips kick up.

Never in a thousand years would I have thought of the name, but now nothing else feels right for our unique, perfect princess.

Which makes it all the better when Maximus nods with scholarly approval but smiles with fatherly love.

Somehow, he seems to read those thoughts with a sweeping study of my face. His lips notch a little higher before he explains, "It's Greek. You probably know that already."

"I didn't," I murmur, stroking a hand along his beard. "But that makes it even more awesome." *And you, amazing man, for thinking of it.*

"The word means *victory*." His tone, newly solemn, has

me inwardly predicting what will follow. "And if we can stack even that odd in her favor..."

I join my other hand to the first, framing his face while nodding my understanding of his trail-off. All the things he can't commit to words. All the *what ifs* we can't dedicate to action. All the control that's thoroughly out of our hands.

But only for now.

I have to believe it. I press the conviction into him too, entwining it into his psyche with my stare.

But nothing's going to seal it better than a kiss. So...I give in.

Not for long. Not very deep. Not the senseless sensuality I'm still craving, but enough to impart him with the point.

We're not going to quit. I won't let it happen, and neither are you.

We will *be victorious, my love. All three of us. I don't know how or when, but—*

I snap back from him, my eyes and mouth wide, as something that feels like my answer already bears down on us.

No. Not down. It's rising *up*—from the lagoon itself.

It's the parade *and* the fireworks. A whirlpool that grows from a minor skipping plunk to a swirl the size of a house in less than ten seconds. But the vortex is more than that. It's a reverse rainbow cone of color, aqua and teal becoming marigold then marmalade, but none for very long.

The beginner hues die out as soon as the persistent red appears. It's not a gradual arrival either. This is like a whole vial of food coloring dumped in the mix.

Or blood.

"Holy sh..."

Maximus doesn't dawdle on the profanities. "Kara." He lurches and hauls me tight against him with the same fierce motion. "Closer," he orders until his makeshift loincloth slips from between us and into the water. "Don't let go of me, understand?"

I nod without a word against the wall of his pectoral. He remains taciturn now, joining me to watch as the shimmering fabric is pulled into the crimson waters.

Into them—but not any further *down*, below them.

The whirlpool isn't behaving like it should. What's left of my wedding gown is just staying there in the violent eddies, rolling around as if it's in a lunatic laundry cycle—remaining as white as it was when I zipped it up at the chapel.

"What's...going on?" I finally mutter. "Why—"

"Huh." Maximus's interjection is an astounding one-eighty from his terse growl. He sounds like we're still simply lying here, newly awestruck at the stars and the fireflies. "The light's coming from *under* the water. From something... that's coming up."

"Holy shit."

It's a joyous feeling to at last complete it—but even more so when I know there's more to add. Better things. So much better.

"Poseidon's back already."

CHAPTER 20

MAXIMUS

I FIGURED IT WOULDN'T take my uncle long to assess the aftermath of Typhoon Wedding and report back but still anticipated we'd be waiting a minimum of twenty-four hours. That was, of course, working in a typical flight time back to LA from Chania or Heraklion—not magic water bubble speed.

I'd blame the mental space-out on naked dock time with my wife, but the first passenger to depart the transport at the dock is better prepared to do the job for me.

"So I see the honeymoon *has* already begun. I mean, we were hedging bets on the way over—"

"And now you owe me fifty bucks," says the second traveler down the water chute—a sight that has me sprinting down the boards as fast as my wife.

"Kell!" she screams.

"North?" I'm ecstatic about blurting my identifier too—layered, no doubt, by several octaves of bewilderment.

My best friend is really here, and really in his trademark wheelchair—only I'm watching him and it as they *float* atop the liquid exit ramp from Po's conveyance. Once he glides safely onto the dock, his wheels work the way they always do, including their rubbery *fwook*s as he pops back and executes a full turn.

"I'd yell *surprise*, dude, but your junk is a serious vibe killer." With a twisted expression, he whips his face away. I laugh, not blaming him for repositioning his chair by the same degree. "*Now* are you glad I suggested we stop in the changing rooms at the sanctuary?" he levels at Kell.

"Should've known better than to argue," she replies good-naturedly. "But you're still not getting more than those fifty bucks. And do *not* ogle my sister."

To her, Jesse's all about the cocky chuff and the roguish grin. But beneath his breath, so low it's not even intended for my ears, he's a much different person. Someone I haven't seen since he crushed on Ramona Stacey our whole eighth grade year.

"Wasn't your sister I was looking at, starfighter."

There's no ground for me to stand on for even half a groan, considering the very bare necessities of the moment. But inwardly I dogear the observation. It *will* be revisited when I'm alone—and clothed—with the idiot.

Damn it, Jesse.

Out loud, my mouth already has sharper axes to throw. "Oh, fuck it all. Seriously?" Four of them, to be exact—which I struggle to wind around more profanities as soon as the bubble gives up another occupant.

Between the sluicing sides of the aquacraft's departure door, it's not my uncle who steps forward. There are similarities, like the messy mix of ginger and blond hair as well as the towering stature and graceful arrogance, but at the point where Po would check his ego, my father's grows on. *And on.*

"Hmmm." He strolls out onto the dock as if he owns everything he surveys plus the whole island beyond. "Not bad, brother. Not bad at all."

"An opinion I didn't ask for nor care about." My uncle stops to hurl the words when he's only halfway out of the bubble, his form rising up and down by gradual inches on the waters that support him.

He can have the swells. I'm claiming the waves. Massive ones that hit the shores of my psyche from right and left, alternating sets between disbelief and rage.

"And why isn't that one hitting like you wish it would?"

The retort barely clears my lips than Poseidon is clearing the last three feet of the water ramp with a lithe leap. But that's not the move feeding my highest irritation. That comes from his expression, continuing a stare at me that evokes a politician who's gotten away with fraud. Wise enough to take the allegation seriously without copping to the lock-me-up-now smirk.

"Maximus. I know what this looks like."

"A lie?" I cock my head. "That the word you're looking for? Though let me know if that one's already been used in this party game. I can get you a bigger list. *Deception. Fiction. Lip service. Whopper order.* I like them all, especially when it comes to gods who promise one thing, like the literal implementation of a concept called *Velo* but deliver on another entirely."

His nostrils flare. "You think I let him ride along because he offered good snacks? Listen to m—"

"You told us we'd be hidden here, from *all* of them! *Especially* from Hecate and him!"

My father *tsk*s past his expressionless mouth. "And I thought you only make odd oaths like that when you want to get in your sirens' gills."

I pierce him with a glare. "Not the time for a *Golden Girls* moment, Daddio."

"Not the time for a *Playgirl* one either, stud. So can you put that thing away so we can all access a much-needed hive mind here?"

Kara jolts. Not by much but enough that I swing up a hand to wordlessly request her restraint.

"This isn't over," I grumble while jabbing legs into the joggers that Jesse's fished out of his chair's side bag. "Damn it, Po. You waxed poetic about why you named this place. How Kara and I would be cloaked until *we* decided when to leave."

"You're right. I did." The apologetic overtone is more effort than expected, considering how the bastard has jettisoned every shred of his cordiality from ten hours ago. That means I'm really struggling to field the curve ball of his follow-up mutter. "But there are bigger decisions to face now."

"Huh?"

I hate how it's the only thing I can find to say. It feels marginally better when Po doesn't have anything to fling in return. He opts for standing there, more discomfited than before, just twirling his trident half a circle one way then back the next. And *now* I'm wishing it was all only monarchal posturing.

Bigger decisions.

Does he really mean bigger than the step we already took in LA?

And why is it so unnerving when Zeus steps forward again, looking better equipped to answer that?

Except that he doesn't.

For the first time since I met him, my father readily defers the floor in a group conversation. To, of all people, my diminutive but determined sister-in-law.

"Hecate isn't done with her fun yet," she declares with a disgruntled head shake. "Seriously. Can someone just offer the shrew a reality show deal and put *us* all out of *her* misery?"

"What is it now?" Kara's interjection emerges in angry spurts as she finishes tugging down the tank top that's still smudged from her wedding makeup session.

I frown at them for a second, unable to believe that was all only yesterday instead of last year. "What's happened? The guests. Everyone in that room—"

"All gone by the time Proteus and I returned," Po supplies. "And, according to the local news feeds, all safely returned to their homes and hotels. I left him behind to double-check the list and make sure."

"I suspect a multi-level spell," Z adds. "After Po fired

up the bubble and sped you out, I turned to see if there was anything *I* could do about the mess. But aside from a reverse wind to suck out the remaining moisture, I couldn't dare anything else. My lightning kills most humans on impact. If I'd tried breaking up the mud that way, with the crowd so close together…" He spreads his hands, indicating the obvious and awful reasoning. "Once I looked toward Hecate again, she had roused Rerek from the muck and hauled him into a huddle along with Hermes."

Kara's cheek trembles against my chest from her vehement shudder. "You mean the shitty shifter in cheap velvet?"

"Big sister for the color commentary win," Kell quips.

"But what about *other* analysts?" Kara stiffens all too quickly, shooting a matching look at my father and uncle. "It's been picked up by the SoCal news outlets. How are *they* explaining it? Did they interview anyone?"

Z meets her gaze without hesitation. Which shouldn't reassure me but does.

"Many," he says. "Who are all relaying the same story. That right after you two were proclaimed legal, a sudden squall hit the sanctuary."

Poseidon precedes his insertion with a brief trident bounce. "The stories all match, nearly to the second." With the second tap, he adds an acrid grimace. "Fucking weird, if you ask me. But it supports Z's theory like the grunion at full moon."

I support his scowl with one of my own. "An amplified spell, likely cast at the same time for maximum impact." I don't want them to see my double-take, but it digs in before

I can help it. "Did you say *Rerek* was in on it?"

"Didn't look voluntary," my father comments. He adds, too low and too fast, "Another reason for the code red speed bubble trip."

Much too low. Way too fast.

Since Kara and I are the only ones who heard the assertion, Po continues with the bigger subject at hand. "I still don't understand why the press is accepting every account without follow-up questions. They're all only interested in how none of the guests observed such an ominous rager approach. Valid concerns, of course, but that's all they're inquiring with their follow-throughs."

"Are the answers just as singular?" Kara inquires.

"More or less." Po doesn't relinquish his frown. "Different wordings but same message. They all say that they were entranced with the wedding itself. That your ceremony was so beautiful, they never noticed the weather freak on the horizon."

A rough tremor takes over the base of my throat. "Freak," I repeat in a sparse growl. "Well, they're not wrong. Except that you're all now looking at the freak."

Jesse's grunt isn't surprising. "Do I need to call Mrs. Ahern out here to order your daily mirror affirmations?" He cups his hand as if inviting Kell to a confidential klatch. "Ahern. Our school counselor. Every day she gave him *I am good enough*s and *I am worthy*s like a priest with the rosary prayers."

"He doesn't need any of them." Kara tucks herself back next to me, all but shimmering with the belief in her words. I'm sure she makes *me* glow with the tender press of her lips to the underside of my jaw. "You're the freak who made it possible for your uncle to mobilize and get us out of there. You saved our family."

I dip my sights down to her, shamelessly soaking up every morsel of that vocal glitter that I can. If I look like a smitten disco ball after it all, so be it. I've got to return to the goth grunge all too soon. It can't be ignored, considering the growing stack of implications to which Daddy Dearest keeps adding.

"But I think this is bigger than you, me, and Niki now." I swing my gaze back up at my father. "I'm right about that, aren't I?"

Poseidon rolls his eyes. "His father's own son."

"Okay, so tell me *how* right." I'm more adamant about that part, despite the latex smoothness that Z keeps pulled across his features. But I pick up enough tells from Jesse and Kell, even after one line of direct insistence, to know the freak himself isn't wrong here.

But I wish the two of them didn't pull out all the stops at once. Between Kell rubberbanding the hair tie she probably brought for Kara and biting the inside of her lips raw, and now Jesse *thwack*ing his trusty rubber hand against a pier piling, I come to an unnerving conclusion.

Poseidon didn't bring his brother beyond his private veil just to score some familial bonding time. And Zeus didn't accept the invitation only to embellish Po's recap of the Southern California news scene.

"Everything Po and I have said is correct," he asserts. "Your wedding guests have been released and are safe."

Before he's finished, I'm clutching Kara harder. And

don't deny the dozen pressure points in my chest, bearing down equally as brutally.

Every one of them points me back to the same revelation. The same word that stands out as if my father bolded and underlined one word of his statement. A word that changes the whole meaning of the damn thing.

"Our wedding *guests*," I reiterate. "But that's not the whole barrel ... is it? A wedding isn't only the guests ..."

Z's jaw clenches like fairies have buzzed both sides of his face. Evil ones. A new breeze wafts across the lagoon's waters, but he's not buying into the gentle wind, even when it lifts his hair away from his rugged features.

"No, son," he utters at last. "It's not."

My wife, already practically bursting with the stress my senses have handed her, lurches toward him by a handful of inches.

"Which means *what*? Zeus?"

He's the king of the gods, but not every king is without certain defeats. I really hate that in this moment, I know—*I know*—this is one of those shitty humblings for my father.

But not just for him.

"Hecate held on to two members of your wedding *party*."

Z stops, clearly not by his own choice. I don't think the deep emotional sheen in his eyes and the stark claws of pain across his cheeks are his idea of a good time. But he swallows hard and pushes on.

"She's kept Nancy and Veronica. Your mothers are her prisoners."

CHAPTER 21

Kara

*W*HY CAN'T I SAY *anything?*

It's not a question I ever fathomed having to answer, always being the one to draw Maximus out of his self-restraint instead of the other way around. But even as Zeus leads the way back up the pier, suggesting my husband follow him instead of trying to dent another piling with the punch-now-ask-later method, Maximus respects my right to pick my way back to words.

Or...not.

If I apply words to all of this, it's a step closer to being real. But that's not possible. Maximus and I have paid our dues already, five thousand times over, at the hideous reality game.

Even if not, this isn't fucking fair. Things like this happen to families who travel around Chicago in big black cars with drivers named Guido who speak in code about breaking someone's knees for the rent money.

And traveling around LA in big black cars is different? With servants who communicate in code you've never heard of, reporting your every move back to an underworld conglomerate that eats the knee breakers for breakfast?

I battle to leave that whole thought outside the door as we all walk inside and then down to the room with the aquarium-style wall. But my effort's as useless as extending a dinner invitation to the fish outside the glass. Every moment I've ever stressed about *that* side of my heritage— the darkness, the violence, the fires, the fear—is rolled up into a disgusting glob and then dumped in the middle of my belly. And it's absolutely refusing to budge.

The pain doesn't get much better when Maximus, bringing up the rear, stalks across the room and then circles a flustered glare around at the others—including my sister and his best friend.

"No way," he spits out. "No *damn* way is this right." He ticks the rage over again, pinning it onto Zeus. Now looking like he wants to hammer it *into* the All-father. "I don't bel—"

As soon as Zeus sweeps up his phone screen, showing an image of Mother and Nancy side-by-side in a cramped car trunk, he chokes to a stop.

"Regina sneaked the shot to me before they closed it up and left the church. It's fuzzy because she was across the parking lot." His expression compresses. "She's still whipping herself for not figuring out how to follow or go with them."

"Because she's that solid," I murmur. "Oh, *Reg.*"

If Maximus follows that part of the exchange, he doesn't show it. He still covers ground between here and the patio door like a caged animal. His agitation climbs so high, I sway by a few inches from its cerebral punch.

"Why would Hecate even...?" he blurts frantically. "*How* would she..."

"I'm sure the room has some working theories about your *why*," Kell offers with ease that creeps toward unnerving—until I behold how hard she's fighting to subdue her own temper. "But the *how* took place right in front of me, and I'm certain I'll be financing my therapist's next vacation home because of it."

The sardonic line only fits her words. During the moments she takes to drawl them, I watch in growing misery as my sister's posture shrinks in on itself and her gaze gains a darkness I've never seen before. She has to clear her throat before giving up her sober recount to Maximus.

"It wasn't long after you two left. We...were all...still in the mud." She stops and punches fresh clarity into her voice. "Nobody was moving or even thinking of doing so. It was like the plaster cast that they made Jaden endure when he was being considered for the space wars movie, except it smelled like wet dogs and a two-month-old oil spill."

She's already taking another break, and I reach for her hand in silent understanding. To Kell's olfactory system, an ordeal in a bog like that was like having to hit the beach with blown pupils.

She accepts my grasp with tight gratitude, a clammy palm, and her continuing account. "The head hag ordered boy toy *numero uno* to shift into something that looked like an orc crossed with the Rock when he still *was* the Rock. Once that was done, she told him to retrieve Veronica and Nancy out of the mud and take them to his car."

I sway in place, wondering if my kouzilina feast is about to claim a dreadful revenge, though am rescued by the weird fact that her concept of an orc is likely worlds different than mine. Once a girl's read *Beowulf* and overnighted in the ninth circle, the reference is as traumatic as a wet dog bog stench. But it's only a mild comfort. Not when every other part of her story plays through my mind's eye with horrifying clarity.

"Did they…fight him at all?" I push past the flash mutism to get it out with low intensity. "Mother…and Nancy," I somehow feel the need to clarify. "Did they struggle? Were they afraid? Did he…hurt them?"

Her wincing glance is worsened by Maximus's pained grunt. I send remorseful stares to them both, and their return expressions are consoling. Someone had to ask it all. I think they're glad it was me.

"Neither of them made a sound," Kell relays. "But beyond that, I can't say. I couldn't exactly turn my head."

"I know." I squeeze her hand harder and reach my far arm over until I'm also clasping her inner elbow. "The wet dog plaster cast. I'm sorry, honey."

During our exchange, Maximus has begun pacing the better part of the living room's floor. His steps have ramped to such ferocity that the lagoon fish have given up on hanging out in this area. But when he pauses and peers over again, I'm surprised to stare into eyes that rival the clear blues of the dawn outside.

"So, there's a chance Hecate's kept them locked like that. In the mannequin-in-mud state. Easier handling?"

Those Aegean blues pay me back with some silent penance of his own. I nod, already forgiving. Someone had to say all of that as well—probably the reason behind our collective and visible relief as soon as Zeus rebuts his son.

"Not necessarily," he offers. "If she had Hermes take them to Iremia—"

"Logical assumption," Kell inserts. "And yes, you can all dagger me for using the dreaded *a* word."

"Why?" Jesse rolls forward though uses only his pinkies to do it. If the crisis at hand wasn't so at *hand*, I'd be asking him all about it, but only on the off chance Maximus didn't first. I already caught his open curiosity about how his buddy glided out of the transport bubble as easily as an action star on stunt wires. "I'm thinking the witchy ashram too. It's not like she can check into the Pendry with Veronica Valari in tow, in *any* form."

"Not with Nancy either," I comment. "She made the pre-wedding press stops right along with Mother and me."

Mother.

The syllables set in, a repetitive knell through my head, striking against one temple then the next. I let go of Kell and push fingertips at the sides of my eyes, begging my brain to stop. Why does it hurt so much when it sounds like something that should blend with an angelic choir?

And why did I even bother with the question?

Mother.

It sounds like seraph's songs because it no longer stands for the underworld's diva demon. Because I now see more than that in Veronica Valari. So much more. It's all so different. I think back on so many moments of my life with such new light...and perfect understanding. A changed viewpoint.

Because *I've* changed.

This time, I'm really enlightened.

Best of all, Hecate's hand is nowhere near the miracle.

This is all my sweet Niki. Already altering me in such amazing ways. In *every* way.

Thank you, little love. Thank you.

I stress the point to her with a soft stroke across my stomach as Poseidon and Zeus take up joint stances on the raised step along the quarry stone wall holding up the room's far end. Neither of them actually needed the assistance with the towering and rugged auras, but the wall is clearly up for the task anyway.

"No matter what she's decided about the where and how, the bitch undoubtedly thought this whole plan through. Carefully."

Though Z's urbane undertones guide the words, it's weirdly comforting to watch some tension sneak over his mien. Maximus's aggravation alone has made it hard for me to take his father's savoir faire with a constant grain of salt, but right now I'm out of all the grains—and glad the All-father seems to be too.

"Hmmm." Poseidon's interjection clarifies that I'm not the one who's noticed. "So *now* she's no longer the honored warrior of the Titanomachy?"

"Let it rest," Maximus snarls. "You've heard of better

late than never, right?"

Zeus has the grace to give his son a rushed but grateful head jog before moving back in on the more important subject. "We've got to assume the imprisonment is as airtight as Tartarus."

"He's right." Kell's mutter, hardly hearable for the rest of them, comes with her new grip to the back of my elbow. "The sorceress supreme is about the details. When Jaden and I were at Iremia, one of the cats needed their claws trimmed by half a millimeter. Morgana was apologizing like the creature had been a coyote snack instead."

Maximus's nostrils flare. His inhalation is heavy but resolved. "Okay. So we'll go in with a careful plan. Arden Prieto already knows how to get past her security perimeters, and I already know the whole compound pretty w—"

"No."

He huffs but hardly lets his father slow him. "A not-so-careful plan, then. Blaze of glory, element of surprise. Between you, me, and Prieto, we'll bring significant cheese to the enchilada. Jaden will probably want in too. That's a good idea. His skills are better than long-distance radar."

"*No.*"

My sharp shout finally speaks to his brakes. He visibly slams them, though with some forced reluctance. Jesse, Zeus, and Poseidon wheel around with him, blunt frowns on their faces.

The only one in the room not looking like I've just blasted all the glass in the place is my sister, who backs up my severe scowl with a don't-even-touch-this sniff. But unlike her, my reaction is homed in on my husband.

I don't care that he's actually sweeping long stares at all the shatterable surfaces. That he sweeps his stare back up to me as if his eyes have deceived him or that maybe he's a few seconds too early. Like I'm only getting ready to smash all the panes but haven't done so.

Like I'll stop if he keeps scrutinizing me with such hardcore energy.

He must know better. And is maybe hoping that he doesn't.

Like he *has* to know better than to turn himself, his father, his uncle, and my brother into SEAL Team Crazy.

"Maximus." I step forward, extending a hand to him, fortified when he wraps his fingers around mine too. "I hate this—I hate *her*—as much as you do. But you're a student of stories, good and bad, as much as I am. You have to already see how she's trying to write this one. The plotline she's boxed us into."

"No." He's entitled to get his turn at the word, except his gritted emphasis takes me aback. Not far enough to untangle his hold, though perhaps I should've gone with that. He's not relinquishing a note of his adamant seethe. "*No*, Kara. *We're* not boxed anywhere. And I'm sorry if you don't agree or approve of this call, since a few of your Iremia friends will probably be collateral damage when this all goes down, but—"

"Stop." It shoots out from between my teeth, which are now as tense and gnashed as his. "*Stop it*. Do you think I—" A jerk backward because the sparks of our touch have never been this hot for reasons other than needy attraction before. After a solid shake of my head, I insist, "I do care about my friends, but not a fraction of a fraction about what will happen to *you!*"

He looks down. Attempts to grab my hand once more. I recoil again, a dozen times harsher than before. During the flight, I ball up my fingers, twisting them nearly behind me.

Though Maximus tries to subdue his answering flinch, there's enough there for me to notice—and rejoice about.

Which is *not* the thing I envisioned getting happiest over just twelve hours after we secured rings on each other's fingers.

Now I *really* hate this. Every agonizing second.

Even the next one, when there's a love-filled rush from deep in my belly—from the being who doesn't want to stay there. But I clamp down my control and keep Nikoleta away, simultaneously urging her to sleep while keeping myself as alert as possible. She has her entire life to deal with fear and conflict. I'm not about to let her start early.

Thankfully, Maximus raises his gaze back up with perfect timing. Though the strife in his cobalts continues, there's strength there too. But not enough to loosen my fists or pull me back to his side. I love him so much. I need him right here. But how can the few feet between us feel like such an uncrossable canyon at the same time?

Harsh air rushes in and out of him. Before he's done, I already know he's thinking the same thing.

But he still tries the leap.

"Kara—"

"Don't."

And I shoot him down in midair. Without a splinter of guilt.

"Just…please don't," I say anyway and reset my shoulders. "Not until you listen, okay?" One of my hands, still clenched, moves across my stomach. "Until you're really *open* about it."

Every furrow that can cut across his forehead does. I don't surrender a flinch of reaction. If all he sees here is his wife weaponizing our previous soul share and not a woman fighting for the literal survival of her family, so be it. I'll be the willing bad guy here.

"Kara." His voice is a ragged growl. "She took our *mothers*."

"Which makes me madder and sadder than you probably think it does."

Desperately, I hope he doesn't think I premeditated the falter in my rasp. It's reassuring when I reach for him again, only to meet his own extended grasp when I'm halfway there.

No. Not reassuring.

It's regeneration.

Cells of my soul built up again when they've been hanging on by threads. My heart refilled, the instant before it felt as drained as a Coachella stage battery on the last encore of the night.

"I didn't mean to imply that you weren't," he murmurs. "But this isn't a high-level stealth mission that we can script out and rehearse for months. Hecate's done being patient."

"And I know that."

"Then you know we've got to figure out a plan for how to respond to this, and fast."

"I know that too. And I agree."

Though—damn it—I prove the point by yanking away my hand again. I can't help myself. Necessity has me desperately splaying my fingers against my abdomen. Subduing the life inside it, who already seems to be begging to help in our mission.

Soon, I silently ensure her. *You've got to get a little bigger and stronger first, my sweet Nikoleta.*

"Hey." Maximus closes the distance between us. Presses his hand over mine. "Beautiful? You okay?"

"Yep. Fine." I rush into a nod, hoping it relaxes his grip. "We both are. She just adores her daddy already."

I long to give him a fast kiss for emphasis, but Zeus has given up the nearby hovering. He's back now, and he's close.

"Then let's make sure she has a pair of wonderful *yia yias* to adore, as well."

Poseidon, hitching a hip against a couch, snorts briefly. "*Yia yias?* Well, everyone mark the moment. My brother's getting sentimental about the grandparenting game. One of the few that the whole room probably agrees with you."

Maximus exposes a mild bristle. "As long as he treats it as more than a *game*, we're cool."

"Not now." Despite the fervency of the declaration, Zeus slips back into a cosmopolitan stance. "Games are a luxury of time. And time is a luxury we do *not* have right now."

Poseidon pushes all the way to his feet. "I live for the

times when you're wrong, but this one has my extra vote."

"This one ... what?" Maximus issues the same demand that's burning foremost for me.

Z regards us with half a glance before sliding out his noncommittal murmur. "A plan," he says. "Maybe."

Kell sidles up, her nose twitching with meaning. "Pine, sulfur, and rubbing alcohol. Ohhh, this is all more than *maybe*."

"I said what I said," Zeus snaps. "And I meant it."

Kell ignores him, already swinging a knowing look toward the old gods. "Holy shit. You guys were really considering it, weren't you? A full-on run at Iremia?"

"What?"

Same word, opposing meanings. My snap is edged with new fear. Maximus's is pure anger.

"*Were* considering?" he bites at his father and uncle. "But you've cooked up a better plan now? Let's have it, then."

Z and Poseidon trade a look. It's harsher than I want to see and darker than I want to feel.

"They don't have one," I go ahead and state. "But they agree with me now. Charging in on Hecate on her home turf isn't going to gain you anything. Or anyone."

Maximus moves back again. Thrusts a heavy hand across his head. As he relents his grip and his hair tumbles against his spine, his shoulders sag too. "Doing nothing isn't an option."

"But neither is doing the wrong thing." Zeus, much braver than I've credited to him, steps over and braces his son's shoulder. He doesn't back down even when Maximus attempts a violent shrug. "You do understand that, Maximus. I know it down to my marrow. Your mother wouldn't have raised you any other—"

With a wide, windmilling arm, Maximus fights himself free. "You don't know a damn thing about me, old man. Or anything—*anything*—about how I was raised!"

On the surface, the god king is still as imperturbable as Yoda and Mrs. Robinson's love child. But I already know differently, even before the dark-blue flames in the depths of the All-father's eyes. And the way he slowly narrows that gaze. And the seething pumps of air, in and out of his nose, so eerily like the way his son processes raw fury.

Wrath that drenches his every utterance now.

"I love your mother too, Maximus. I'd walk into Iremia through the front gate and let Hecate laser me through the heart if it meant Nancy Kane could walk over my body and out into freedom. But that's not how the bitch is going to let us do this."

There's a low *thwick* from my far left, drawing my attention to where Jesse is trying to snag grapes from one of our leftover kouzilina orders. He pauses to join his serious stare along with Z's.

"Dude…he's right. Not what you want to hear, I know, but I've never dealt you dirty with the honesty, and I'm definitely not starting now."

In any situation other than this, I'd be actually hugging the guy instead of hoping my small nod does the trick. But Jesse's answering smirk conveys enough of his answer to ease my mind. I just wish we could work together to do the same for my husband.

I combat the nervousness with my favorite new way to fidget, by impatiently rubbing my middle. The space beneath my fingers warms, and I imagine our little girl smiling from the caresses.

For some reason, the moment seems exactly what Zeus has waited for. He straightens and ratchets back his shoulders before pivoting and confronting Maximus again.

"With Prieto's help or not, the only way we'd get past Iremia's border is with your wife—and child—in tow."

Maximus slashes his arm so hard, it's almost a fresh windmill act. "Absolutely not."

"And if, by some magical miracle, that we *do* succeed, she'll have you pinned and paralyzed faster than a gnat in flypaper." The god pauses only fast enough to get stricter. His eyes no longer glow. They're as black and stony as cinders. "At which time, she'll use whatever means necessary to slice into your mind and access where you've hidden Kara from her. The bullshit you went through with Hades's boys is going to seem like an hour at the Charlie Cheese Pizza Port."

"No," I cry out. "Maximus!"

"*Kara*." His tone is a petition, but his stance is a mandate, his rigidly stretched hand sending me into silence. "We'll figure this out," he murmurs, now leading with the voice I usually hear during quiet mornings in bed. "I promise."

I breathe in deeply, longing to believe him. *Having* to. He has as much here to lose as me. *Everything*. Together, we knew all these risks and took them. Now together, we'll fix things.

We'll get them back. No matter what it takes.

"All right. Jesse and Kell can take charge of it, then." Maximus wheels his gaze around to them both. "You both know I trust you."

"And guess who else does?" Poseidon drawls before I can dig my tongue out of my throat.

During the same pause, I watch a hard swallow take over my sister's throat. Jesse's reaction is similar, his plastic stress rope winding crazily around his hand.

Aloud, he quips, "I'd really just prefer a trip to Charlie Cheese."

"Better than square one," Maximus growls, dragging back his hair with renewed frustration. "Which seems to be where we're headed. *Again.*"

Beneath his breath, he adds more words that I'm glad I can't make out. Probably for the best. This isn't the time or place to spout statistics about everything a *human* infant can hear in utero, let alone a special girl with demigod DNA.

Bigger priorities have to be stacked first. Along with them, arduous comprehensions. Glaring logistics that I can't ignore so easily. That none of us can. Not if we want to see our mothers alive again.

Not if we also want one more shot, however sparse, at keeping peace between the realms.

I'm ready to meet Maximus's stare when he finally turns back. It's not easy, but I do it. He deserves to see, and to know, how much I love him, despite what I'm about to propose. But we don't have a billion options here, and the strategy that rises first to my mind is going to be our best shot.

And his worst nightmare.

It has to be done. It's the most solid way. But even after a dozen more similarly worded pep talks, I can't open my mouth to dredge it into words.

I'm about to start pacing, praying that quick steps will shake loose the stubborn words, but Kell makes me the world's most grateful sister by pacing forward with an adamant nod my way. She's ready to jumpstart this engine on my behalf, ensuring I'm already jotting a few things on the brain as possible thank-you gifts. Twenty pairs of Ferragamos. Ten nights at her favorite Bali resort. The new Panamera she was eyeing at the shiny showroom in the mall.

"We have to burn her out. Yank the hag into the light," she pronounces. "A light *we're* controlling."

Maximus releases a suspicious growl in tandem with his father and uncle. "I already don't like the sound of this."

"Well, I don't like the sound of delivery dudes who pump their bass at five a.m.," Jesse inserts. "But it gets me up for predawn workouts."

"We're not talking bicep curls, damn it."

"He knows that." The defense bursts out sharper than I planned, but I don't back down from a single note. It's as much a stand for *myself*, since my senses are already blazing with the direction of my sister's intention. Now I've got to brace for Maximus's reaction to it—in every way I can.

Zeus hikes his head toward Kell. His gaze is as clear and searing as the August sky it invokes, looking like he's already peeked at my sister's flight plan, as well.

Still, he murmurs, "All right. What's your play?"

Before responding, my sister swoops one more look my way. I send an approving nod.

"Hecate's only going to budge for one reason." She secures her gaze on Maximus with more strength than ten men. Damn, how I love her. "For one *person*."

I've seen my husband in the throes of rage before. When he confronted Hades in the castle at Dis. The moment we learned that Nikoleta might've been exposed by a paparazzi's stray flashbulb. Even a few times during the wedding planning, when rude or close-minded people got on his last nerve.

All just silly flickers compared to this.

How he spins on everyone like a cornered warrior with a sharpened broadsword. How he glares as if there's already blood coating the blade but it isn't enough. How he's ready to take down the rest of whatever we're calling a kingdom here.

Which is why I pull in a deep breath and push out the next words in the room.

"She's right. Maximus—"

"No." It's a feral, awful sound from the center of his chest. "*No*, goddammit!"

"*Maximus*."

He turns again, crouching low to face off at me. "I won't allow it. You're not going to do this, Kara."

"You're super right." As I level it, I refuse to let *him* up. The steel in my bloodstream can triple-fill every cargo container on the docks at San Pedro, though he refuses to acknowledge it even as I guide his hand across the middle of my body. "*I'm* not going to do it. *We* are. Together."

Nikoleta breaks into a soft but joyful pummel at my abdomen wall as if we're kicking off down a metaphysical yellow brick road. Though I'm sure she's responding to our little family embrace and not my motivational speech, it's impossible to ignore her enthusiasm.

Maximus does just that.

Well…tries to.

With stiffened muscles and a sharp grunt, he keeps it up, insisting on clinging to his control like Oz's silly wizard hiding behind his green curtain.

Refusing to see that his stubbornness is dragging us back more than helping us get home. That we're not getting anywhere—when there's so far left to go.

"What…are you talking about?" he demands from between his teeth. "I can't…I *won't* let either of you be at risk. Not for this. Not to lure *her*."

"Not even for the sake of the realm?"

I double down on the point, flattening his hand tighter on my belly. I'm as unrelenting with my other one too, desperately tangling my fingers in his hair.

Because I'll do anything for my cause too.

Anything for the world that's given us this love.

"Maximus," I whisper, my lips less than a gasp from his. "The stars didn't give us to each other only to let us crash and burn."

He's still rigid in my hold. Unyielding to my touch.

"I also don't think the stars enjoy unprepared pilots on the manifest, wife. And purposely making yourself the target of a witch on a cosmic vendetta—"

There's a blast in my senses that I can't identify, let alone control. It's as ineffable as the presence that moved through me back in Palos Verdes. A power as old as the stars but as new as our baby. Wisdom that's circled right back around to its core: pure innocence. And energy. And life. And light.

So much light.

Flowing up through me. Deafening in my ears. Thundering in my veins. Reminding me of the surge that took over when I first levitated, only multiplied tenfold. Twenty. Thirty.

Until its intensity isn't just burning inside me.

It changes the air *outside* of me.

Erupting. Enflaming. Rolling into the form of a blazing fireball that pings around the room, like a superpowered cat toy pounding parts of walls and half the hanging pottery in the kitchen, before zooming out across the lagoon.

And then into it.

After a couple of seconds, the ball finally strikes down. There's a noticeable, if muted, *boom*—followed by a waterspout that erupts with more passionate fervor than the finale of the fountains at the damn Bellagio.

"Ah…well, then," Zeus utters, losing his urbanity with a shake on the last syllable. But his brother doesn't bother with any suavity.

"*Shiiit.*"

"Look, Jack. I'm flying," Jesse jests in a soft choke.

Kell's reaction takes a couple of seconds longer but is well worth the wait. "And I smell a sassy little girl who's already giving her mommy some fun times."

Maximus adds a commiserating grunt. Or so that's my interpretation. I resist firing back a disclaimer, because they'd both see through my lie. I truly have no idea if my light show was a mysterious helping hand from Niki or not, but since we've got many more months to go before the possibility of a confirmation, I'm going to save us precious minutes now.

It's easier to keep the commitment than I first expect—from the second my husband swivels his gaze back to me.

And at once scours the breath from my lung with his twin blues.

Should I be terrified? Turned on? Or maybe unnervingly dealing with both, as they take me in with more dark intensity as ever before—without any apparent inkling to stop.

He dares to plumb even deeper, all the way down into me, past all my usual boundaries. As if he's seeking something specific. As if he's confident he's going to find it.

I don't hesitate about letting him do exactly that.

Letting him discover.

Letting him *see*.

The brilliance of the life that's growing inside me. The warrioress who's already so bold and brave—and willing to bypass her mama to prove it.

Maximus sees it too. Not for long—a second or two at best—but as soon as his grin becomes a wide smile, I'm sure of it. As certain as I am of the words, plentiful and stern, I'll have for this kid later.

Good freaking heavens.

What kind of discipline is in order when one's rowdy little rebel is still kicking at the umbilical cord? Worries for another moment. For now, I lean half an inch closer to celebrate how much joy I share with this incredible man of mine. I absorb the warm safety of his form. The dazzling sparks in his stare—and soon, between our laced fingers, as well.

The sun is cresting over the gorge's far ridge, and the lagoon has a far way to go to calm again, but that's what makes the view twice as captivating. The waves are like dancers, dashing liquid streamers of aqua, amber, and white through the whole canyon and its lone building.

I snuggle closer to him. There's a pleasureful rumble from the center of his chest, made better by the soft kiss he presses into my hair. More energy flows between our senses, as perfect and pulsing as starlight.

Almost.

The stars take millennia to modify. We have minutes if not milliseconds here. Moments barely longer than a blink to remember that we're their celestial equals, and not only because Hecate and the diamonds forced them to make room. We've fought hard for this place. Defied demons for it. Survived hell for it. Faced even the ugliest sides of humanity, like bullying frat boys and snide tabloid writers, for it.

And now, we'll do it again. With every force of our strengths and belief in our souls.

But this time, we won't be alone.

Though the defiance brimming from Jesse and Kell already says as much, my conclusion is based in a more profound truth. The irrefutable connection that now ties me to more than just this man.

The life—and love—inside me, as well.

The extraordinary being that already fills me with her brilliance and boldness—and inspires the words I give to her beautiful daddy with my most loving look.

"So … what was all that, about being unprepared?"

CHAPTER 22

MAXIMUS

LESS THAN TWENTY HOURS after my wife and sister-in-law broadsided me with their action plan in Velo's living room, I'm still attempting to get back into practice on this quirky little hobby of mine—called *thinking*.

But there's the biggest joke of the day.

The trophy for most insane guy on the planet goes to . . .

I chuff for a second, envisioning my ugly grill etched on a plastic award like the ones Mom always saved from my elementary school years. I'll never forget that first one, with its funny little tragedy and comedy masks. Guess I was a damn good spear carrier in the play that year.

None of this makes any more sense.

A truth made that much clearer by remembering how fast I agreed to this insane game plan.

No. Not that.

"Because game plans are for football movies and date nights, asshole," I growl to my reflection in a mirror that's too brightly lit while jerking back my too-tangled hair.

The queue is hardly worthy of the occasion I'm prepping it for, but I also hardly care. I close my eyes and inwardly whip myself with the insult again.

I'm busy wondering if adding a growl will tighten or loosen the knot in my gut, when Jesse's sarcasm breaks the silence instead.

"Well, you look snappy. But *not* happy."

He's begging for a return zinger, however bad it'd be. But *snappy* isn't happening right now. My brain stays as chaotic as my hair. I'm only pulled together from my neck down, courtesy of the white designer ensemble into which I've buttoned myself all the way.

Buttoned up being subjective. For that matter, *designer*.

I keep wondering if said couturier was just having a bad day, needed something for the presentation meeting, and grabbed a drawing off their three-year-old's coloring table. I'm dressed in a layered look that's supposed to be all the rage right now. It's certainly all of…something. Deciding exactly *what*… There's another dilemma altogether.

"I don't recall *happy* being on the punch list for the plot here, so I guess we're still good on the script?"

As comebacks go, it's not my best. But proving friendship really is magic, my buddy rewards the line with a bigger chuckle than it's worth. "We're always good, Kane. Even if you did forget the Funyuns again."

Another great tee-up, but I only borrow one word of it to reply.

"But *you* didn't forget to safely stow the thumb drive I gave you, right?"

I turn and lean against the mirror, bolting a look on him across the spacious bedroom of the resort villa that we've decamped Velo for. Through the window behind him, the sunset tosses an AI-perfect orange glow over Spinalonga and Upper Mirabello Bay. But the scenery has nothing to do with how dapper *he's* looking too. Plainly said, Greece agrees with my friend. If it's possible, Jesse's cover boy kisser is even more striking here.

"It's stowed and safe, Professor Kane," he reassures. "Cross my heart, hope to—"

"Oh no, you don't," I snarl.

"Dude, figure of speech," he retorts. "One we've always treated like a good luck charm, if Po's speed bubble didn't suck out *all* my memory."

"It didn't." I push away from the wall, clamping my arms across my chest. "But tonight we've got to take things a hell of a lot more seriously."

He shows me both his palms like I've ordered him to hand over his wallet. "I know, man. Say no more. The verbal rabbit's foot is officially stashed, along with the horseshoe, the dreamcatcher, and the seven ladybugs."

"Thanks." I don't hide my furrowed brow. "I…think."

He dips an affable nod while resettling his elbows to his wheelchair arms. It's an effort to wait now, anxious needles goading my brain, but I let him have one more moment before shoring my stance.

"So, as long as we've added a little weight to the prologue here…"

"Oh, man." He rocks his head back. "I *really* should've

known you weren't going to let me get on with the ballad for the Funyuns loss."

"*North.* Come on. Focus up." Accepting the stiffer set of his shoulders as the best I'm going to get, I lower onto an ottoman with my hands on my knees. "You remember everything we discussed at lunch, right? You're clear about what do ... if all this shit goes south tonight?"

"Maybe just a haiku?" he persists. "*Little rings, so pure. Flamin' hot, the taste I fave ...*"

I slump my head between my own shoulders. "I worry about your brain sometimes."

"Better that than the plan we've reviewed twelve times, and *that* you need to park at the back end of *your* cranium, Professor." He's glaringly sober about it now, and I don't want to be so overly relieved. "One, because you personally hovered while I put that memory stick into my room safe—"

"Because my advanced directive, updated will, and final letters to everyone are on it?"

"And two, because the entrance to Olympus itself is on this same island and is being scarily reinforced by your dad—the *king* of that whole damn kingdom, just in case you need a refresher."

He pulls out one of his sticky rubber ropes, appearing to aim the small hand at the end toward the middle of my face, but he turns at the last minute and snares one of the sample ouzo bottles from the room's hospitality basket.

"In short, your hand wringing is null and void right now," he adds. "Do something more useful, like chugging this."

My glance is broody as I wave off the aperitif. "Go ahead," I encourage, jogging my chin. "Said the hand-wringer hurtbag to his matching nimrod of a best friend."

"*Unhhh?*" Jesse protests before downing the clear-colored shot. "Nim *what?*"

"You're right. Forget *nimrod*. Let's go for *shyster*, instead. Because nobody's buying that you're twitching harder about Funyuns than the possibility of Hecate's crosshairs tangling around the woman you love."

Within seconds, he's shoved all his sarcasm off a very high cliff. "Leave Kell out of—" And then his indignation too. "*Shit.*"

I'm almost whipping back with a double take. I lobbed *my* comment only as an informational fishing trip, not expecting him to smack back so fast and so clearly.

Now, in the pause I greedily grab to form a new reaction to the revelation, fate rubs in the discomfort tenfold. A new sound breaks into the air. The central vent system broadcasts some musical magic from the bedroom directly over our heads. The combined giggles of the Valari sisters.

Jesse drops his head—but not fast enough to hide his heavy gulp from my sparked attention.

I drop my own head, succumbing to its heavy shake.

"Jesse." I don't sugarcoat a note of it. "Damn it."

"*Don't,*" he spits back. "Okay? I know what you're going to—"

"Do you? I beg, not so deferentially, to differ, Professor North. Because I actually *did* say it, straight to your face, at least six weeks ago. Do you remember, dumbass? The part where I said she's promised to someone else?"

"And you knew, more than *eight* weeks ago, that Kara was promised to the same incubus asshole," he bites back.

I fume for half a second. "Prieto's done some growing."

"That's supposed to make everything okay?"

I snap away from him, already ripping a hand through my hair. It doesn't help the thousand knots in it, but the choice is already made for me. Half an hour with the detangler, or tell my best friend what I know now. What I've seen. The tentative but meaningful steps that Arden and Kell have been taking toward each other. *With* each other. No actual connections yet—not the kind I'd call essential for a lifetime together—but better than the animosity of a few short weeks ago.

But better than what I've observed between her and Jesse? Their humor and ease and mutual respect?

"Fuck," I rasp, really meaning it. "Maybe I shouldn't have designated the signed Tom Clancy collection to you, after all."

I hate how good it feels when his answering snort layers over some of the new laughs from the girls. "Who's your Jack Ryan, bee-otch?"

"You, baby," I return, though a rote smile breaks through.

"And you're mine, man," he replies, reverting me back to discomfort that has nothing to do with my Jared Leto-meets-Obi Wan getup. "You've always been my solid. In many ways, my eyes and ears and brains."

I shake my head. "You have all three, and they work just fine."

"Not like yours," he asserts. "Especially not during the times when I didn't give a shit about them. When I wanted to kiss them all goodbye along with the rest of this ridiculous shell."

As he gestures up and down his form with a furious hand, I release an audible seethe. "Not acceptable, man. Not *ever*."

His hand smacks into his lap. "I know that now. And I believe it too because of the Jack Ryan in my life." With his other hand, he stabs a finger my way. "Who taught me that no matter what shit looks like, there's a way to victory. There's a *chance*."

Another minute in which I hate the guy again, though legitimately this time—especially as Kell seems to finish off his pep vent with another giddy shout from above.

"Yesss!"

Nooo.

But this isn't the moment to be telling the guy that Jack Ryan isn't always right. That even the world's most formidable Eagle Scout has to recognize the elephant—or the underworld power brokers—that'll quash his rally cry into the world's crappiest breakup ballad.

One day I'll have to be the guy holding out that violin, but it's not this day. Not in this moment that already feels too unreal, and not in any of the good ways—except for whatever has my wife and her sister continuing to yell at each other like they're getting pumped up for a rock concert, not a face-to-face showdown with the most powerful witch goddess in the known realms.

"One more of those cute whoop-dee-doos, and I say we order them down here at once," Jesse declares.

I answer with a definite nod, almost wanting to take him up on it now, but there's another subject here that gives me pause.

"In the thirty seconds we have before that, I want to ask you something."

A frown from my buddy. But he counters with a smooth drawl, "Of *course* I'll be happy to look after the signed Stephen Kings too."

"Asshat." I narrow my gaze. "You peeked."

His hands are already up again. "That would be unethical and illegal. But thanks for the confirmation." And then flashes his most engaging grin. "But I *won't* be making room on the bookshelf quite yet. You're going to get through this, man. We all will."

I nod again, though his smirk dips. The guy sees through me nearly as clearly as Kara. He senses the perfunctory economy of my move, and I don't dishonor him with another polite preamble to my curiosity.

"Speaking of peeking habits..."

He breaks in there, his expression already vacillating again. And holy shit, is he blushing? And is this a new thrum in my chest, already dreading the conclusion my instinct has jumped to—because of a place *he's* gone to?

"Okay, so you did see what happened on the pier. But I swear, man, Kell initiated things. And it was only the one k—"

"Uh, yeah." I practically bark it out, ordering him to

silence with the force of my new stomp across the room.
"But *no*. The only thing I saw on the pier was whatever
happened with your chair."

It's agony to turn back around, already seeing that I've
handed him at least the violin bow for his heartbreak ballad.
Or maybe that's the part he's already had in hand for nearly
twenty years, thanks to me.

Shit, Jesse.

Shit, shit, shit.

"What…was…the deal?" I persist, albeit with a couple
of awkward start-stops. "You were floating more than rolling
out there."

"Floating." He considers the word like it's about to be
another haiku, the edges of his face crinkling with a blend
of mirth and contemplation. "Okay. That's a good way of
putting it."

"But it never surprised you? Or freaked you out?"

"Of course it did." He resettles in the seat, rolling his
shoulders with that same mix of watchful humor and cocky
strength. "But times like that are when you go for the inner
Jack Ryan, right? And after Poseidon ex…plained…"

It makes no sense to ask where his finale, and his voice,
have run off to. I already take a well-educated guess once
Kara and Kell hit the midpoint landing in the staircase. I
follow the lively little thumps, already thinking the last hour
has been long enough to be away from the other half of my
soul.

But apparently not the remaining parts of my voice.

My volume…as depleted as Jesse's.

My air...as nonexistent as every thought in my head.

My strength...willingly surrendered to the glorious female before me.

I didn't think she'd entrance me more than the moment she appeared at the end of that aisle in the cliffside church, with that gown of mermaid crystals, that veil of diamond stars, and the promise of my every tomorrow in her huge and magnificent eyes. But now...

This feels like more than tomorrow.

Because it's just today.

Just right now.

This complete moment, flowing into the next, which feels even better than the one before it. We grasp them all with everything we have, which turns them into bigger, brighter treasures.

Like the gift of her reaching out for me, an impish smile kicking at one side of her lips, more stunning than the ornate Valari earrings on her lobes. How those things have survived through the last day and a half is beyond my comprehension. Like her, their shine seems more enhanced now, even without the matching gemstone headband and the crystal-studded flowers. Perhaps *because* of that.

Nothing is getting in the way of her beauty anymore.

My clutching vocal cords are still attesting to that.

"Well, good evening, Professor Kane."

With a gritted gulp, I beat my throat into enough submission to croak something back. It might even make some sense.

"It *is*...a good evening, Mrs. Kane."

Her eyes slide shut for a moment. The thick fans of her lashes send my gaze down the fitted V of her long-fitted dress. There's no jewelry gracing her neck and torso, but the bold white lace pattern doesn't need it. Ironically, this gown is cut lower but shows less cleavage than the high-necked organza of her LA look. It's demure but damnably sexy.

Who am I kidding?

Sexy?

As soon as she takes in my greeting with those closed eyes and parted lips, it's nothing short of erotic.

"Oh, God," she rasps, nearly for my ears alone. "I want to hear you say that, again and again and again."

I switch the angle of our handclasp until I'm pulling her arms around me. Until I'm bending in and she's tilting back and there's only inches left before I'm through with merely ogling her and I'm sealing the deal on conquering her.

Again and again and again…

Mrs. Maximus Kane…

Her lips taste like a little Retsina and a lot of desire. Her skin, completely exposed by the gown's back, is like a swatch of dark cream and sun-warmed satin.

And her pulse, throbbing against the place where I brace the curve of her neck, feels like home.

Until a pair of amused coughs break in, reminding us that tonight isn't for pizza, Netflix, and chill.

Damn it. Far from it.

"Well, kids. I'd usually grab some popcorn and tell you go for it all about now, but there are twenty waiters outside just waiting to make sure my *dakos* and tzatziki quotas are filled for this trip."

Kell's gibe is a perfect representation for her look: a burgundy-red pantsuit with attitude to spare. But dragging my lips away from her sister and reacquainting myself with the sight is a rougher journey than expected. I was so busy dropping my jaw at Kara's romantic elegance that I missed the tight waist nip of Kell's jacket—and the cleavage gap that ends in about the same place.

No wonder my poor buddy is still sweeping the floor with his own scruff, which heightens my gratitude for his mature move the next moment.

"What I think she's trying to say is that the show must go on, you guys. At least if we want to flush the right guest out of the target audience."

"Thanks, man," I say. "Though with these two leading the way with *these* fashion statements, I'm sure our show is about to hit much bigger than this circus tent."

"That'd be the general goal," Kell says, curling a hand to Jesse's shoulder and rubbing as she leans in. "Why do you think we were tittering like naughty peahens?"

Against the don't-do-it screams of my self-control, Jesse and I do a tandem eyebrow dance. He ends it all too fast to swing a worshiping look up at his brunette companion.

"You two *don't* look like peahens."

Just when I think Kell's going to take her answering swoon even further, she yanks back and braces into a runway-ready pose. "Then that must mean it's time to channel the inner egrets." With another half-inch of confidence from that defined Valari jaw, she directs her attention back our way. "You two ready to do this?"

As Kara nods, she reaches for my hand. She takes a long breath, her air as shivery as her fingers, but her smile is steady. She sets her head higher, readying for the camera flash explosion that assaults us as soon as Kell pulls on the door that opens onto the pool deck.

Sure enough, there are the twenty tuxedoed waiters with their lupin-garnished hors d'oeuvres trays. The pool, a sparkling sprawl bested only by the vast sea beyond, is enhanced by a constellation of floating candles. Crowded around it are about a hundred people, dressed shockingly formal despite our exhortation on the email invitation that nobody needed to worry about attire. But the girls warned Jesse and me that the media wouldn't listen. When the most bizarre Hollywood story of the season is about to be explained in one of the world's most glamorous destinations, everyone in town grabs the emergency formal wear from the back of the closet.

"Here we go, crew," Jesse murmurs as Kara and I continue to wave, smile, switch our angles, and repeat. "Cue the highfliers in Speedos and the pretty ladies on tightropes."

"Damn," Kell softly quips in return. "Right when I thought it was okay to leave the calliope at home."

"Doesn't matter. They showed up anyway. Now we have to hope the box office returns our investment."

I pivot long enough to toss my friend an affirming look. He's spoken a lot of truths today and tonight, but none so searingly accurate—or scarily important—as that one.

CHAPTER 23

Kara

"*K*ALISPERA, EVERYONE."

I'm shocked by the composure lining my voice, considering the number of flashbulbs still throwing off the edges of my equilibrium. Though I've been through the strobe parade before, it's never an experience someone gets used to. Except, perhaps, my mother or the White House Press Secretary.

Mother.

I blink frantically, hiding my twinge of torment by expanding my smile. *Weakness isn't an option.* And borrowing those perfect words from the Veronica Valari bible, making myself a perfect apostle of her ultimate ministry. The image. The impression.

Don't fuck with us. We're the Valaris.

But apostles also know when to pray. And this entire minute is mine. I plead to whatever power there is, with every strand of stamina I can spare, for a power that my abilities don't cover. The magical muscles that only this throng can wield for us.

Global communication.

The flashbulb barrage calms to a dull roar, making it possible for me to speak again. The resort here on Plaka Beach has thought to provide a microphone on a stand, but I hope I don't have to use it. This might be the strangest circus on earth right now, but it has to be one with heart and sincerity.

"Good evening, everyone," I say, repeating the greeting in English. "Thank you for dropping your lives and flying out here, to Elounda, Greece, to be with us. Maximus and I"—it's a perfect place to pause, making sure they properly note our location as well as my kittenish grin—"or should I say my *husband* and I, are floored by how many of you made it in such a short time."

A spatter of applause follows, though everyone's generating the sound around their holds on champagne glasses, so the sound isn't ripping the air apart. It's easy enough for someone at the far end of the pool to shout out and be heard.

"Don't think anyone's calling this a sacrifice, Mr. and Mrs. Kane."

There's the one that gets some louder claps, though a reporter near the front with a Radio France identifier box is fast on the draw for a follow-up.

"*Is* it?" she asks. "Mr. and Mrs. Kane? Were the nuptials actually commemorated before the storm bore down?"

"Affirmative." As Maximus states it with alpha-style emphasis, the group laughs. "If they weren't, do you guys think we'd let a stupid little squall stop the ceremony?"

"A *little* blast that nearly took the roof off the place," reminds someone else from down front. "And, as many initially thought, made off with you two, as well."

"But it didn't," I inject before scooting against Maximus with mushy affection. I kick out my back heel, ensuring that my gown's small train is accentuated: a move that Veronica taught me years ago. The crowd surges forward, their swoony *awwws* layered over a new flurry of flashbulbs to capture head-to-toe shots.

"Fortunately, there was an experienced mariner who happened to be on site," Maximus explains, somehow managing to ignore the small snicker that Kell and Jesse share. "And that individual quickly shuttled us to safer ground."

Mistress Radio France absorbs that with a knitted brow and a glance at her smart pad. "There are many ceremony guest accounts, monsieur. None of them mentioned this mighty hero of yours."

By the skin of my teeth, I hang on to neutral composure as Maximus regards her like a student who's debating the social relevance of Dickens.

"Curious," he returns, still going for the you're-stepping-in-it-more-than-me bearing. "But maybe it had to do with people being afraid for their lives and all. I mean, just a theory."

As the journalist obviously opts for holding her tongue,

another hand goes up off to our left. The man it belongs to is swarthy and stylish enough to likely be from here or Athens, but his question bears a London accent.

"And, as you are certainly well aware, all the guests *are* now accounted for, save both your mums. Any flint for that fire, eh?"

My husband's gaze takes on a new flare. Though he disguises it well, flipping on the switch for a larger smile, others have probably noticed his hitch if I already have. *Media loves the minor stuff.* Yet another Veronica-ism to make me long for her in more ways than I ever thought I would.

"Sorry," I offer, almost too cheerful about my own front. "No flint at all, I'm afraid. The steel's not much either. Veronica Valari and Nancy Kane are both…resting." I'm able to look as many of them in the eyes as I want. It's a stretch, but not a lie.

"Exactly." Maximus thanks me in the best possible ways, with a comforting constriction at my waist and a sincere stare of his own. "Most of you know that things were a whirlwind *before* the wedding. And then, with the day itself making a NASCAR crash look like a fun alternative…"

Quiet but nervous laughs join the rustles of the Mediterranean winds through the palms and cypress trees. The Brit is kind enough to assure, "We can all only imagine. Please accept our collective wishes for their comfort and continued vitality."

"We'll relay that," Maximus says, tipping his head with sincerity. "Thank you. Honestly."

"As long as we're on that subject…"

I hinge away from him to reach for the microphone now, summoning the boldness from one more golden nugget from my mother. *When there's a real point to be made, don't be afraid of your megaphone.*

"We want to again convey our thanks to all of *you*," I state, making sure the amplification is on. "I see a lot of familiar faces here, because you were so supportive and happy about everything despite Maximus and me going for that NASCAR speed record on our courtship."

After everyone indulges in some volume with their laughter this time, I conclude, "Since the wedding was probably…ermmm…a little tricky to write about, we wanted to make up for it by inviting you all to share in a little of the honeymoon instead. We hope you've had a chance to sign up for some of the activities tomorrow, though you only get Maximus and me for the reception and dinner tonight. It's still a honeymoon, after all!"

More rounds of happy cheers are in order, and a good part of the crowd salutes me with upheld glasses. But when their free hands shoot up too, demanding they be next pick for interview questions, Kell strides over to take the mic from me.

"Mingling time now, ladies and gentlemen. My big sister was trying to phrase it more tactfully, but the dakos is screaming my name."

I lead the legions in applauding her for the honest humor but am amazed she means every word, down to flagging down the nearest waiter and the appetizers he bears.

"Yesss. *Efcharistó.*" She beams an enchanting smirk at

the already smitten server while loading up a napkin with the bruschetta-style mini toasts. "How many does everyone else want?"

"Load me up, starfighter," Jesse says, instantly giving me a new fixation—my sister's flustered flush—in place of at least half the sharp twinges along my nervous system.

But only half.

The other ones still grab me with frequent fire, but I don't try to fight them. I need the heat more than ever now. The prods that remind me this part is only the beginning of our plan. The setup of our fight.

The bait we've placed in the trap.

Luckily, chomping down some appetizers, as delicious as they smell, is not a requirement for this to work. Even Kell gets that after downing only two of the cheese- and tomato-covered toastettes, opting to give hers away to some willing reporters as we move through the crowd for more gripping and grinning with everyone.

"Ugh," she utters in my ear. "I was ready for those all afternoon. Why do I want to throw them up now?"

I give her a sympathetic glance. "Because you're discovering that stress eating isn't as fun as they all say?"

"Valid point." The feedback is from Jesse, who rolls up next to us on a stretch of the patio overlooking the resort's amphitheater and yoga lawn. "Unless Flamin' Funyuns are part of the mix."

Kell loops a tight frown at us both. "*Stressed* isn't a usual part of my vocabulary." Though she looks like it'd feel better to snarl it, she leans into the contemplation with a thoughtful sip from the flute she grabs off another grinning waiter's tray. "I don't think I like it very much."

"One out of ten stars," I drawl. "Would not recommend for daily usage."

My sister arches a brow. "Yet one whole star anyway?"

I shrug. "Because stress sex is kind of fun."

It's a level-up from our normal sibling banter, but no situation in our lives has justified it more. Since we can't both wait on Hecate's response with half-gallon glasses of wine in hand, Kell will understand my conversational equivalent.

Or...not.

I look on, wavering between amusement and bafflement, as my little sister lets my quip fall to the ground along with her stare. At the same time, Jesse rubbernecks his concentration toward the sky.

While I'm still wondering whether to harbor hope or worry about the development, Maximus is my awkward-moment savior. "What'd I miss?" he asks, pressing a kiss to my forehead and a glass of club soda into my hand.

"Hmmm. Intriguing question." I finish with a small frown when his reaction tops Kell's on my surprise meter.

But as thoroughly as my mind wants to write *The Tale of Kell and Jesse*, complete with a Madame Voracity original of her own and lots of pretty cousins for Nikoleta, it's my sister herself who yanks us all back to the harsher reality of right now.

"So how long do you think this is going to take?" She raises her head for the sole purpose of nailing me with the stare that practically matches her kohl makeup. "I'm serious.

On a realistic one to ten. I mean, it's not like the Iremia crowd is sitting around comparing social feeds…"

"Unless Circe needs the *Hathaway Harbor* recap," Maximus supplies.

"Ah, damn it," Jesse mutters. "Did you have to tell me that? Commonality with one's enemy is dangerous, man."

"They're not our enemies," I rush to protest. "Not all of them, okay?" I push that part directly at my husband's instant glower. "We spent significant time with them, Maximus. You helped Liseli and Kiama with the animals. Morgana baked us the best morning scones on earth, and Marie can sing like Beyonce and Ariana's love child. And *you* just spoke about Circe with more than a little affection."

Jesse clears his throat. "And she *is* a fellow *Hathaway Harbor* addict. So there's that."

Maximus grunts. "Why are you right about the weirdest things?"

"The diamonds aren't monsters. Yes, their leader has careened right off the deep end, but I choose to believe the rest of them, women I called my friends a short month ago, are still struggling to stay on the better side of the ledge. Their fingernails might be bleeding and the tears might be stinging, but they're *there*. Trying to hope. And trying to make sure that our mothers do the same thing."

I've never been more grateful for my little sister's ability to hopscotch over my head and wrestle away the social reins. While her usual sweep of a smile isn't in place, at least her flawless call to action is.

"I vote for taking a quick walk down to the beach." She

nods toward Jesse. "You've got the all-terrains on right now, and the shoreline here is pebbly." And I was wrong about the smile. It appears tentative but gorgeous at the far edges of her shiny crimson lips. "If we have to be in Hecate's waiting room, let's middle-finger the receptionist with ocean breezes and dolphin sightings."

Maximus juts his bottom lip and lifts a grin of his own. It's one of my favorite looks from him, so I'm too busy dealing with my somersaulting heart to catch the beginning of Jesse's reaction. But wow, do I notice the end. His reverent gaze up at my sister is trumped only by the soft admiration in his voice.

"Now that's an even better idea than looking up today's *Hathaway Harbor* recap."

"Damn right," she counters, handing over her wineglass to him. As Jesse secures the vino in his chair's cup holder, Kell steps around to rest hands on his shoulders as we start down the paved path with its curved approach to the shoreline.

The closer we get to the waterline, the better and calmer I feel—whatever *calm* can truly be in circumstances like this. I feel Maximus trying to do the same, inside and out. Though his aura is still pensive and tight, his palm is warm and strong against mine. In return, I thank him with a long squeeze of my fingers, though I know they aren't repaying the favor for steady reassurance. We're all dealing with the tension in our own ways, even if that means we're all putting up with Jesse's off-key rendition of the *Hathaway Harbor* theme tune.

Until, suddenly, he's not.

As we round the last corner of the path behind him, around a tall crop of boulders and trees—

And see we're really not in the waiting room anymore. She's there.

She's here.

Hecate.

As luminous and daunting as the first night I ever beheld her.

Only, when she was floating over my family's swimming pool, facing off against the king of hell, her serene smile glowed even more than her magical energy. Now, Hades is standing *with* her, positioned just beyond her left shoulder—and there's not a single trace of a smile near the firm, stern line of the goddess's lips.

Still, she croons as if we've decided to meet up for a friendly look at the moon, "Well, here you are indeed. So lovely to see you once more, sweet one."

I twist my lips and triple the force of my hold on Maximus's hand. "Wish I could say the same." I gulp hard, battling not to expose the surge of my dread and the nausea through my belly. Nikoleta already isn't fond of the bile, or so I conclude from her flurry of painful jabs. I'm so busy attempting to regulate it all back to normal that I'm too late with a cautionary arm as Kell steps up to our line.

"Wow. I've seen some desperate moves for attention in my time, but this has to be a new record. You're freaky *and* fast, girl."

Hecate doesn't react. Every prism in her gaze remains on me, unaffected and unfaltering.

"Perhaps we should talk."

CHAPTER 24

MAXIMUS

ONLY A LIFETIME OF holding down a long list of emotions saves me from running forward with my hands aimed for the witch's neck. That I keep things curbed to a vehement jerk and a vicious snarl is still a shock, for which I reward myself with the words that spew past my jammed teeth.

"Talking was an idea for yesterday. You chose to turn our friends and family into sludge statues instead!"

"I believe the sludge was *your* part of the party, demigod. Just so we're correct on the credits scroll."

When Hecate dots that by pulling her posture higher, looking like she's somehow still worthy of the opulent green dress and all her magic symbol pendants, I think of yanking my eyes out for relief from the sight. But that'd make it impossible to jolt my scrutiny to the black-suited prick next to her.

"Nephew," he acknowledges, tilting his head like a Ninth

Circle Ken doll. The comparison fits, since his lacquered-back hair doesn't budge by an inch. "Nice evening for a family reunion, hmmm? But where's everyone else?"

"Fuck you." I soak my glare in as much disgust as I can. "Who am I kidding? *Damn it.* Fuck us all."

Hades swings his black brows so high, they resemble the beginnings of question marks. There's definitely no replacing the metaphor, since a thousand of them are barraging the chaos in my brain.

"All right, then," he murmurs smoothly. "If you insist . . ."

If his remark didn't crank up Kara's anxiety by several noticeable notches, I'd really be screwing the self-control for a go at *his* throat. But again, I dig deeper than I ever thought conceivable, scooping at stores of composure that I didn't know existed. They're helpful for tightening the seams on the outside—but inwardly I'm a mess of frayed edges and burnt seams.

We thought we were resetting the stakes. Loading the fates in our favor. Bringing the witch here so we could control the plot twists. Change the narrative.

Has she stolen the script? Reconfigured our rewrite?

She's fought side-by-side with Zeus. Few Olympians, if any, know his thoughts and quirks better than she does—which means she also knows a billion moves that might throw him off.

Like letting us think she's swimming in for our lure but arriving at the pond with a housebroken Hades in tow. Why? How?

More hideously: for how much?

Deep in my gut, the answer already rises on well-sharpened blades. Knives dunked in acid. The stuff taints every syllable I openly spit at my uncle.

"You. Disgust. Me."

Hades leans back on one heel, barely an alteration in his expression. He's equally as stiff down to his toes, like Hecate's dipped *him* in some of her wicked paralysis juice, keeping only his head free of the elixir. All of that is still very much him, including the savoring simmer of his gaze and the cultured coil of his lips.

"I. Don't. Care," those lips drawl at me now, bringing sickeningly clear delight to his new gal-pal. By maddening degrees, Hecate is increasingly in her element on this dark stretch of rocks and sand—a nauseating view but an equally troubling observation.

What the *hell* is happening here?

What aren't we seeing yet?

Or even worse: what's the witch queen still hiding from us?

We're not going to get that answer if I stand here rocking and seething like some video game beast. *Words, asshole. You remember those? And how to use them for more than insults and shit talk? Expletives that your* daughter *is likely taking notes on?*

"But you're obviously caring about some new things now," I push out, but only by zeroing sights on the asshole's bloodred tie. "Things you didn't split a fingernail about after you tore open LA that night. You remember that, right? When you told *her* to basically go suck eggs?"

Hades is as wooden as before, hardly acknowledging

my brutal thumb toward Hecate. "Times change, nephew. Sometimes faster than one expects. And closing oneself off to advantageous alliances just because the gears of history are spinning instead of turning, is like, well, reading a book that's no longer relevant."

I shift in place and even glance down to make sure that I've still got Kara securely held. Such simple words from my uncle are suddenly weaving such complicated meaning on the air, but I can't discern any of it. The book he's talking about…there are no pages inside. No meaning to be grasped. And yet I'm still searching for it. Jumping my scrutiny back up to his whole face, examining all his rugged ugliness for it.

I don't see a damn thing.

Until—holy shit—I do.

Kara gasps, sharp and scared, as she beholds the change in his eyes as well. It starts out like the photoreal blazes that often claim her own stare, with heftier kindling that fans his own version of molten flames. But it swiftly turns into more: a power that even my uncle doesn't seem to expect at first. As it crackles and glistens, inciting an intensity that rivals the center of the sun, he blinks to accommodate the formidable new load.

But he also smiles.

Wider. Crueler.

Another crackle. Another sizzle.

It takes over the air around him now, expanding with licks of fire and white-core heat, until I'm stumbling back by a couple of steps just to reclaim some air. Kara's breathing hard too, using her free hand to shield her stomach. The protective move clutches at my gut, but it's what she has to add to it that makes me wonder if I'm capable of self-combustion. The soft, fast murmurings that in a normal world would make her look like a kooky rich girl reciting self-affirmations before a jog around Hollywood Reservoir with her bodyguards.

But I know the reality. She's frantically battling to reassure our *baby*, maybe even trying to explain that the goddess of magic and the king of hell won't actually harm Mommy, Daddy, or her...

Promises she can't completely guarantee.

A realization that really combusts me.

Enough to enrage my veins, clench my every muscle, and make me relate more to the video game ogre than I ever thought possible—including the words that scorch their way past my lips.

"All right, asshole. Let's talk some relevance."

I pivot, ready to release my self-inflicted handcuffs and enjoy the pleasure of going for every hit point I can get to on the preening asshole, but Kara's urgent tug sets me back. I turn back, confronting the raw conflict across her whole face, as if she's reached inside me and taken it all as her own burden. But that's not all. There's an even deeper conflict for her, beyond the love for Niki and me. I know it as if it's *my* own, as well. I feel it into my marrow—and it hurts.

I shake my head at her, conflicted and confused—but now terrified too, as the tears threatening to well from her eyes are suddenly just dry salt against her wider gape. The stare she's no longer focusing on me.

I spin around, following the arrow of her stare past my shoulder. It's a willing choice anyway. Anything to set me back on the drive toward fulfilling a dark dream since the afternoon Hades sidled up next to me at Honey Bacchus's bar. The goal of physically tearing the bastard's head off his shoulders.

The second I take in the haughty cant of his nose and the unctuous smirk across his mouth, I'm ready to go. Ripping off the cuffs. Snapping the damn bit in half.

One tromp ahead. Savoring the scent of his blood already.

Two. And now wondering if it'll taste as disgusting. And not caring.

I never take the third.

I'm a human retreat bugle, nearly tripping over myself to halt. Only after the siren dies in my head do I realize part of the wail was my wife's doing. The terror of her outcry lingers in the stilted whines of her panicked breaths. I wonder if my own respirations sound similar. They sure as fuck feel like it. I'm unable to fully tell, since a raging wind tunnel has started up again in my head. The mental thunderheads aren't far behind.

Neither are the ones in the sky.

Though I hardly notice them, past their ominous silver streaks, as I fully focus on the actual importance here. The real priority that's just tumbled at my feet—manifested from my uncle's blazing aura.

The asshole wasn't playing nuclear glowworm with us.

He's brought some extra cocoons for his sadistic fun.

They're like a pair of oversized chrysalises, still bound by strands like magma-dipped barbed wire. Whatever's inside is twitching and shivering, as if battling to get their cremaster hook out and get to freedom, but they're either too weak or terrified to do so. I don't understand at first, because there's no folded wings or spun silk to hold them back—

Until, like Kara, I *do* see it all.

"Mom?"

Now I do get tangled in my own feet, twisted until I've crashed to my knees in front of the wriggling pupa on the left. Just as quickly I slide over to check on the other mound, my nausea cutting off my air along with the rapid recognition of Veronica Valari's scuffed and beaten face. Her lower lip is double its normal size, and only one of her eyes pries enough to return my shocked gaze.

But she's looking at me.

She's *alive*.

They both are.

A fact that needs to go in my positivity column right now—but fails to get there.

"Max? Oh my God…is it really you this time?"

Not even my mother's weepy joy can tick it over. If anything, her emotion supports my wrath by digits on an exponential climb. The only tethers that keep me from ordering one of the lightning spears out of the sky and through Hades's chest are the ones still wrapped around my mother's tremoring, whimpering form. The fire ropes that are clearly under his control, not Hecate's—a factor that introduces conflicting implications.

Hades has been tasked with handling the clout they have in hand: Mom and Veronica. I *will* put that part into the advantages lineup. Like it or not, a fraction of the dickhead's DNA runs in my own veins, and I've spent more time in the trenches of his world. Reading him is less of a slimy chore than deciphering—or not—the nuances behind Hecate's coy games. But Hecate herself heads the disadvantages list. Why has she passed off the big responsibility to him? What's she clearing her slate for?

And why can't I admit that I already know that answer— and am being a full wuss about facing it?

This isn't the time for weakness. Not physically, and especially not mentally.

"*Mom.*"

And yet here I am, still on my haunches in a rising tide, battling to find a way through the chains that have left terrible welts all over her exposed skin. There's a lot more of it now too: the chiffon of the gown in which she felt so pretty is a collection of remnants now, fried and torn across her hunched and defeated limbs.

"It's going to be okay, Mom. I promise," I grate. But I can't even touch her to enforce the point. I can't reach her.

I can't reach her . . .

"I—I can't talk right now, Max," she soughs past quivering lips. "I—I just—it hurts too much . . ."

Her strange drop-off has me looking over to Veronica. For a bizarre moment, I expect—or hope?—the always-elegant woman to fill the pause with a pithy line from her unending supply, if not borrowing from a favorite like Coco

Chanel or Vera Wang. But my mother-in-law only hits me with a hollow stare that's a tormented thumbs-up on Mom's summation.

It hurts.

"All righty, then."

The contrast of Hecate's interjection, along with her demure handclasp at her waist, slams my teeth together with enamel-whittling force. I swing a glance around, confirming that the extra heat I feel is blazing straight from Kara's glare, already prepared to become a full flamethrower at the goddess.

Hecate drops her chin like my wife is merely a pouty child with a tree branch sword. "Are *you* ready to talk now, darling missy?"

At once, I hate what that does to Kara. Part of my soul sinks as her shoulders do. Not all the way, but enough that I hazard a strong guess about what's going on beyond the surface. My confirmation comes with the flicker of her gaze toward her own mother, along with Veronica's responding moan.

Conflict digs into her face. But not for long. It's full torment within seconds, the force she needs to power a response that the arrogant sorceress can hear. When she lifts her head higher to speak it, I'm damn sure that my flamethrower comparison is about to become reality—but my incredible bride delivers a better blow. A stronger force. A conviction that she pulls from a deeper power.

"I'm not going to give you the words you want to hear, Hecate." She shakes her head, actually lifting a rueful smile at her former champion and mentor. "This child isn't yours.

Not now. Not ever."

As she speaks, I push back to my feet. After the last four weeks, I can't predict a single thread of how the goddess will stitch her reaction. In a couple of seconds, we could be locked up back in our cottage back at Iremia, chained on the sand next to our mothers, or even marooned among the stars that the witch manipulated for us in the first place.

At least fifty more scenarios join my what-ifs—all of which I'd readily register for in place of what she actually does. I make the conclusion even before she's done with her soft, eerie smile or readjusting her stance like a gaudy, contemplative monarch.

"Now, Kara," she chides. "You must know that I don't want only her."

Against my will, a long growl rushes up my throat. My wife herself is the sole reason I swallow it back down, a new portrait for me to fixate on when self-control feels like an impossibility.

In excruciating moments like now.

"I'm sorry, goddess." There's zero regret in her enunciated murmur, and I've never loved her deeper or harder. "I'm not a diamond for your collection either."

I'm pulling in a lot of air as the witch queen does, though I admit it's more fun to watch the pinch of her nostrils as the salty sea air moves through me. But her fury keeps churning, whipping up beach pebbles in its wake.

"Foolish chit!" she stabs out, ramping the tempest higher. "Do you still think *any* of this is about *me*?"

Incredibly, Kara is able to spit a small laugh. But there's

nothing mirthful about it. "If any of it isn't, then stop teaching me foolishness by example. You can stop all of this, *right* now!"

The links of a chortle roll out of Hecate in return. *Damn.* This can't be good.

"You have no idea what you're asking."

"No?" Kara snaps. "When you're standing here, demanding I bow to your indentured servitude? With my own *child* as the barter?"

No laughter from the goddess this time.

Instead, with a high roar, she scourges more of the shoreline to life.

The shrapnel is brutal enough to make us all shield our faces, but past the spikes of my fingers, I can't ignore the very new and noticeable changes to this bizarre power balance.

One: the shoreline rocks aren't the only force of nature skip-hopping across the Aegean shallows now. The lightning party I started is becoming a celestial rave, with a pair of constellations that can't be named—or mistaken.

Two: as I wave in welcome to the humanoid formations, hoping Dad and Po touch down here sooner than later, there's no mistaking the hinky happenings with the relative I'd rather forget. Hades looks…worried. And his stress has everything to do with the invisible force that's ripping open his black dress shirt—then pulling out the book he's been hiding underneath.

Three: that's not a book.

It's a grimoire.

And as it travels through midair, gaining a brighter and brighter glow on its way to Hecate's outstretched hands, the tethers around Veronica and Mom start to waver.

Suspecting Hecate is too riveted on Kara to notice, I inch into the small area between Mom's head and Veronica's feet. They're both still getting cut up by the wild-flying rocks, so I hunch as much as possible to protect them. It's better than nothing, which is exactly the support I'm able to lend my own wife right now. The witch queen is clearly looking for any avenue into Kara's resolve, and I'm one of those obvious mechanisms. *Support from afar* isn't nearly as poetic in real-life application.

Especially as the power seesaw tilts back in the goddess's favor.

From the moment that her grimoire lowers into her arms and resettles against her bosom.

A chest that rises and falls with the heft of rising dominion. Knowing sovereignty.

The upper hand—in ways that I now wish were actually poetic.

Because as she lifts hers, with fingers splayed and palm curved in around her invisible door knob, the searing straps around our mothers are back to full force. And she's completely celebratory about it.

"You want me to set them free, Kara?" she charges. "I can do it, you know—with nothing but a small wave and a tiny wish. And I *want* to do it for you, my sweet one. More than anything, I want your beautiful little *louloudi* to know and love their grandmamas as they grow up. We shall even build them a special villa next to yours at Iremia—"

"Bullshit." Kara screams it over the tempest, her eyes filling with flames again. Some of the pebbles still flying past her face are ignited like specks of flint before flickering out in the wind. "That's bullshit, and we both know it. Once you take Olympus—"

"Then you'll have *another* home to call your own," the goddess says, reminding me of some movie producer desperate to land a big star for the show. But this isn't a negotiation for a bigger dressing room. It's the future of the realms as we know them. The worlds that this witch is willing to burn for the glory of just one. The misguided purpose that continues to flash in her intense gaze.

"You won't be the only one, Kara. Everyone you love will have a stunning villa too. We'll all live in the *aither* and bathe in pure waters. We will drink nectar and dine like kings and queens. Best of all, your child will never know grief or suffering or sadness—"

Kara slashes up a hand. "You mean after she helps you attack the gods' realm and assassinate Zeus?"

"After *we* take the necessary steps to rise … *together.*"

Now I'm ready to say something again—loudly—except that my astoundment's cutting me short before I can start. More exigently, I don't even know if I can find the right words. What's the right way to call out a creature talking about turning against their king—*murdering* him—as if she's getting ready to gift him with the Holy Grail instead?

"Bullshit," Kell declares, marching past me with furious purpose. Along the way, she yanks her hair back from her face before ponytailing it like a sadistic pirate knotting a tow line. Her energy punches my senses hard enough to render me speechless.

But not useless.

I haul up my own determination, ordering myself to stay vigilant. If necessary, to ruthless degrees. Painfully, vehemently aware that I'm now the only protection between my treacherous uncle and my best friend. Also aware that my *other* uncle and dear old Pops should've finished their descent from the horizon a while ago.

Did you stop for cocktails and flirting, fuckheads?

"Bullshit." Kell's reiteration yanks me back to the dilemma that has to take bigger priority. Like why she's still attempting that line when it obviously failed for her sister. And emphasizing the whole point by continuing her advance on the sorceress with the ultra-powered grimoire in hand.

"Guess what, bitch witch? You don't get to do this anymore," she dictates, waving Kara back as she bears in on Hecate. "*None* of this."

I almost abandon my post when my wife ignores her sister's heed. "Kell! Are you freaking—"

"Pissed off?" she cuts in. "Fed all the way *up* with this broom rider messing with you? With every one of us?" She turns back around to spit at Hecate, "I get it, all right? Going for the high road all the damn time, especially after getting jerked around and disappointed, time and time again...you must be wiped out. And angry. And probably *dying* to let your bitch flag fly."

Hecate huffs, bristling but confused. "I didn't ask for things to go this way."

"Uh-uh." Kell wags a finger. "You *did* ask for this. You have to *look* at this. The wreckage *you've* chosen, Hecate. Is this really how you want it to go down? Is this really the way you want to be remembered?"

"*Kell.*" Kara steps over again, scooping a hand toward the back of her sister's elbow. "Please—"

Hecate takes a big stride as the wind catches her hair and dress. "*Goes down.* Your phrasing fascinates me, Kell Valari. My intention has always been, and remains forever, to raise Olympus *up.* Your sister is exclusively qualified to be the center star of that new order. Venerated forever in the history of the realms. Why do you want to hold her back?"

Kell doesn't flinch. "And why do you want to use her up?"

CHAPTER 25

Kara

FOR THE FIRST TIME since I was a little girl, I can't turn myself off. My sentience is on overdrive, gunned its highest gear by the agitated passenger in my belly, and I feel them both. Hecate and Kell.

All of them.

The anger. The outrage. The vexation. The indignation.

Neither one of them ready to turn anything down. Their dual commitment to choosing the opposite is what makes me rush forward again, ignoring Maximus's protective growl.

Instead, I run into my sister's stiff back as she confronts the goddess fully face to face. *No, Kell. You foolish, amazing vanguard. No!*

"She's already made herself very clear about your offer," she states without hesitation. "*Several* times. And yet you keep pulling these new stunts—"

"*Conditions.*"

The goddess is as sure with that as a fresh-sharpened knife through chiffon cake.

"Excuse me?"

"Not stunts. I choose to call them *conditions*, darling."

The final word feels like anything but an endearment, especially as the magic queen draws up her posture on a new blast of wind. The layers of her skirt mix with flying stones and metallic moonlight. The centers of her eyes flash like diamonds—matched by the unblinking stares of the human versions, who suddenly materialize behind her.

"Circe?" I call out. "Morgana? Kiama? Aradia?"

All seven of them are here, but none of them blink for me, let alone answer.

"Hecate?" I charge. "What's going on? What are you doing?" I accept the idiocy of the demand. The clarity of its answer.

They're here because she commanded them to be. Because they're marrow-deep in their mistress's thrall now. Alive but not free. As imprisoned—and likely in as much agony—as Mother and Nancy.

The exact same way she'll capture and torture Nikoleta.

The shackles in which she'll trap your daughter if you don't agree to do this with her.

She'll never accept a compromise, Kara. So you have *to.*

"Conditions." I force myself to say it, though bile claws the back of my throat. The bitter tang is still there as I step to one side and let the goddess see my full, trembling stance. "You call them conditions," I grate. "And many times, conditions change."

A higher set of my jaw. A harder pound inside my brain. A huger clench throughout my spirit.

"And we ... have to change with them."

Hecate's smile fills out, valiant.

Kell's stare twists deep, horrified.

"Kara?"

"*Kara.*"

My spirit is sliced open. My soul is a centrifuge, spinning my cells apart. All the moments of my existence to this point, good and bad, awful and awesome, separated into the vials they'll have to live in for the rest of time. Stoppered out of necessity. *All* of them. From now on, I can't allow myself to feel any of them.

From now on, I'm only a diamond. Stunning. Sharp. Decadent. Deadly.

Cold. Dead.

"No! *No!*"

I step toward Hecate, barely hearing Kell's shrieks. Shrugging off the pain of her nails digging into my shoulder and pulling at my hair.

"Kara! Damn it! Nooo!"

"Kara. *Yes.*" Hecate's croon is louder despite its velvet lining. The book beneath her arm gets brighter, its gold symbols pulling at the talismans around her neck. Aligning her ultimate power. Weaving *me* with it too ...

"That's it, my sweet one. Almost ..."

"*No*, Kara!"

"Hey. It's okay."

I wince as I push out the whisper, already knowing she

won't hear me. Achingly aware that she'll only be able to witness my shaky steps and smell the sharp burn of my fear.

Because I *am* ... terrified.

But I don't hold back a single drop that stings its way down my cheeks. I'm grateful for each and every one that mists up the edges of my vision. They're reminders of my heart and soul. Of how human I remain ... at least for now.

"It's okay," I recite again ... and again. And all the way to the point where I don't keep track anymore. Committing to the litany means I don't have to think of other things. The depth of my dread. The bleak vista of my eternity. "It's okay. It's okay. It's ok—"

"Kara!"

Until I halt, as his bellow booms through the air.

As I knew it would. As I prayed it wouldn't.

"No, Maximus. *Please.*" But I'm unable to push enough volume into it either. The wind snatches it all away, charging the shore with more intensity, so I shoot the message by refusing to look back at him. The act will likely kill me long before Hecate does, but I crunch my steps harder against the rocks, forcing myself forward. With every step, leaving him farther behind me.

Forever.

It's okay. It's okay. You'll be okay because you have to be. Because Niki needs you to be.

It's okay ...

"No! *No*, damn it!"

I don't want to stop again. I *can't*—

But I do.

Sheer shock is a more powerful force than I've ever given it credit for.

It's not Maximus's shout on the wind this time. Or Kell's sobbing cry.

"No! Not now. Not *ever*, Hecate."

This time, I do turn. And blink. And gape. My wide eyes are filled with a sight more unbelievable than a trip under the sea to a sea king's secret villa. Or a visit to the center of hell. Or an escape from it.

The vision is ... my mother.

Who's not just broken free from her white fire bands. Now, the remnants of those ropes are *bolstering* her.

As in holding her up, a full four to five feet above the rocky ground. But more than that. The glowing ashes fly and float and sparkle along with her, flowing all the way *through* the red outlines of her fully healed form. Though, like Nancy, the remains of her wedding outfit are still dirty tatters around her body, every inch of skin is bruise-free and every broken limb is fully functional.

"What ... the *hell* ..."

I'd almost elbow my sister with congratulations for once again summing up a situation with brilliant brevity, but what even *is* the situation? What has our mother done to herself? Who has she become? Or, more brutally, has this always been her truth? Something she never felt she could share with us? Why?

"Get out of the way, girls," she orders, and I'm weirdly comforted when Kell stays as frozen as me.

Finally, we stammer in tandem, "But—"

"I said get out of the way."

"*No*, Kara!" Hecate shrieks.

I grab Kell by the elbow, hauling her back as Veronica takes our place in the witch queen's direct strike field. Once she zooms into place, hovering like a she-hawk about to dive in at a rat, the crimson forcefield around her begins to pulse with audible energy and angrier heat.

"No more, Hecate. We've all had enough!"

I can't rip my stare away from the witch queen's face. I have damn good reason. Her features start clenching and twisting.

She's…afraid.

Of…our mother.

Veronica freaking Valari has the goddess of sorcery quaking in her shiny green boots.

What. The. Hell?

But my careening mind has no conceivable answer for it. Not even one vague theory.

I peer around, wondering if there's anything I can discern from Maximus or Jesse. They look just as helpless for suggestions and equally petrified in place.

Crunches on the rocks have me wheeling to look the other way. But the footsteps belong to Zeus and Poseidon, now arriving to the scene. I can welcome their presence but little else. Their auras are off-limits to me. Then again, their glowers aren't—and they're speaking volumes.

Things like *oh shit*.

And *this isn't going to end well*.

I shove it all away when real words scythe the air again.

My mother's scathing snarl.

"That's it," she spits with vehemence I don't even recognize. She's Veronica but not. Our unrelenting, uncompromising family monarch, only hopped up on demonic drive that's almost unreal. Even Hades is stepping back, inch by sneaky inch, until he starts blending in with the shadows. "You don't get to do this, Hecate. You're done, bitch."

Kell's stunned stare is already waiting for mine.

Hecate's wielding the grimoire.

Bracing it like a soldier gripping a grenade launcher. With a grim sneer to match.

"Then you don't get to do this either."

Before I process any of it, she's done it.

Before I can comprehend that my heart's still beating, Hecate has put a giant hole through my mother's.

Before I can consider that the earth is still turning, Veronica Valari has fallen to it, no longer concerned with how our family will dominate it.

Before I can process the sight of my sister running and dropping to her side, still muttering solutions like she's reading from a first-aid manual. As if packing a grimoire-sized wound is going to stop all this blood. And put back every one of her vital organs, which we can now see entirely too much of…

"She…needs…help." I plummet next to Kell as I choke it out. In the same motion, my head shoots up. My frantic stare rakes the beach again. "She needs *help!*" I scream at Zeus and Poseidon, hating them with the same breath.

Their expressions are as harrowed and hopeless as before.

"Mother. You have to hang on," I intone, now wondering why I'm going for the same fruitless mindset as Kell. What stage of grief is this? The denial? When does that come in?

No. I'm not grieving, because this isn't grief. Because Veronica is still looking up at us both. *Focusing* on us. Reaching for us.

She's here. She's *here*. She's as formidable and driven as ever. I take her hand and pull in on its strength, so tough and tenacious that she's shaking with it. And she can still breathe. Deep and fast. Whatever she did to herself, before flying up to Hecate…it must have been some kind of forcefield she never let us know about. The secret behind her tenacity on the Hollywood battlefield.

Blood is only for the makeup team to stress over.

How many times did she use that one on all three of us? After every skinned knee, snapped fingernail, and blown audition. A hundred more examples are bombarding my spirit as Kell spews the woman's own words back at her now, and I even compliment Kell with a watery laugh while waiting for Mother to do the same.

She doesn't.

Not even the smallest version of her humor, a half smile that had the power to make whole days for me, seems near her thoughts. She holds us both a little harder before an answer finally does tumble from her.

"Kell. Please shut up."

My sister sags, a mountain of emotions dropping on her at once. But her lips quaver with gratitude as she nods in acquiescence.

"You girls…have to listen to me. We don't…have much time."

The lightness leaves Kell's mouth. The rest of her posture slips lower as well. "Now *you're* coming with the bullshit, Mother? Seriously? When we're back home and it's your turn to pay for lunch, we're buying out the Delilah. *And* ordering caviar."

"And I'm getting champagne," I put in, unable to control the shivers that set in from my toes up. "Well, the most expensive apple cider on the menu. And the lobster rolls. And *three* desserts."

"Just…as long…as one of them is the pear crumble."

The last of it spills from her on a collection of heavy huffs, increasing my conflict. I don't know what to say now. What to do. Who to scream at. *Pear crumble.* That can't be her finale. Why does it feel like the finale?

"Of course," I say, increasing my clutch as hers starts slipping. "Crumble for everyone, Mom. With extra ice cream. *Mom?*"

Kara echoes me as Mother's gaze slides shut. Her eyelids flutter once our shouts sink in, but she gulps hard when forcing her eyes back open.

"Oh, look at you two," she whispers, jumping her glassy gaze between us. "My gorgeous…amazing…girls…"

But while her voice swerves all over the energy spectrum, from strong to weak and back again, her grip wavers. Her fingers turn to sticks of ice. Kell and I wrap our hands around hers, but it's no use. The red resilience and bold strength upon which she literally flew across this shore…are draining from her as fast as the blood that's staining the stones beneath her.

"The fire…it's not mine anymore."

She jerks her head higher, which angles her face into the moonlight. The extra illumination makes it possible to view so much more of her face now—and the one thing I've never seen on it before. Tracking down across both her temples, there are tears. Not many. But too many.

"You two…have the fire now. The gift."

I shake my head.

Kell does the same. "Mother," she bites out, then louder. "*Mother.* What are you talking—"

"It's a *gift*, Kell. You understand…right? It *must* be cherished. Valued…"

She obviously wants to say more but is strangled by her own inhalation, which turns into violent coughing. I pull down gobs of air, longing to yell at her to look up again and see me breathing for her—*I can do it for us both, Mom; look at me, look at me*—but she drops her head back to the ground and concentrates solely on the stars overhead.

"It's really beautiful, girls…isn't it?"

"Mom," Kell demands again, moving one hand to her shoulder. "Mom?" And then shakes it. Harder. Angrier. "Mom, *no*. Don't you dare. Don't you fucking *dare*."

"Don't waste the gift, all right? Both of you promise me…you won't waste the gift."

I'm thankful for her cryptic words only because they force her to finally take in new air with me. But in my mother's throat, the sound is wet and labored. I'm sure she only gets half of what she needs. And her stare never veers from the constellations over our heads, so vast and luminous in spite of the lights from the village and resort.

"Damn it. *Damn it.*" Kell's voice pitches louder and harsher. She rocks back on her heels, gulping hard—but only once. After that swallow, which distorts every curve and plane of her face, she tosses back her head.

And screams again.

"*Help!* We need fast medical *help*, damn it! Or was my sister speaking Nepali to you all before?"

I'm too desperate to try reining her in anymore—though desperation might be all we have left, since I look up with her to see that Hecate and the diamonds haven't shifted their daunting position by one inch. That rules out any kind of call for help from Maximus's or Jesse's part—and for reasons I still can't discern, Zeus and Poseidon look as stuck and miserable as before.

But suddenly I'm double-taking.

Because something *has* changed here for the better.

Though Maximus's mom is unable to call on a half-demon superpower to heal from her singes and bruises, she's already able to stand.

But better still, she's able to walk.

"Tell her to hang on. I'm on my way!"

Correction. The woman is pushing herself into a run. Right toward us.

"Mother." I lean over, joining Kell in trying to shake her back to consciousness. "Did you hear that?" I yell. "Help is coming!"

"Not if we're doing this one by the book."

There's no chance to check on Nancy's progress as soon as Hecate's calm quip takes over the air. The kind of serenity I'd liken to Annie Wilkes. Or Hannibal Lecter.

Or a witchcraft goddess with an even grander purpose in the center of her demented mind—and a high-impact automatic weapon still in her white-knuckled grip. The book that's glowing again. Pulsing, stronger and brighter and hotter, as our grinning taunter steadily turns.

And lines up her aim with Nancy's path.

"Shit!"

I gasp it the same time that Maximus roars with his reaction.

"*Mom!*"

His torment drills into the center of my soul, lodging there with a painful dent. But a gouge I welcome, since it's the only element of the next minute that I'm able to keep track of.

I watch every step of Maximus's run toward Nancy, the wind whipping his mane around his horror-filled face.

I comprehend that before Hecate's done recalibrating at him, Jesse's zooming for his best friend like he's been shot out of a cannon. And that he's already halfway across the war zone before Kell bolts to her feet.

"No! *Jesse!*"

But just as swiftly, she's *not* on her feet.

She's...surpassed them.

"Oh my God," I croak.

"Holy fuck," Jesse and Maximus snarl together.

The crimson force that we witnessed around Mother...

Now it's under my sister.

Swirling around her feet like a zillion ignited rave club lights, bouncing and zooming and—

Flying.

I keep one hand on Mother while twisting around and up as thoroughly as I can, mouth agape as I watch her rise even higher than Mother's cruising altitude.

"Kell!"

But the power of her launch is her miracle *and* her bane. My sister, so full of conflict and sorrow and fury, doesn't have any concept of how to balance herself or hit reverse. She wobbles wildly in the air, dipping and weaving, until leveling enough to descend safely.

But that's just what I think.

She doesn't want to come back down at all. Her purpose is to remain at exactly that height, with precisely that angle over the beach. I can see it in the determination on her face now, but even more from what she does with the rest of her body.

The arch of her back. The backward hooks of her hands. The way she scoops them both along the side of her body, gathering the red energy like it's a collection of the sludge in which she was buried yesterday. But once it's balled up in front of her, formed into the size of a mega beach ball, we all see that it's *not* mud. Not even close.

My sister is a comet bearer.

A star wielder.

But most obviously: a really mad magic bringer.

The star—comet? light orb? fireball?—lights up her hands as she raises it high, using the thing as a counterweight for her swinging legs. I stare at her with a mix of dread and awe, but also with the agonizing wish that we could flip back time by a dozen years, when she was pulling off stunts like this on the climber rings in the playground.

But Kell's not playing around anymore.

She reminds me as much as soon as she hauls the ball behind her—and then, as her body rocks back to take its place, hurls the thing straight at Hecate and the diamonds.

From the red star, sickening snarls and sizzles.

From Kell, a scream of agony and avengement.

From the depths of my throat, moans of primal fear.

I duck low, flattening myself across Mother while waiting for the awful explosion.

Which is, despite my frantic prayers to any god that might be listening, exactly that.

A blinding, deafening blast. A searing, terrifying pulse. Inside of seconds, I'm horridly aware of every inch of my skull—along with the conviction that it's about to crumble apart. Worse, that all the pieces will be washed away into the sea by the stinging rivers that well up from my soul.

Because I know, before raising myself back up, that the woman beneath me is no longer breathing.

Veronica Valari is gone.

Which means it's no surprise to drag my sights back up and find that Hades is too. Where he was just standing in deep shadows, there's now only the wind and the tides.

The certainty of it should be an ease on the weight over

my chest. But everything only feels heavier.

A soft sob tumbles out of me. It's not any louder because at least I can claim one comfort in this bleak moment. Mother is totally gone—but so is Hecate.

Except that she's not.

Aside from a layer of dust along the bottom of her flowing skirts, the goddess is still standing before us as if her grimoire has turned into a sippy cup of cream and she's the feline who sucked it down.

With a quirk of her head, the witch glances to where my sister has tumbled to the sand. But Kell, agonized and drained, can't summon one spare spark of defiance.

"Hmmm. Word to the wise, Kell dear?" Hecate sing-songs. "If you're flinging fireballs, make sure you're not going to miss."

I don't give the witch the satisfaction of a return sally. Hecate hardly looks expectant of one anyway, as she shrugs and turns toward the diamonds with a minor twirl of one finger. Clearly she's over the fetish to blow apart this beach and everyone on it.

I wish I didn't understand that fact so completely.

As far as Hecate's concerned, her mission has been accomplished. The game has been officially and irrevocably changed.

Kell did miss her.

And blew Zeus apart instead.

**

For the next eight hours, even after we're all secured by

the police into our villa at the hotel, I reject the actuality of it. The reality of what I witnessed, second by astounding second, no matter how many times my mind forces me through a loopback of the whole awful scene. Every blood-drenched detail of the results.

I'm not the only one.

"It was like *Rouketopolemos*, only worse," someone stammers out to the police officers, who seem determined to gather a statement from every one of our pool deck guests. It's a local female referencing the famous Chios fireworks fest, though I recognize the voice of our friend from Radio France as her quiet comforter. But the charity doesn't detract *la femme* from ensuring she's on record, as well.

"My friend describes it well. The chaos and fire from the beach had us screaming, running. As if a war had been declared, beyond our knowledge."

There's a short grunt, likely from the patrolman whom Jesse has unironically nicknamed The Brooder. "And you say it lasted for several minutes?"

"*Ressenti comme une éternité.*" The woman succumbs to a shudder that could be considered melodramatic—in any moment but this one. "It felt like forever."

"Understood." It's the closest thing to empathy Brooder will likely get. "These kinds of incidents can be most jarring."

Incidents?

The poor woman on the patio won't ever know how much empathy I treasure from her responding huff. "Officer, respectfully"—her obvious code for the exact opposite—

"an *incident* is someone deciding to take a naked midnight dip or a waiter dropping a tray. Do you hear me on this? Are you listening?" She barely waits for Brooder's respectful platitude before pitching the polemic by three octaves. "We were *attacked*. Things were *exploding*."

"And a woman is dead."

Madame Radio France is abnormally subdued about the insertion. But some things, like a truth that feels like a boot in the gut on its own, don't need dramatic help.

I sag onto a hassock, wishing the boot would stop expanding. Spreading my ribs, rearranging my organs, stopping my breath—not even stopping when it gets to my sweet Niki, who fights back with instinctual fervor.

When I'm positive she's going to send me to the facilities for a nauseous visit with the *toualéta*, another policeman ensures I'm driven back to my backside again. His form moves in front of the drawn curtains, his captain's stars winking atop his uniform's epaulets. He focuses his attention on our French reporter friend.

"You are grieving," he says. "So, you knew the deceased?"

There's a long pause. I imagine the Frenchwoman inhaling deeply to compose herself. "In passing. I interviewed her once, a few years ago, and we always complimented each other at Paris Fashion week. Veronica was always flawlessly arrayed. Every hair in place, every accessory en pointe. *Mon dieu* …" Another pause, half of the first. "I cannot believe she is …that she *was* …"

Now I *am* on my feet, though not to dash for the bathroom. To pace clear across the room, wondering if the hands I smash to my face will be enough to clamp my agonized scream.

My mother, with her fierce spirit, unstoppable fire, and determined dreams, is being remembered for well-lacquered hair and picking out the right earrings.

I cross the threshold between the villa's living room and bedroom. I may be needing the thick bolsters against the headboard, after all. But after digging a fist into the largest one and then clutching it to my chest, I'm torn between sobbing into it or ripping it apart.

Before I make the call, Maximus appears in the doorframe. With the intensities of the night slammed on a one-to-ten scale, I still remember him down on the beach, at his incensed eleven. To look at him now, that level is barely a six—but it's also a lie. It has to be. I search his aura, seeking for where he has to be hiding his shock and grief, but every new path has me hitting a wall. Deliberate ones.

To him, necessary ones.

My teeth grind hard as I turn my probe inward. My fury has to be here somewhere—this isn't the way to start a marriage; even the man's most stoic inner Rambo has to know that—but when I finally find the emotion, I discover why it took a while.

I'm not mad at my husband. I've skipped ahead to the monster who's really responsible here. The bitch who took my mother *and* his father from this realm. Though she flipped the fuse only once, both the detonations are on her. I don't care what court of law or powers that be go and declare it otherwise. For now and for always, Hecate of Olympus is the harridan who murdered our parents.

"Hey. Are you okay?"

Maximus's murmur is my needed lifeline out of the torturous thoughts. I want to nod at him, but the action emerges as something closer to an anxious tic.

After giving up on that effort, I confess, "I have no idea." It's an ideal excuse to step over and burrow against his chest: a huge improvement over the cushion I drop to the floor behind me. Beneath my ear—*far* beneath—I finally detect everything he's fighting to shield me from. The stressed rush of his blood. The millions of neurons still firing through his thoughts.

But I don't reveal my discovery. His control is his safety—and right now, since he's *my* safety, unhooking him is inhumane to us both.

"Is your mom still upstairs? Did she finally get to sleep?"

"Yes," he answers to the first part. "And no," he says to the second. "But she wants to be alone right now."

"Of course." I shift so that I can see his face. "And what about everything with you?"

I utter it as openly as I can. Giving him the space to admit stuff if he needs to.

"The same," he replies for my ears alone. His breath is warm in my hair, and his hold is strong around my waist. "I mean, I think." He bends his head until our cheeks are pressed together. "Everything's mostly…numb. To be honest, I hate it."

In any other time and place, I'd likely be lobbing a cute tease about the mighty Maximus Kane admitting he *misses* his feelings. Instead, I say, "That's okay. It's *all* okay. I think I'm reaching for the Novocain too." But as soon as I admit it, an icy tremor takes over my whole body. "But I'm so afraid it's not working. That it won't work when the police have their turn with *us*."

My husband pulls back far enough to infuse my gaze with the dark azure authority of his. "Listen to me. You're going to be fine. We all are. Our cover story isn't so far off of what really happened. That a gang of odd guerilla locals surrounded us on the beach and were furious when we didn't give them what they wanted. We can claim the language barrier for a larger misunderstanding." He waits for my rickety nod while steeling himself to finish. "It'll be okay, Kara. We won't be lying so much as ... omitting."

"Right." I battle to say it like an actual agreement, but when the man says *omitting*, it's not a blithe triviality. "Like the parts where we don't mention that the goddess of magic and her preternatural posse vanished off the beach before they got there. And that a whole other body was missing from the beach by that time too ..."

My own ragged choke dices the rest of it short, but not because of what Maximus clearly assumes. After a few seconds, even his gentle hums and tender rubs at my nape have slowed—pulled by the changed energy in our area.

It's impossible for Jesse *not* to have that effect on a space, though this is the most somber version of his aura that I've ever experienced. He rolls his chair with expert grace despite the gravel and beach sand still stuck to the wheels. Though his shoulders are set and proud, his handsome face is grave.

The man definitely hasn't prepped a host-of-the-party one-liner for the moment.

Because this is nothing close to a party.

"I'm worried. About her."

His qualifier isn't necessary. Maximus and I already prove it by staring past him, straight toward the figure on the couch in the other room. As I take in my sister's eerily still presence, I almost tell Jesse that his first two words weren't needed either.

I'm more worried than him.

No. I passed *worried* at least three hours ago.

The cloying foreboding that's taken its place is the drive beneath my feet now, carrying me back over to sit next to Kell on the overstuffed couch. The big thing reminds me of the one we picked out together for our LA place, envisioning a lot of sisters-only gab fests while watching the sun rise or set over the Hollywood sign.

With every fiber of my being, I wish this conversation was going to be that easy.

Kell looks up when I don't move after a long minute. In the searching shadows of her exhausted stare, I see the same wish.

But there are different things…in her spirit. She gives them to me more willingly than she ever would in LA—or maybe that's her fear at work, dropping all the usual barriers that are her standard operating procedures.

The fear *is* there—though not in the ways it was even an hour ago. She's resigned to it, though struggling to embrace it. I don't know how to tell her this isn't going to be as easy as pinching her nose to accomplish a reality show eating challenge or ignoring the heights when she first tried the Santa Monica Pier trapeze. There are ramifications of what just happened, far beyond the bedlam of what's happening outside the villa doors. Things that happened on the shore … that still have no explanation, even to us.

Maybe Maximus is right. Omissions, not prevarications. After all, that's what the cosmos just pulled on *us*.

There's no point hiding my vexation about it. I'm probably sweating frustration and dread, as my sister's lifted head and wiggling nose clearly prove out.

It's not surprising that the rest of her face tells me nothing. I want to weep from the comforting familiarity of her typical stoic aspect. As it is, I manage half a smile—though it fades fast as she reaches for my hand and grips in tight.

"K-demon?"

"Hm?"

"You think the mini bar has any good vodka?"

The heat at the backs of my eyes is like a furnace now. Does she know what she's doing to me, tempting all this emotion with a chaser of pregnancy hormones?

There's the indictment I keep to myself. Instead, I ask, "Want me to check?"

"No." Her protest is another Kell classic: rapid but intense. "Stay. Please."

And just when I think I can relax into all our normal rhythms, she has to hit hard with the entreaty. My throat burns, yearning to lash back with twice the force. *No. You don't get to* please *with me, damn it. We're Valaris, damn it. We do* please *with reporters and agents and hairdressers, not with sisters. Not ever with sisters!*

But her chin notches higher, as if I've just ranted all of it aloud—and she doesn't care. She's sticking by the *please.* Somehow, it's helping with her terror. Karmic brownie points for a situation that, with every passing second, overwhelms my comprehension. Digs deeper at my soul. Even worse, to the parts of me that are reserved solely for magic and spells. The powers that are connected to much higher powers. So many things I still don't comprehend and can't even begin to embrace...

"K-demon?" she murmurs again.

"Hm?"

"Do you think I really killed him?"

I've got dual longings. To pull her into a hug or stab her with a glare. She'd abhor me for either, especially because they won't help the situation. But it's also impossible to give her what she seeks. An actual, factual answer. Or even an educated guess.

"I know as much as you do, Kell." I shrug but try to give it purpose. "I mean, it wasn't *murder.* You didn't take the aim on purpose. Plus, speaking to the obvious, He's the king of the gods. Actually obliterating him has to be harder than it looks."

"Or impossible." Her fingers twist tighter around mine. "Right?" There are more dueling shadows in her eyes as they search the whole of my face, a modern Fantine begging Javert not to arrest her. "That's why he vanished off the beach. They took him away ... back to Olympus ... so they could sew him back up. Doesn't that sound right?"

I tilt my head, letting her supposition set in. "It doesn't *not* make sense." The concept really is valid, but we have zero ways to validate it. I can't even ask Maximus to shoot a text to Regina, since we now have tangible proof that a goddess grimoire beats high-end cell phones in supernatural rock-paper-scissors.

But waiting on the answer is starting to feel like a thousand rounds of everyone pulling scissors, over and over again.

Until suddenly, someone—or something—is taking actual sheers to the air itself.

"But speaking of things that *don't* make sense ..."

The grate spills from Kell as she scrambles closer to me. Her thundering pulse is strangely perfect punctuation for Jesse's more colorful expressions of shock. He's stopped in the middle of one when the atmospheric Ginsu knife gains a soundtrack, *thwing*ing ruthlessly through the oxygen daring to stand in its way.

Only after I've given up on ever swallowing comfortably again do I blink and see that the spectral sword is materializing into its mortal realm counterpart. It's an impeccably restored *xiphos*, also known as the preferred battle blade of the ancient Greeks—or, so I assume, until my gaze travels to the ornate hilt and the burnished hand around it.

"Holy shit." Definitely time for assumption retraction. There's a good chance that sword has had only one owner since the Spartan age. And Regina Nikian has taken very good care of the baby. "Uhhh...hey."

Reg only dips a curt nod before finishing her slice all the way to the floor, an Olympian Grace Jones gashing her way into our realm. She resheaths the blade before pushing the edges of her aperture open and then stomping through. By her second wide step, Maximus charges all the way in to face off with her, looking as dazed as I feel.

"How long have you known how to do that?"

"Since she was ordered to travel with me."

And suddenly, I realize I judged *dazed* too hastily. It's gone without getting my heartfelt goodbye, though I'm positive my lungs have squeezed my heart to dust anyway—as my mind identifies the speaker of that qualifier before he ever appears. Kell's in the same stupefied desert as me. There can be no other explanation for why she's trying to rip my arm out of its socket with the new torque of her hold.

Sure enough, the top of Arden Prieto's head appears in the portal. He's ducking to accommodate the difference in his and Reg's heights but doing so with the elegance of a sheikh climbing out of a limo for a vital business meeting. He's dark, calm, and arrogant—and clearly expecting everyone in the room to heed every syllable from his lips.

In this moment, I'm not sure if that's a wholly bad thing.

I'm unable to tell who else is still with me on that page, though I'm grateful Maximus has the composure to step over like the incubus has merely stepped in from the pool deck.

"Ordered," he repeats, shoulders hitching back as a logical reaction to its implications. "By whom?"

"My leadership," Arden supplies. "But yours, as well."

"Mine?" My husband's posture heads toward the cast-in-concrete category. "What do you mean? My boss? Elizabeth McCarthy sent you? Or *the* president...Capitol Hill time?"

Arden looks ready to roll his eyes. "Mount Olympus time."

That has Kell rushing to her feet. "So...Zeus? *He* ordered—"

"No."

Though the word is a verbal gavel, Arden pivots to her like a tender barrister. The move and its aura, though fleeting, are more terrifying for me than every moment we spent on the beach. If Arden's being that overtly sweet, then nothing of the news he brings can be.

"Zeus is dead," he declares with stunning neutrality—though his gaze on my sister is a determined blend of strength and encouragement. It's so forceful, turning his mild grays into fierce charcoal, that even my trembling form is girded a little more. "As applicable as the term may be in these circumstances."

"Applicable?" Kell blurts, her own stare a dark whirlwind. "Applicable...*how*? In *what* circumstances?"

My husband steps forward, nostrils pinched and forehead furrowed. But his nod is full of comprehension. "Nothing's as clinical for the pantheon as it is for carbon-based creatures. Life has a thousand different meanings for them, which probably also applies to death."

"All right, then." Reg nods too. "Pretty much simplifies that one."

Kell throws her fisted hands up, and I'm sure something's going to actually get punched. She doesn't even notice the glowing red sparks that escape from between her fingers.

"Not a fucking thing is *simple* here yet," she seethes. "Can someone just tell me—"

"He just has." Regina jogs her head toward Arden. "And he's not bending it, love. We knew it as soon as Zeus was rematerialized in Olympus." She stops, breathing in and out with heavy intention. "He was there...but he wasn't."

I shoot to my own feet, ready to join my sister in demanding a hacksaw through the explanations. Just as quickly, Arden arcs a finger, dictating my silence.

"You blew him up, Kell," he says, again so placid and lawyerly. He cups an equally gentle hand to her shoulder, but she smacks it down with a hiss.

"I'm more than aware, Arden."

He ignores the rebuff, though tucks his hand into his pocket. "So, he's in pieces," he explains with enunciated care. "And though all those pieces are, technically, still alive, they can't be put back together again. Zeus is existing, but not alive."

Kell rocks back with a grimace. "I...didn't mean it."

Arden's chest fills with a visible breath, even from beneath his three-piece suit. "Everyone is aware."

"So." My sister's gulp is thick with her trepidation. "What happens now? What are they going to do with him? Or...what's left..."

"Cronus."

Maximus has been so stiff and still that his sudden

interjection startles me. After a second's worth of an atoning glance, he refocuses on Arden with eyes like twin blue lasers.

"Damn it. I can't believe I didn't put that together sooner."

"Same mind track," Jesse puts in, his voice sure but his mien deflated. Though Arden's arrival is the last thing we all expected, it's clearly the last thing that the poor guy *wanted*.

"Why?" Kell asks. "What does Cronus have to do with this?"

"He's Zeus's father," Jesse fills in. "And, once upon a time, was the acknowledged ruler of the gods."

"Until what?" My sister's composure teeters between desperation and agitation. I feel it all from her soul before it reaches her voice. She always scoffed at me for loving the last-minute romance movie saves, but now she's gunning most of her spirit for one. "He abdicated, right? Fell in love? Decided to plant an herb garden and binge true crime shows in his old age? Bought an RV and rigged it for cross-cosmos adventures?"

Maximus fits his hands together, only giving away his dread by rubbing the knuckle of one thumb with the pad of the other. "He was killed. By Z himself."

I'm up on my feet again too, moving quickly to steady Kell's backward stumble.

"Also … by accident?" she stammers.

"Depends on your viewpoint." While the answer is amorphous, my husband isn't. His stance is still firm but attentive, his version of acknowledging the conflict Kell's own composure is losing out to. "The move was premeditated but nobly purposed. Cronus had already eaten Z's five siblings and would've done the same thing to him if not for some fast thinking on his wife's part. After Zeus used poison to make his father hurl the family back up, he realized he had no choice about what to do next."

I stick to my position behind Kell, here to help if the story just made her stomach do the same gymnastics as mine. I even grab my middle for a long moment, inwardly begging Niki not to ride the acid flumes. The child isn't listening, of course, but I'm relieved to observe that my sister's attention is better.

"No choice," she repeats, her nod as deliberate as her voice. "Yes. I get it."

I just lived it.

The wordless addendum might be somewhat different through the filter of my senses, but the overall meaning is the same. And its follow-up feelings inside my sister's spirit. That surely, if Zeus's motivation was properly preserved, hers will be equally acknowledged. *Forgiven.*

But now that Maximus has recounted the first part of his story, my mind readily pulls up the rest of it—and quails.

Because the pantheon, while probably ready to understand and absolve, is probably ready to do something else with my sister. Something that even a Hollywood upbringing didn't prepare her for...

A shock that makes me weirdly grateful to Arden for stepping up again. If this next part is going to roll out like I predict—and dread—then our friendly neighborhood incubus and his acrylic-coated delivery might be the best call.

"After the Titanomachy sealed Cronus's political fate, Zeus diced him into small chunks. The pile was taken to the center of hell, where the pieces were scattered across the icy lake around the castle."

A disgusted groan spews from Kell, saving me the trouble. I'm pretty sure she's actually turning green around the edges, which has me wondering if *I've* become the first pregnant mutant ninja turtle. A month ago, I was gazing out over that lake from my prison suite in Hades's castle. I'll never forget that awful expanse of ooze and how it was like a living beast with the moans of the hopelessly damned ...

Including Maximus's grandfather.

I'm ready to frantically excuse myself, certain the few bites I had at the reception are about to hit the ejection button from my belly, when Arden is again my unknowing benefactor.

"Hades is meeting with his counselors as we speak, deciding how it'll all go for Zeus. Obviously the Lake Cocytus ice makes the most sense from a security standpoint. But mingling father and son in the same wasteland, where they'll have nothing better to do than stir and bicker ... Well, we can all write the stories from there."

As he adds the inference, discomfited grunts vibrate out of Maximus. His throat clenches with them until the tension radiates up, also claiming the bold outlines of his jaw. "Tell me they're not just going to make him a fancy keepsake urn and stow it in the library."

"Pandora has actually been summoned as a consultant, but no," Arden returns. "I've been authorized to inform you that they're considering the backswamps of Styx or the third circle slush. I'm certain the decision will be made soon."

I push my hand tighter across my abdomen, notifying the acid it'll now have to wait for its turn. Maximus, and the increasing tension on his face, take much higher priority. I stand next to him as he forces his shoulders to roll back, a contrast to the probing regard he maintains on Arden.

"You've been *authorized*, eh?" he states. "But that's just the warm-up announcement, right? It's not really why you've just zapped yourself thousands of miles with an armed Olympian guardswoman at your side."

"Shit," Kell cuts in, her chest pumping harder with every passing moment. But through some miracle, there's not a single waver in her voice. I'd be secretly fist-bumping her if I wasn't so consumed with stressing out for her. "I knew it." She impales Arden with an unblinking glare. "You've come for me. To ... *collect* me. Right? I'm already a wanted woman in Olympus?"

Regina's lips play against each other, almost as if she's suppressing a wave of mirth. "If that were the case, I'd be here with my commanding officer, the goddess Themis. Who, incidentally, smells a lot better than this bloke."

Arden pushes forward, snubbing her remark. "You're not wanted, Kell. You're *needed*."

"Needed? How?"

She rocks back farther, scrutinizing the new look on her fiancé's face. I admit that the subtle change in Arden's mien is baffling to me too, especially because Maximus and Jesse seem to have already figured out the demon's direction.

The thing is ... they don't look comfortable about it.

"Arden, I need more to go on here," my sister demands. "I'm not getting *any* of this ..."

Until, with an abrupt jerk, she does. The jolt she gets courtesy of the incubus that pulls a monstrosity of jewelry out of his pocket: in actuality, only a single purple gemstone, though it's the size of a decent river rock and set in enough gold filigree to line several hallways of Versailles.

It's a piece only made for figures like popes. And kings.

"Oh, holy *shit*," she reiterates from between clenched teeth. "All right, I get it now." She whips her head back and forth. "And no, I do *not* want to get it. No, no, n—"

"Kell."

"I said *no*, Arden."

"You don't have a choice, *megaleío*."

His tone is tolerant, but his intention isn't. My chest throbs with the surety as soon as he brings out that word.

Megaleío.

Majesty.

Arden doesn't waste time to speak again. He abandons his quiet croon for decisive declaration.

"The king of Olympus is dead."

He circles around, directly meeting each of our stunned stares, before positioning himself before my sister once more. He holds out one hand, the huge purple stone nestled in his palm. He lifts it higher while dropping to one knee.

"The king is dead," he intones again—with a new addition that drops my stomach. "Long live the queen."

CHAPTER 26

MAXIMUS

"HELLO, EVERYONE. I HOPE you all enjoyed your winter break and time away from campus. I'll start on a personal note by saying I see many familiar faces in the room right now. A lot of you turned out to help with the fundraisers for rebuilding downtown after the earthquake, and I'm grateful."

With a nervous swipe, I slide my glasses on. They're just as unnecessary as they were back in August, unless my clattering nerves count as new sight impairments. I wasn't ready for that quick part of class, but Kara urged me to try shedding some of my growly exterior to build rapport with the class.

I'd say that's tiny enough.

"With the housekeeping taken care of, let's begin. Welcome to Advanced Studies in Ancient and Classical Literature, the spring semester version."

I'm comfortable enough to now look up from the

podium at the front of the lecture hall, only to straighten my posture with a pointed look from the brunette in the front row. It's her same expression from this morning's lecture about letting my guard down. Still, I oblige gladly, since I'm wearing the decadent dark-blue sweater she gave me for Christmas. Though the garment makes me feel like my torso is being dipped in spun angel tears, Kara says it makes me look like a hot modern Lancelot.

I like being her Lancelot.

Better than that, I *love* being the object of the adoration in her smoldering eyes. Despite everything we've been through, especially figuring out our lives after the chaos in Crete, the woman still gazes at me in that incredible way—and I've given up trying to find gratitude for it.

"Uh...huh?"

My own stammer is my interruption, directed to a student about five rows up. He's got the look of a goofball, but his all-here attention has me concluding otherwise.

Looks are hardly ever what they seem. And books are definitely not their covers.

I've been learning that lesson in interesting ways. From a witch on a beach, holding a nuclear isotope disguised as a grimoire. Then from a Hollywood princess suddenly planted on the throne of Olympus. Best of all, from the wife who's declared she wants to become my peer in the ranks of academia.

The mental tangent has me comprehending only the last half of what the pseudo-goofball has queried. I'll have to take a stab at the first part.

"Uh, yeah. I'll get to grading criterion in a few minutes. But first, the important stuff. The content you're going to learn and know better than your favorite *Rick and Morty* episodes."

There are a few appreciative laughs, including one from my wife. The poor goofball doesn't join in.

"Not exactly my jam," the guy mumbles.

"All right, then. How about Luke Skywalker?" As soon as I hook his smile, I go on with matching optimism. "It's a better segue anyway, since the works we're examining are related to an important theme. The hero's journey."

I pause to gauge the entire class's reaction—and suppress a pleased grin. Not only is nobody sneaking a glance at their phones, but over half the room is still listening. Even engaged.

"Now, of course, *The Odyssey* will be our largest module. But you should also get your hands on copies of *Beowulf* and *Sir Gawain and the Green Knight*. The editions from which I instruct are in the online syllabus. Since we'll be starting with the former"—I ignore the tight groans and heavy sighs that extend up to the back doors—"I'd advise hitting the student store as well as a number of shops around town that offer student discounts. My favorite is Recto Verso, which isn't too far from campus."

How I forget my cardinal rule about control during class time, already flinging a quick wink toward Kara, is past my understanding—and apparently, my judgment. Awareness dawns as clear as the late-January sun that makes its way past the high windows and across my wife's gorgeous head.

We've fought damn hard to be here. Faced more disgusting adversaries than a hundred or so college smartasses. So if anyone in the room wants to throw shade—or spitballs, or phone camera clicks, or snide side-eyes—because I'm flirting for half a second, they can absolutely bring the shit on.

To my shock, even after one sweep of the room and then another, not a single face is staring back with less than respect. And they're still looking back at *me*. Not phones. Not website searches on laptops. Not even any adoring looks at pseudo-goofball guy.

Finally, I wave a figurative white flag—and make it evident in the new look I swing over to Kara. But my open curiosity is bested by hers. With wide eyes and a bashful smile, she clamps both hands across the perceptible swell of her middle. Her wonderment flows out to me, swelling my heart with its entrancing junction of darkness and light. Filling my world with as much magic as six months ago, when we stood in this same room and tried to assume that everything would be the same when we left it.

Nothing—*nothing*—has ever been the same.

Nor would I ever ask for it to be.

All the plot twists and the identity revelations. The hell dives and the rocket-launch highs. The red-carpet dramas and the paparazzi invasions. And so much more ...

Even what happened on that beach in Crete.

I wouldn't trade any of it if Kara and I weren't guaranteed a moment like this in the end. Even with all the eyes on us and the subtle giggles around us. Even with a lot more swelling than just my heart. Even though I can't do anything about it in this moment—though I cast a longer look at my wife, promising it'll happen once we can get out of this lecture hall and into my office…

Opportunity is often what you make it, Professor Kane.

I have no idea if the challenge is mine or Kara's, but I'm a much less patient man than I was when the school year was new. But the plus side? My humility has climbed the other way. Growly Kane is nothing but a myth for the day, and I'm unafraid to fully own it.

"So…ermmm…I think the *Beowulf* announcement is enough trauma for everyone today. There's reading on it due by the next time we see each other, a week from today. Look up the pages online and *be prepared*. My wife is also my teacher's assistant for the semester, and I guarantee she's tougher than me."

I tack a puzzled scowl to the end of my statement, starting to wonder if there's a hidden reality camera crew somewhere around here. Not a single member of the class accepts my generous bye by bolting for the door or pumping up a fist. Instead, after a collection of buzzy murmurs, a lavender-haired girl in the back raises her hand.

"Excuse me, Professor. Did you say a *week* until next class?"

I nod, including Kara in the motion. "We've got imperative family events to attend out of the country."

"Like a wedding?" someone else calls out, accompanied by some hefty whistles and hoots. But another girl, wearing a Broadway show shirt that gives her away as a boisterous theater geek, breaks through the din.

"Your sister's a lucky wench, Kara. Arden Prieto is one of the hottest of the hotties."

"Uhhh, you forgot who you're talking to, wench?" says her curly-haired friend. "The girl's last name is *Kane* now."

There's a last-day-of-school air that takes over, not as corruptive as I'd expect, when the room erupts in laughter. The mirth is more *for* Kara now, not about her. It all feels even better when my wife jabs up her left hand, ring finger lifted in much the same way she'd wield the digit next to it. As the crowd erupts in louder laughter, they also reward her with a round of raucous applause.

The energy of it all persists though my senses, even after the last student has exited the lecture hall. Knowing my early dismissal has bought Kara and me some uninterrupted privacy, I beckon her to the front of the hall with a slow smile and a slyly crooked finger.

Once she's by my side, I use that pointer to gently tug at the underside of her chin. And then my mouth, and then my tongue, to slide selfishly along hers. Tasting her until I get my fill…

And who the hell am I kidding?

I'll never have enough of this woman. Of her beauty and passion and fire…

Blazes that are dimmed by a few degrees as soon as I let her draw a few inches away. I meet her gaze in full, wondering if my own energy is fringed by the same melancholy.

"I'm sorry," she murmurs, her quiet tones reaching into the corners of the big empty room. "It just feels so weird, being as happy as we are ... when they aren't."

"I know," I rumble back, stroking one hand to her stomach while the other comforts her spine. "Have you talked to Kell today? How is she?" I add the last as soon as she nods to the first.

"About the same," she replies. "Morose, bitter, angry. And Jesse?"

"The same," I confess. "To all the above."

A small huff escapes her. "How did they expect this to go? Even before ... well, what happened?"

"Maybe they harbored some hope. I mean, you and I ran the gauntlet of true love. And now ... miracle magic baby, anyone?"

Her lips, stained with some shade that's probably named after a princess in red but has me thinking of doing *un*-princessy things to her, twist with rueful intent. "Maybe if we had sat down with them ... after we started really noticing the signs back at Velo. If we'd been brutally honest about all the times we barely thought we'd make it ..."

"And we'd have had time to do that *when*?" I counter. "After they got to the villa, Velo turned into Crazy Town."

Another little sigh from her. I know they're her way of trying to tame the frustration of the upcoming situation with her sister, but how do I tell her that they also remind me of other sounds she makes? Sounds that I'm dying to get out of her now before we have to meet Poseidon at the coast and jump back into the aqua bubble once more?

"Yeah," she husks out. "You're right."

"It's not like we could've really changed the situation."

With another cute huff, Kara pushes her forehead against my sternum. "I know, I *know*."

"Your sister is going to be an awesome queen. And I think Arden's really going to step up as consort. Maybe this will be a new era of better relations between the realms."

She chuckles, warming the area over my right pectoral. "So…wedding day mission accomplished, right? We just took the scenic route to get there."

I pull her in closer, tucking her close and warm against my heart. She swivels her head in, nestling until I know she can detect every beat it gives to her. Every pulse that has belonged *to* her, since the first day she woke my blood in this very spot. Since she ignited my soul and captured every corner of my heart…

"It's still not going to be simple," I murmur into her hair, breathing deep of her every essence. The cinnamon that's like her fire, so sensual and right. The roses that are like our love, forever in bloom. "And I don't know if I can ever offer you that, beautiful."

Kara pulls back so fast that I startle. I shoot a worried look at her belly only to be yanked up by her hand under *my* jaw, pulling at my beard and forcing my gaze upon the dark intensity of hers.

"You think I want *simple*, Maximus Kane?" She slowly shakes her head. "Simple is never going to be us, okay?"

Her lips are suddenly mashed to mine as she hauls me down for a kiss that crisps my veins from the inside out. *Holy fuck.* Someone's got to add kissing to the woman's list of magical skills. Not that I'm going to remember that, if she's ever done blazing my every sense with her passion and engorging every inch of my cock with answering need.

When she finally does drag away, I'm such a sensory mess that I'm damn glad she's taking new breath for new words.

"*This* is what we are, Professor," she whispers against my lips. "Creation and connection. Might and magic. Demigod and demon. Something that was never meant to be but *is*—because our love wouldn't accept any other answer. *Maximus*." Her fervent rasp flows over my face as she slides a strong, magnificent hand into my hair. "You and I are a miracle. An enormous gift from the edge of the stars themselves. And do you know what you've got to remember about gifts?"

I dip my head, smiling down into the perfection of her expressive face, and growl lowly, "What?"

"You never waste them."

She presses her mouth up to mine once more, as if to seal every one of those words into the center of my spirit, the fiber of my soul, the core of my heart.

And, oh damn, how my sweet little demon certainly does.

ACKNOWLEDGMENTS

What a ride this has been! I can't believe we're here, letting Maximus and Kara drive off into their pretty Los Angeles sunset.

Never would have made it here without the support, talent, and amazingness of some special people.

First and foremost, a shout to the most incredible spouse a girl could ask for. Thomas, you keep everything else moving when my head is too far in the clouds of Mount Olympus to worry about the little stuff. You are my incredible gift from heaven, and always the man of my dreams.

On the subject of super men: a special and heartfelt swath of gratitude to Scott Saunders, editor extraordinaire. It takes a very special individual to follow along with the crazy machinations of my mind, and you have been here every damn step of the way. Your talent makes mine a thousand times better. I am so thankful for the blessing of working with you.

To everyone on the Waterhouse Press team—Meredith, Haley, Jesse, Jon, Amber, Kurt—your support is appreciated, always! I've grateful for you all.

Victoria Blue, Rebekah Ganiere, and Carey Sabala: you're the three who kicked my backside the most throughout this one. I cannot begin to thank you enough.

Most all, I want to thank every single reader who believed in this series enough to pick it up and read it. Maximus and Kara are so precious to my soul, and it means the world that they've perhaps touched yours in unique ways too. Thank you so much!

ABOUT ANGEL PAYNE

USA Today bestselling romance author Angel Payne loves to focus on high-heat romance starring memorable alpha men and the women who love them. She has numerous book series to her credit, including the action-packed Bolt Saga and Honor Bound series, Secrets of Stone series (with Victoria Blue), the intertwined Cimarron and Temptation Court series, the Suited for Sin series, and the Lords of Sin historicals, as well as several standalone titles.

Angel is a native Southern Californian, leading to her love of being in the outdoors, where she often reads and writes. She still lives in Southern California with her soul-mate husband and beautiful daughter, to whom she is a proud cosplay/culture con mom. Her passions also include whisky tasting, shoe shopping, and travel.

Visit her at AngelPayne.com

Photograph © Regina Wamba